SAINTS & STRANGERS

A Sam Warren
Private Investigator *Extraordinaire*
Mystery

RICHELLE ELBERG

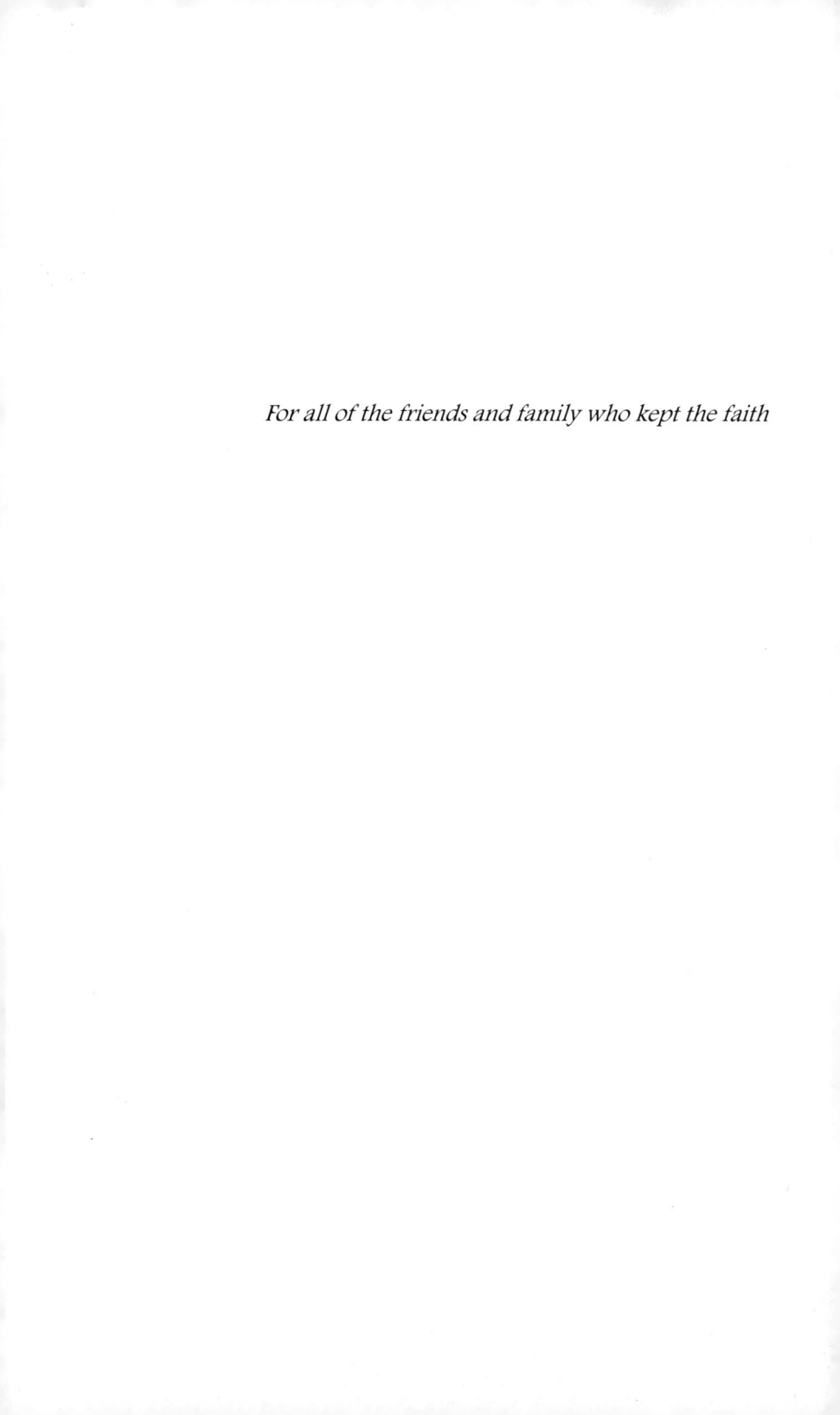

For all of the friends and family who kept the faith

The Mayflower Compact
Cap Codd
November 11, 1620

In the name of God, Amen. We whose names are underwriten, the loyall subjects of our dread soveraigne Lord, King James, by the grace of God, of Great Britaine, Franc, & Ireland king, defender of the Faith, etc., haveing undertaken, for the glorie of God, and advancemente of the Christian faith, and honour of our king & countrie, a voyage to plant the first colonie in the Northerne parts of Virginia, doe by these presents solemnly & mutualy in the presence of God, and one of another, covenant & combine our selves togeather into a civill body politick, for our better ordering & preservation & furtherance of the ends aforesaid; and by vertue hereof to enacte, constitute, and frame such just and equall lawes, ordinances, acts, constitutions, & offices, from time to time, as shall be thought most meete & convenient for the generall good of the Colonie, unto which we promise all due submission and obedience. In witnes whereof we have hereunder subscribed our names at Cap Codd, the 11 of November, in the year of the raigne of our soveraigne lord, King James, of England, France, and Ireland the eighteenth and of Scotland the fiftie fourth, Anno Domini 1620.

Mr. John Carver
William Bradford
Mr. Edward Winslow
Mr. William Brewster
Mr. Isaac Allerton
Capt. Myles Standish
John Alden
Mr. Samuel Fuller
Mr. Christopher Martin
Mr. William Mullins
Mr. William White
Mr. Richard Warren
John Howland
Mr. Stephen Hopkins
Edward Tilley
John Tilley
Francis Cooke
Thomas Rogers
Thomas Tinker
John Rigsdale
Edward Fuller

John Turner
Francis Eaton
James Chilton
John Crackston
John Billington
Moses Fletcher
John Goodman
Degory Priest
Thomas Williams
Gilbert Winslow
Edmund Margeson
Peter Prowne
Richard Britteridge
George Soule
Richard Clarke
Richard Gardiner
John Allerton
Thomas English
Edward Doty
Edward Lester

In the name of God, Amen

"I suppose, Ms. Fuller, you think I've brought you here to rape you."

The man crouched and pulled a coil of thick rope from his bag. He wore black and a cheap ski mask obscured his features.

"You may even be praying that I'll rape you and then leave you here to lick your psychological wounds. And you tell yourself, 'I can survive this. This isn't my fault.'"

He strapped on a headlamp. A pale red beam bounced off the floor and walls as he moved, sending eerie shadows about the small room.

Anna struggled to breathe through the duct tape wrapped around her head and mouth; he'd hogtied her after they reached the cottage. She lifted her head from the gritty floor and clawed frantically at the bindings.

He stood and faced her, then shook his head. "That's a double constrictor knot. You won't be able to loosen it."

He measured the rope out, folded it on itself and began to wind the end around the two halves.

"But as I was saying, you might already be planning your recovery. You take comfort in knowing that the victim isn't to blame."

He continued adjusting his knot.

"As it happens, Ms. Fuller, I would agree with you. Rape is a vicious crime and women too often feel shame where none is warranted. But Anna, I don't intend to rape you." He turned and stared down at her. The red beam shone in her eyes and she closed them. Seconds passed before he spoke again. "Fornication is a sin against God."

Anna opened her eyes wide and renewed her efforts with the ties. She rolled to her side and tried to scoot away, her screams muffled under the tape.

The man turned and threw the rope up over a cross-beam and secured it, then backed away from the noose.

"And so tonight, my unfortunate girl, you must die. In the name of God, Amen."

Chapter 1

"And....you didn't see any sign that he's been seeing another young man? I mean, er, romantically?" Harvey Mattison lowered his voice when he said 'romantically.'

My jaw dropped and I stared at the phone. I'd put Mattison on speaker so I could easily refer to my notes while I outlined the findings of my surveillance.

"Because my wife and I, well we—"

"Mr. Mattison," I interrupted in my best professional voice, "as I explained, over the past week I observed your son at home, at school and with his regular group of friends. Four or five young men and at least three different young women. My report includes details on my observations. But frankly—"

"So there were—" Mattison tried to butt in, but I forged ahead. This time though, the professional voice stayed behind.

"Frankly, if I'd known exactly what you were digging for, I never would have taken this case. You told me you thought Andrew was into drugs. I saw *no* sign of that whatsoever, which I did think was strange since you seemed so concerned, but now I realize that you weren't worried about that at all. You can't just hire a private investigator to spy on your son because you're curious about his sex life. It's....it's...repulsive."

Mattison was silent.

When I finally spoke again, my voice was tight. "I will mail out my report along with photos and an invoice this afternoon. If you have any further questions, ask Andrew!"

I punched the speaker button off, stood up and yelled.

"Unfuckingbelievable!"

I grabbed all of my carefully compiled notes and photographs and wadded them up into little balls. Then I pitched them, one by one, at the wall. Cy Young would have been proud.

"Stupid." Throw.

"Lying." Throw.

"Bastard." Throw. Pause.

"BASTARD!" Throw.

My cat Pepper opened his eyes and watched from where he lay. He was on his back with all four feet in the air. When I stopped throwing things he rolled over and ran out the door to the deck.

"Sure, Pep, that's great, just leave," I yelled after him. "Next time around *I'll* be the spoiled rotten house cat and you can be the stupid private investigator. And I want the expensive kibbles from the pet store."

Pepper licked his paw.

"Maybe I should get a dog."

He stopped licking, squinted at me and then ran down the stairs.

"Yeah, you go hide under the house," I muttered. I considered joining him. I wasn't just angry that my client had lied to me, or that he would actually hire a PI to find out whether or not his son was gay, although that was certainly reprehensible. I was also angry with myself. How did I miss the lies? I might be a whiz on a computer, but if I couldn't read *people* I was going to suck at this whole PI thing. I flopped down on the couch and exhaled.

From where I sat I could see Mrs. Trimble silhouetted in her kitchen window, watching me and probably preparing to duck. I'd pulled my 9 mm on her a week ago when she showed up and let herself in my back door, the way lifelong neighbors around here sometimes do. She was bringing me a piece of Mr. Trimble's birthday cake. She hadn't popped in since, which was a shame. That was really good cake. I waved and smiled a big smile and she darted away from the window.

What the hell? I'd had my PI license for almost six months and I hadn't even tailed a single cheating husband yet. Wasn't that the bread and butter of PIs everywhere? Not that I'd been looking forward to it, but I'd assumed that following mid-life crisis-ers who couldn't keep their dicks in their pants would be a cornerstone of my new career.

But no. There wasn't a single horny pecker to be found in my case list. Nor was there one in my personal life, but that was another matter. My list of investigative successes included such triumphs as one recovered sound system—the man's teenaged step-son hocked it—and one recovered baby boa constrictor— behind the client's dryer.

And then there was Mrs. Jansen. Two weeks ago I went to see this wealthy eighty-year-old woman who'd made some vague comments about a problem with her children when she called for the appointment. I showed up expecting a nice juicy estate problem—maybe she needed intelligence so she could cut someone out of her will. Maybe her kids were conspiring to take control of her money. Maybe they were trying to off her. I was excited.

When I got there she invited me to her back yard, where I raked and bagged leaves for four hours while she drank iced tea and whined about her negligent offspring. She paid me a hundred dollars.

Now it turned out that I'd spent a week tailing this kid, eavesdropping, taking pictures and getting hit on in a testosterone-filled college bar, only to realize that Mattison Sr. was a liar and a homophobe.

Sam Warren, Private Investigator. What a joke.

I sat on the couch cursing aloud for a little while longer. Finally, I stood and said, "Screw him."

I went to put on my running clothes.

The tide was low as I jogged along White Horse Beach in the warm, Indian summer air. I wore tight black running pants with one of my dad's faded grey hoodies over my sport bra. My carrot-colored hair was pulled back in an elastic band, which did little to control my long curls. *Ha.* Curls was my mother's word. I called it frizz, especially when sweating in the humid Atlantic air.

I ran down the hard-packed sand, ignoring the homeboys and pretty young things in their low-slung shorts and bikinis. I guess they didn't get the memo announcing that summer was over and the beach should be handed back to the locals. *Like me.* At least the really fat, red-faced weekly renters were gone for the season.

("Enough, Miss Pissy.") My father's voice. He sometimes

intruded with unwelcome comments. My shrink said it was my subconscious trying to tell me something, but I knew better. Even dead, my dad was a bossy SOB.

I grunted and kept running.

Just past the homeboys and girls a flock of seagulls gathered; they always stood together in that same spot when the tide was low. Hundreds of them. Why did they do that? It was like an ornithological happy hour. Except it was only eight-thirty in the morning.

I turned off Taylor and headed up Manomet Point Road toward 3A. Traffic was light, but every other car was doing forty in a twenty zone. *Assholes.* ("Pissy," Dad repeated.)

After another mile or so my breathing evened out and my pissy thoughts waned. I continued northwest on 3A to White Horse Beach Road and turned back toward the ocean. By the time I finished the four-mile loop my anger had faded. I ran up the front steps into my bungalow, went into the kitchen, got a big glass of tap water and walked through the living room to the deck overlooking the beach.

White Horse Beach is part of Plymouth, Massachusetts, tucked between the Plymouth Harbor and Cape Cod to the south. It's less than two miles long with lovely fine sand and a lot of big rocks that stick up at low tide. The largest of these has an American flag painted on it, though this late in the season it was tough to make out, what with all the bird shit that had accumulated. The shoreline is a patchwork quilt of older bungalows and newly built homes trying to look like they're old too. There's a lot of that around Plymouth. "Olde" is cool here.

My weathered cedar-shingled home sat almost directly in front of Flag Rock. I stared out past it to the horizon and gulped my water. An angular gray tanker shimmered in the distance; nearer to shore a graceful red and blue sailboat glided toward Duxbury Point.

I stretched and got down on my yoga mat. I did sit ups and pushups and then I stretched some more. Pepper came along, his long tail straight up, and rubbed my nose with his cheek. No hard feelings.

"I wouldn't really get a dog, Pep," I whispered. "Not a real one anyway."

Pepper is a solid black Bombay cat with species-identity issues. He walks with me along the beach, retrieves thrown objects and enjoys car rides.

I sucked up to him for a few more minutes and then went inside. I picked up all of the crumpled papers and photographs off the floor, smoothed them out and put them back on my desk so I could send them out later. Then I hit the shower.

"You know, Pep, I wasn't always pathetic," I said, as I rinsed the conditioner from my hair. "I used to be a professional. I had a real job; I was *respected.*" Pepper had pushed his way into the steamy bathroom as soon as he saw the closed door. Pepper hates closed doors.

"I owned *suits.* And I made real money. I even had health insurance." I peeked out from behind the shower curtain. Pepper looked up at me with a puzzled expression.

"The stiffs at Fort Meade couldn't get enough of Sam Warren. They called me Miss Mitnick, which honestly, I didn't appreciate." I turned off the water, climbed out of the tub and grabbed a towel. "I'm a *way* better hacker than he was. Mitnick got caught."

I still remembered the absolute thrill I'd felt when one of my favorite professors called me to his office near the end of my sophomore year at MIT and suggested I apply for the NSA's Cryptanalyst and Exploitation Services Summer Program. He stroked my ego and set up a meeting with the agency's recruiter.

I breezed through the program and two years later I'd marched across the podium, accepted my diploma, returned my cap and gown, drank a toast with my dad and gave him an awkward hug. Then I jumped into my old Ford Falcon, bursting with my meager wardrobe and an abundance of computer gear, and left for Maryland and my grand career with the National Security Agency. Six years after that I'd made the journey back to Plymouth with what would fit in my tiny Mini Cooper. That car was the only really good souvenir I had from my abbreviated professional life.

"I shoulda run when I heard the program was called exploitation services, Pep," I said as I toweled off. Shaking my head, I went to find clean shorts.

Thirty minutes later I was back at my desk. I had the police scanner turned low as I alternated bites of glazed donut with bites of sausage egg bagel from Dunkin Donuts.

The scanner was belching its usual mix of staticky squawks and chirps and military alpha codes mixed with numbers. Very little intelligible conversation came through but, best I could tell, it was a quiet morning around Plymouth. Someone called in a raccoon behaving strangely. A few minutes later the responding officer reported that the raccoon was fine.

Well, that's a relief.
    I prepared an invoice for Mattison. I was disgusted and indignant but also dangerously close to destitute. Pride is expensive. So are Pepper's kibbles and all the little luxuries I enjoy in life. Like electricity.
    "Officers in the vicinity of Plimoth Plantation, please respond. Possible 10-54, reported hanging victim. I repeat, all officers in the vicinity of Plimoth Plantation respond, 911 caller says there's a body there."
    I inhaled my bagel, dropped my head down between my knees, gagged it up and then lunged across my desk to turn up the volume. Did she say *hanging* victim?
    I was still hacking up sausage chunks when I ran out the door.

Chapter 2

I did forty in the twenty zone up White Horse Beach Road and burned rubber pulling onto 3A. I had to get there before they closed off the entrance. Before some wet-behind-the-ears uniform shut me out. I was only four miles away.

I was shifting the Mini into fifth when I rounded a bend and nearly plowed into our local vegetable stand, which was being towed by a pickup doing thirty in a forty-five. It was Farmers Market day. *Shit!*

I hit the brakes, came within inches of the colorful trailer and stayed there. For a full mile I cursed the bright tomatoes, corn and strawberries painted on the back door. I cursed the farmers with their holier-than-thou produce and I cursed the yuppies and vegans who bought it. *Fucking organic!* Finally we hit the two-lane stretch before the left exit to Highway 3 and I floored it, careened around the veggie wagon and cut over onto 3A as it bends right toward town. In another thirty seconds I was skidding left into Plimoth Plantation.

I hit the museum's long winding driveway and lifted my foot from the gas pedal; seconds later a squad car zoomed past me, lights flashing. I hit the accelerator again. I held out little hope of glimpsing the crime scene, but on the off chance...I tore into the employee parking lot, kicked open the door, hefted my backpack onto my shoulders and jogged to the main parking area.

Three empty black and whites sat like scattered dominos in front of the main entrance. I wove between them and mounted the stairs. Below the rough-hewn archway, a crowd milled on the paved path that wound through the forest to the welcome center.

I descended and discreetly joined the group. Some thirty people were gathered, many in period dress. Others sported khaki shorts and cameras. All of them twittered like excited jays.

"Ron said Mrs. Smit nearly *fainted.*"

"Who found it?"

"Are we gonna get paid for today?"

"Marty said John walked right into her!"

"This is *way* better than a bunch of stupid Pilgrims! You see that cop with his gun? Bang! Die, muthah'!"

"Jason!"

"There's really a body in there?"

"In the Billington House. John just went in to get set up and Bam!"

"Is Melissa here? I think she's doing John."

"Marty said John thought it was a joke at first, like a fake. He was laughing, you know, trying to pull it down, when he realized it was real."

I snuck my tiny private-eye camera out of my backpack and took a few pictures on the sly. I glanced down and hit preview. For posterity, I'd captured four butts and one toddler's snotty nose. Back at NSA, I had been confined to a desk; my only field experience had been with the intermural soccer team. And I wasn't very good at that.

I was peering around trying to memorize faces when one of the tourists hoisted his camera and took a picture of the group. *Outstanding.* I raised my cell phone and followed suit. Some of the actors put their arms around each other and smiled and pretty soon all of us tourists were snapping away.

I was laughing at a couple of actors mugging it up when Dennis came through the wooden archway and descended the steps. He glanced over, did a double-take and frowned. *Uh-oh.* He said something to his partner, Turk, who nodded and continued down the path. Dennis veered toward me.

Dennis Sheffield was in his mid-fifties. He'd been a detective for nearly as long as I'd been alive and he had lines on his face for each and every case he'd ever worked. Maybe a few more for his three ex-wives. His eyelids drooped over his brown eyes, which had puffy bags underneath. His thinning grey hair was combed back and slicked down. He was a grouchy, gnarly old guy, but he'd been my dad's partner for twenty years and was one of my closest friends. He was also the one who suggested I put my over-the-top curiosity to work as a private investigator. I wondered if he now regretted that gem of fatherly advice. ("Probably," said Dad.)

Dennis clutched my elbow and marched me away from the crowd.

"Just what the *hell* do you think you're doing?"

"Soaking up some local culture?"

"Sam! This ain't a joke; we got a body down there. Get your ass out of here."

"But Dennis, I can help! Take me to the crime scene with

you."

"No fucking way. This is a police matter, Sam, you know that."

"Dennis, you know I have certain…skills. Let me work this with you."

In the past Dennis had occasionally given me 'research' projects on the sly, usually when he was trying to nail a particularly slick suspect. But he'd never involved me in anything this serious.

"And lose my job? Get kicked back to patrol? Sam, it's a murder, for fuck sake."

"I know, I know, but *you* know I can get twice as much info in a fraction of the time that it'll take you and Turk pounding the pavement. You know I can."

He sighed. "Yeah, I know you can. I also know I should arrest you for what you do to get your info."

"Come on, Dennis!"

He shook his head. "I'm not taking you to the scene and you need to get the hell out of here, Sam." He lowered his voice. "But if you happen to be out for a drink tonight, say you just happen to be at the Trap, around ten, then you might just happen to overhear a few details about the case. You might get a look at a few photos."

"Right!" I was grinning from ear to ear.

"*Might,* Sam. Depending on where this thing goes, I may not even make it."

"Okay, okay, fair enough. I'll start on my research."

Dennis snorted. "That what you call it?"

He nodded at the uniform who'd just told all my new friends to go home.

"You too, Sam. Outta here."

He turned and hurried down the path.

I climbed the wooden stairs back to the parking lot and meandered toward the employee lot. I studied the surroundings. Except for the paved parking area, the landscape was hilly and densely forested. And not fenced in.

I knew the history of Plimoth Plantation; I'd come here on countless field trips as a kid. In 1955 Hattie Hornblower (I swear, that was her name) bequeathed 140 acres of land on the north bank of the Eel River to Plimoth Plantation, Inc., which was established to create an open-air museum. There was a Wampanoag settlement and an English Village where "interpreters" in Seventeenth Century dress interacted with tourists and school children. They grew crops, chopped wood, cooked over fires and tended to livestock. It was considered one of the most authentic open-air museums in the world.

The museum was a huge tourist draw for Plymouth and with Thanksgiving less than two months away, I was pretty sure the town elders wouldn't welcome any negative publicity. Murder's pretty high on the negativity scale; they'd want an arrest ASAP.

As I reached the far side of the lot, a big guy sitting in a minivan called out to me. "Hey, you a reporter?"

"Umm, sort of?"

"Cuz I work here. I'm part Indian; I work in the Wampanoag home site. I can tell you some stories, for background."

The guy was huge, maybe 350 pounds. He was wearing a

red beret and had long thin grey braids coming down on both sides of his fleshy face. His dark eyes were intense. Except for the eyes he looked nothing like an Indian, but I decided to go with it.

"What kind of stories?"

He lowered his voice as I approached.

"This place is filled with spirits. *Loaded.* You can hear them at night; I've heard them myself. Many times. Some people have *seen* them, but I was baptized when I was two." He sighed heavily. "Closed my third eye."

He looked at my blank face and shrugged. "It's an Indian thing."

"Spirits? Are you saying these spirits had something to do with the murder in there?"

He blinked. "What are you, *stupid?*"

I blushed. "No, I am not stupid. What *about* these spirits?"

"I just think people should know, if you're writing a story on this, if you're doing any background research *at all.* You need to make sure and tell the whole story, including the Native American side. And there are spirits here of the Wampanoag that were wiped out by English disease."

"Go on." In for a penny, in for a pound.

"Even before the Pilgrims landed, and they weren't called Pilgrims then, by the way, English fisherman came to these shores. Up in Maine a disease spread among the natives and it worked its way down the coast. Something with the liver, they think; the White Devil hasn't been real good for Native American livers. Anyway, the illness was very painful and made them hot, so the sick ones would go lie in the Eel River. And they would moan in agony."

He lowered his voice further. "I've had reason to be there

at night, down by the outlet to the harbor. I've *heard* the moaning."

"But these spirits don't have anything to do with someone getting murdered in the English Village?"

"Nah." He shook his head. "You ask me, that's just another crazy white man who lost it."

I nodded. He was probably right about that.

"Anyway, gotta go, I'm getting a satellite dish installed. Ciao." He closed his window, cranked the engine and pulled out of the parking lot.

Okaaayy. *That* was weird. But I committed the guy's plate to memory, just in case.

Ciao?

Chapter 3

Back home I buzzed around my living room. I cleaned the white board that hung behind my desk and pulled all of my bills and personal photographs off my bulletin board. I brewed coffee. I thought about buying some cigarettes, but I don't smoke. Probably a bad idea to start. Scratch the cigarettes.

Ten minutes later I sat down with a steaming mug of coffee, my nerves tingling. I rolled my head around and cracked my knuckles. I got out a clean legal pad and dug around until I found my favorite pen. Then I laid into my keyboard.

First I hit the Plymouth PD. Technically, this didn't even require hacking; I'd figured out Dennis' password months ago. But, as expected, there was very little in the system yet. I wouldn't be able to research the victim until they figured out who it was. With luck Dennis could tell me tonight at the Trap. An autopsy might take another day, although I was pretty sure they would rush it, given the sensational nature of the crime.

I switched over to the company that handles 911 calls for Plymouth County. About ten minutes later I was in. I found the recording from that morning's call and listened.

"911, please state your location."

"This is...Plimoth Plantation is the location. 137 Warren Avenue. In the John Billington House."

"What is the nature of your emergency?"

"Um, we have...there's a...woman...a woman's body in one of our buildings. She's hanging from a beam. I mean she was hanged."

"Please stay on the line. I'm dispatching police and emergency personnel....Is the victim still alive? Has she been cut down? Can you tell if she's breathing?"

"No, no, she's dead. She's....stiff. She was tied up. There's duct tape around her mouth. She's still hanging where she was found."

"OK, stay on the line with me please. Officers and EMTs are on the way. Who am I speaking with?"

"This is Elizabeth Smit. I'm the Executive Director of Plimoth Plantation."

"And how long has it been since you discovered the body, Ms. Smit?"

"Mrs. Smit. Um, one of my actors called me on my cell about ten minutes ago. John Clarkson. I was nearly here. I told John to wait for me before doing anything."

"So, the actor discovered the body ten minutes ago?"

"Yes. He called me on his cell phone."

"Can you hear the police yet, ma'am?"

"No...uh, yes, yes, I hear sirens now."

"OK, just stay with me until the police arrive. Did John say if the woman was definitely dead when he called you, Ms. Smit?"

"*Missus* Smit."

"Uh, Mrs. Smit. Was he sure the woman was dead when he called you?"

"Yes! There's a message. In an envelope. John opened it. It says 'In the name of God, Amen.' Don't you see? She was murdered!"

"Mrs. Smit, please stay calm. Have you seen anyone strange in the area? Anyone that doesn't belong? Are you and your staff in a secure location?"

"I...uh, I don't know. I didn't see anyone strange. I'm in my office. I sent the staff and the visitors up by the parking lot, near the Welcome Center. We open at nine; there were already some guests here, I mean tourists, when the body was found."

"Okay, ma'am, can you move back to the area with the other employees until an officer arrives? I'm going to stay on the line with you."

"Um, okay. I hear more sirens."

"Okay ma'am, I want you to go outside now and meet the policeman and take him to the body. All right? I'm going to hang up now, okay?"

"Is this call going to be made public?"

"Ma'am, please go outside now and stay with the officer."

"Yes, fine. Okay." The line went dead.

I listened to the recording twice more and transcribed the call. I read it through until I had it memorized.

I made some notes. Elizabeth Smit, Plimoth Plantation Executive Director. John Clarkson, actor. Marty Somebody, who'd spoken to John after he found the body. Melissa Somebody, who was doing John....Who else?

I got back on the computer, hacked into the DMV and found the fat Indian in the minivan, the guy who lost his third eye when he was baptized. Robert Hopkins. *Injun Bob?* I wrote down his address.

I decided to work my way through the Plimoth Plantation employees next. Fifteen minutes later I was surfing the company intranet. For the next few hours I trolled every subdirectory. I learned schedules and read performance reviews. I got names and addresses. I read emails and culled the financial statements. Finally, I logged out and leaned back.

I had a handful of names to examine; some because they seemed discontent in their position, others because they were new. Marty Atherton was hired in early September, just four weeks ago, and he'd apparently been there just after Clarkson found the body. Returning to the scene of the crime?

The financial director, Aaron Stevens, also caught my eye. Revenue at the Plantation in the first half was under budget and he and Smit had exchanged numerous terse messages. In the latest, Stevens suggested that "perhaps someone more talented— or less scrupulous—could serve the numbers up to the board in a more palatable way." He might be scrupulous, but he also sounded quite angry.

And then there was John Clarkson. He'd been reprimanded for turning up late, and Smit, more than once, voiced suspicions to her colleagues that Clarkson was drinking on the job. He'd been there for more than a decade and played John Billington, one of the character roles in the English Village. Smit's last email about Clarkson indicated that he would be fired right after Thanksgiving. Could he know?

I made a note to print out their DMV records and then moved on to the message left with the body. Dennis and the forensics guys would be working on the paper, the envelope, the ink and prints. But what about the message?

"In the name of God, Amen." Pretty generic, but I was

assuming that Plimoth Plantation wasn't chosen at random. The victim was probably hanged there for a reason. I fired up Google.

The first reference I found was in the Mayflower Compact. "In the name of God, Amen," was the opening line of the famous document drawn up by the forty-one men who crossed the Atlantic aboard the Mayflower and landed at Cape Cod in November of 1620. The Mayflower Compact was considered by some to be a precursor to our American Constitution and to democratic rule in general. For a hanging at Plimoth Plantation, this seemed like the most obvious source for the message left with the body.

I printed out the text of the Compact and continued checking for other references. "In the name of God, Amen" was used in the body of a lot of wills that for some reason had been transcribed and uploaded to the Internet. Some dated back hundreds of years. After reading a couple, I decided that the wills were probably a dead end, so to speak, and there were too many of them anyway.

The other reference that bobbed to the surface was a book entitled *In the Name of God, Amen*, by a Daniel J. Ford. The subtitle was "Rediscovering Biblical and Historical Covenants." One gushing reviewer gave a mile long homage to the book. A few quotes stood out:

"The history of the world, of nations, and individuals can only be understood in terms of those who kept covenant with God, and those who did not… Never before in our history have American lawmakers, pastors, and students been more ignorant of who they are and how they got here….there is little time to remedy this problem…It must begin with the people of God. We must embrace these truths and argue the case on behalf of generations yet to be born."

    The hair stood up on my arms. Would the people of God try to remedy the problem with murder? Pro-lifers had been doing it for years. The book was offered on a website run by Sight Ministries, which promoted "Discipleship & Scholarship for the America Christian Family."

    I looked up Daniel J. Ford. He had another book, *The Legacy of Liberty and Property in the Story of American Colonization and the Founding of a Nation*. Sounded more historical than religious. Also, incredibly boring. I found his bio. He lived in St. Louis and was a collector of historical documents.

    I went back to the Sight Ministries page. In addition to offering religious and home-school texts as well as educational toys for sale, the site offered a blog, written by the same man who'd given his glowing review of Ford's book. His most recent post was a defense of David Barton, a questionable religious historian who'd recently come under fire after a book he authored, *The Jefferson Lies*, was pulled by the publisher due to inaccuracies. I clicked around some more until I found the blogger's name. Charles Prescott Smit. He lived in Plymouth, Massachusetts and was married to Elizabeth Jane Smit.

Chapter 4

It was going on eight when I shut down my laptop. I pinned a bunch of printouts to the bulletin board and jotted several notes on the white board. I stood back and looked it over with satisfaction. My very first murder board. *Hot dog!*

I scarfed down my last microwave burrito, twisted the frizz up in a clip, and pulled on my favorite jeans with a tank-top and another of my dad's hoodies. Sandals and hot pink toenails were my only concession to femininity—a girl's feet can tell you a lot, especially if she has a thing for her dead dad's old sweatshirts. I tucked my 9 mm in the small of my back. I probably wouldn't need it at the Trap, but I was working, sort of, so I took it.

I had my head down and was lost in thought as I walked out to my car, when someone grabbed my shoulder. Pulling my nine, I spun around.

"Jeeeesus, Mrs. Trimble! You gotta stop sneaking up on me."

"Well, Sam, maybe you shouldn't have a firearm. You're awfully jumpy with that thing. Now put that away. I want to ask you about the murder at Plimoth Plantation. With all your cop friends, you must know some details. So, what aren't they telling us?"

She stood there, all five feet of her, in her pink calico housecoat and green flip-flops, tapping her toes. She was obviously braless. I made a mental note to shoot myself if my boobs ever descended below my belly button.

When I didn't reply she narrowed her eyes. Behind her coke bottle lenses, they nearly disappeared.

"Don't you hold out on me."

"Mrs. Trimble, I'm a *private* investigator, I don't get involved in police cases. I follow cheating husbands around and get their wives good alimony." I had my fingers crossed behind my back. "You should talk to Jenna Jones down the street. Lenny's a cop, remember?"

Mrs. Trimble pursed her lips.

"Your mother was a cop. Your father was a cop. Your father's best friend is still a cop. Chief Hastings is your *godfather*. You expect me to believe that you haven't spoken to *anyone* about this murder? Where'd you rush off to this morning in such a hurry? I didn't just fall off the potato wagon, Sam."

Maybe I should have Mrs. Trimble on my payroll. If I ever had enough work to hire help, she'd be a real asset.

"I'm sorry, Mrs. Trimble. And I'm sorry I pulled my gun on you. Again... But I've got to get going."

Did I lock the back door? I could just see her going in and studying all my notes and printouts. Handing out copies up and down Taylor Avenue.

"Where are you going now? It's nearly nine o'clock."

"I...have a date. And I don't want to be late, so..."

She burst out laughing.

"Sam Warren, you haven't had a date in two years. Really, what do you take me for?" She was still laughing as she walked back through her front door. "A date..."

Everyone's a comedian. I went back inside, made sure the back door was locked and left.

Twenty minutes later I turned into the parking lot at the Trap and slid the Mini in between a newer Harley and a beat up Ford pickup. I checked my face in the rear view mirror, picked at the frizz, grabbed my backpack and jumped out of the car.

The Lobster Trap Tavern is a local institution on the edge of town with a rundown look and clientele. Its darkened cedar shingles are framed by peeling red trim; a handful of mildewed lobster buoys hang across the front. Tall weeds grow around the walkway and matching dead geraniums bracket the front door. The occasional lost tourist might venture into the Trap, but they seldom stay. There's no wine that any educated nose would accept and the Trap's owner Jimmy didn't seem to notice when the No Smoking law was passed eight years ago. No one pointed it out to him either.

The regulars at the Trap were mostly fishermen and lobstermen, with a smattering of local cops. My dad was a fixture here before he died. I often came on Wednesday nights; Wednesday was really the only night of the week that I didn't sit home alone, thinking too much and unsuccessfully resisting the urge to hack into corporate or government databases. Like at Proctor & Gamble or the DOD. Sometimes boredom got the best of me.

I went in, bellied up to the bar and smiled through the

haze at the bartender. A gaggle of old men with bald heads, shiny eyes and hairy ears nodded at me from both sides. I was reminded of those seagulls.

"Sam, looks like the freckle factory's been running overtime."

I laughed. "Every summer, Tommy."

Tommy hadn't worked at the Trap for long, but he knew my drink. He grabbed the Dewars bottle, poured me two fingers, added an ice cube and pushed it across the bar.

Then he leaned over and got in my face. "So, when you gonna let me count 'em?"

Tommy had a salt and pepper crew cut. He had dark, close-set eyes and the barrel-shaped body that comes with a lot of years of weight lifting combined with a lot of years of beer drinking. He was pushing fifty and, I heard, had done some time. He was always cracking a joke, but there was a hardness about him that made me a little nervous. I didn't back away.

"When I'm suffering from the advanced stages of Alzheimer's you *might* have a shot," I fired back. The gulls at the bar squawked and Tommy threw his head back and hooted.

"Keep the change," I added, as I slapped ten dollars onto the bar. I felt a flush rising in my face. These guys needed to understand that Sam Warren wasn't just Jack Warren's little girl anymore. More importantly, *I* needed to believe it. I'd been a hotshot back in Maryland, but here in Plymouth I was still the geeky girl I'd been in high school.

I had another hour before Dennis was scheduled to show. I took my Scotch and squirmed through the flock. I headed over to the corner where Grady Cooke was hooking up his mike and speakers. Grady was an old family friend. He played his banjo at the Trap every Wednesday night.

"Grady Cooke! How's it going, old man?"

Grady untangled himself from an impressive mass of cords, stood, grabbed me and mashed my nose into his sternum. Grady was 6'4" tall. His face was weather-lined but still handsome and his muscles were still strong. He had thick white hair and he'd probably been wearing his black corduroy Levi's since high school.

"Samantha!" he yelped. "You're a welcome sight. Where were you last week?" Grady was the only person alive who could get away with calling me Samantha.

My mind flitted to the conversation I had that morning with Harvey Mattison.

"Working for a stupid, stupid man on a stupid, stupid assignment."

Grady's smile faded but I slapped him on the back. "Hey, at least I figured out how to use some of my new PI gadgets."

That was really the only good thing I could say about the job, so I stood there smiling stupidly for a few more seconds. I wasn't about to elaborate on the reality of my glamorous work as a private investigator. Not at the Trap. I was working to cultivate a reputation as a Tough Bitch, not a Whiny Bitch. And if I spilled even one little bean about helping on the murder case, Dennis would have my ass.

After an awkward moment I leaned in and asked, "How's Laura doing?" Grady's wife was fighting breast cancer.

He took a deep breath.

"Ah, you know, Sam. She's cheerful as always most of the time, but I know when she's hurting. But the doc's optimistic." Grady's eyes twinkled. "She's laughing more now, too." Laura had the best laugh on the planet.

"Grady, that's great! I'm so happy to hear it."

Grady leaned down and just about blew out my eardrum. The old man was too vain to wear a hearing aid. "*Milo's* the one who's a problem. Working the traps with me instead of finding a real job. I just wish he'd get his ass into the city and use that degree of his."

I glanced over at Milo, who was playing pool in the corner of the bar. He'd nodded at me when I came in, but we didn't talk much anymore.

"Cut him some slack, old man."

Grady shook his head with a frown. "That's what Laura says, but I can't understand it. Degree from Harvard just collecting dust. That sound normal to you?"

I laughed a little, but Grady didn't and neither did Milo, who took a big swig of beer and turned away. Lobstering had been Grady's life for more than forty years; if he said he didn't want his son on the boat, he meant it. And Milo had heard it, probably not for the first time. Grady wasn't one to mince words.

Grady nodded at someone behind me and said, "Gotta get this road on the show, Samantha. You take care and stop by the house some time. Laura'd love to see you."

He turned back to his equipment and crouched down. I leaned over and squeezed his shoulder before working my way back to the bar.

For the next hour I sat with the flock nursing my drink, listening to Grady's gravelly voice and tossing my two cents in with the gulls' banter.

I knew all of Grady's songs by rote. When I was young, he'd bring his banjo over to my house and he and Dad would drink and sing together late into the night. Those songs brought back good memories, for me anyway. I had some suspicion that Mrs. Trimble would disagree.

I avoided Milo's gaze but periodically I could feel him staring at me. Milo Cooke was tall like Grady but pretty like Laura. Handsome might be the gender-correct term, but really, he was pretty. He had Laura's dark hair, big brown eyes, a straight nose and wide full lips. He had smooth, freckle-free skin. His shoulders were wide but not too bulky and his waist was narrow. And that butt....

Milo and I had a thing when I was sixteen, but we never even rounded second base before my mom was killed in a convenience store robbery. Dad had asked her to pick up beer and she went in in uniform. A nineteen year old gangbanger panicked and shot her in the neck. She was dead in less than a minute. Dad never forgave himself, and, for a long time, I didn't either.

After that I'd pulled away from my friends, including Milo. Over the next few years my father learned the fine art of pickling himself and I discovered the security blanket of the online world. Milo got on with his life. He went to Harvard on a scholarship, travelled Europe for a year and then returned to Cambridge for an MBA. Here in Plymouth, everyone had expected big things of Milo Cooke.

Then, just before I quit the NSA, the golden boy lost his mojo. I didn't know why. He quit school one semester before finishing his MBA, although it had been decided that Grady didn't need to know that a degree was never bestowed. Milo moved back home and took up lobstering with his dad. At the time he said he was just 'taking a break,' but the months passed and then Laura was diagnosed with cancer. Milo was still living at home and lobstering and Grady was none too happy about it.

I felt awkward around Milo, but I felt even worse about how long it had been since I'd been to visit Laura. The Cookes had been a surrogate family to me after my dad died, and Laura in particular had seen me through some rough spots. I promised myself I'd go see her soon.

Chapter 5

I ordered another drink and Tommy served me wordlessly. With any luck he'd found some other woman to honor with his charm. I was sick of his creepy comments and manner.

I checked the time on my phone every five minutes. By ten-fifteen, Dennis still wasn't there and I was getting discouraged. I bought a bag of Fritos and sat there shoveling them into my mouth, thinking about what I'd learned so far.

I'd watched the press conference that afternoon on TV. Dennis would have flipped if I showed up in person, and anyway it was your typical information-free affair, with a bunch of frantic, Teflon-coated journalists asking stupid questions.

"Do you have any suspects?"

"We're pursuing all avenues of investigation but we have nothing to report at this time."

"Did the victim die from being hanged?"

"An autopsy will be performed tomorrow morning."

"Chief Hastings, do you think the murder at Plimoth Plantation has something to do with Native American animosity over Thanksgiving?"

He nearly rolled his eyes. I saw him. But the Chief just said, "No, we don't," and took the next question.

In its statement the PD hadn't mentioned the note found with the body; I figured they were keeping that tidbit to themselves so they could filter out the bogus tips and confessions that might come with a case like this. At least that's what they did on TV.

I thought I was on to something with Sight Ministries and Elizabeth Smit's husband, but I needed to know about the victim. All I knew at this point was that it was a she and that duct tape was wrapped around her mouth and head before she was tied up and hanged. I shuddered, thinking of her final minutes.

"Hey." Milo was leaning over the corner of the bar looking at me. He grabbed some Fritos and crunched on them.

"Oh! Hey." My heart flipped. He always had that effect on me; it was one of the reasons I avoided him. I looked down at my drink and took a sip.

"You waiting on someone? Saw you checking the time…"

"Well, uh…..no. Not really. Nope."

I ate some more Fritos. I studied the bag. The silence dragged on; I felt an irrational need to fill it.

"Did you know there are only three ingredients in Fritos?" I tapped the bag. "Corn, corn oil and salt. They're practically good for you."

Milo blinked. "Really? Huh. That's cool."

For God's sake, where was Dennis?

"I'm going to get another bag, you want a bag?" I hopped off my bar stool.

Milo put his hand on my arm and I felt a jolt that would have jump-started an eighteen wheeler. I looked up. Behind

Milo I could see Turk leaning in through the front door. He caught my eye and waved at me to come outside, then slipped back out. *Thank fucking God.*

"Shit, sorry, Milo, I've got to go. I just realized what time it is."

"You've been checking the time every few minutes for the past hour."

"Right, well, yes, and now it's time for me to go. I'll see you...."

I slid around him and made a beeline for the door.

Dennis and Turk were in Turk's Lincoln at the edge of the parking lot. I jumped into the back seat and Turk pulled out and headed up the road away from the bar. I leaned forward between the seats.

"So, do you have the name of the victim?"

"Whoa, whoa, slow down, Nancy Drew. First I want to hear what *you* got. I'm still not convinced I should be talking to you at all. This is a major case; the state police are involved and we've called in the FBI too. Somehow I don't think the Feebs would be too impressed by your...techniques. Then there's the media; they're fucking foaming at the mouth. Tell me why I should even be talking to you right now."

I blew out my breath. I had to make this good. For the next forty-five minutes I walked Dennis and Turk through all of my research and findings, building up to the clincher: Sight Ministries and the writings of Charles Smit, husband of Elizabeth Smit, Executive Director of Plimoth Plantation.

They were quiet for a while. I was holding my breath.

Turk spoke first.

"That be some good shit for one day."

Turk's a tall slim black guy who looks a little like Eddie Murphy and talks like he's from the ghetto, even though he was born and raised on the Cape. But he's no joke on the job; Turk made detective before he was thirty. Dennis once told me Turk was the best partner he'd had in thirty-five years on the force. ("Bull*shit*," said my Dad.) Dennis was drunk when he said it, and the next day he made me promise never to tell Turk. He said Turk was a cocky bastard as it was. I was starting to like Turk.

Dennis still didn't reply.

I couldn't take it anymore. "So, do you know who the victim was?"

After another excruciating minute, Dennis exhaled.

"Anna Fuller."

Yes! Yes! Yes! I would have done cartwheels if the back seat were just a little bit bigger.

Dennis continued. "Twenty-eight years old, worked in Boston at a financial firm." He shook his head. "Just got married. Husband's name is Alan Perkins. She kept her own name. Here, I put everything we got so far together for you."

He handed me a thick manila envelope.

"You knew all along I'd come up with the goods, didn't you, Dennis?" I punched him in the arm. "You're a real shithead, you know that?"

"Yeah, well....I've got a bad feeling about this one, Sam. I'll take all the help I can get. Do what you do and update me every evening. Call my cell, not the station. And don't. Get. Caught. No one can know what you're doing. More importantly, no one can know that *I* know what you're doing. Don't fuck up my pension, Nancy Drew."

"Not a problem, Dennis, you watch. I'll find your man. And consider your pension completely unfuckable. I don't *get* caught." Cockiness must be catchy.

"You go, Sister," said Turk.

I turned to grab my backpack so I could put away the envelope. I came up empty handed. *Shit.* I'd left it on my bar stool when I fled Milo. I looked at my phone. It was after eleven. They stopped serving at eleven, but Tommy would still be at the bar, closing up.

When we pulled back into the Trap's parking lot, there were a couple of cars besides mine and a pickup truck still there. They probably belonged to old gulls that Tommy put in a cab.

"Um, can you just wait for a second and make sure I can get back in? I left my car keys in the bar."

Turk laughed and Dennis snorted.

"We right here, Sister," said Turk.

Clutching my precious envelope, I jogged over to the door and pulled. It didn't budge. *Shit!* I knocked on the door. Nothing. I knocked again harder and Tommy opened the door. Whew. I signaled OK to Dennis and Turk and they pulled out of the parking lot.

I stepped into the bar and hurried past Tommy.

"Thanks, Tommy, sorry about this. I left my backpack—"

I moved toward the corner where I'd been sitting, but I didn't see anything on the back of the stool. I walked around the bar, crouched down to the floor and looked under the tables and chairs.

"Tommy, did anyone turn in a lost backpack?" I yelled. I thought he'd gone into the back room. But as I stood, I felt his breath on the back of my neck, and then he spoke in a low voice. He was right behind me. And too close.

"Nope. The only one lost right now is you." I turned around and he grabbed me by the back of my neck. He pulled my head up to his face and forced his tongue down my throat. I tried to squirm free. With his left arm he pushed me back over the bar and then pinned my arms down with his elbows. His breath reeked of alcohol. I could feel my 9 mm; it was wedged between my back and the bar, still inside the waist of my jeans. With Tommy's full weight on me and my arms pinned down, there was no way I could get to it. I tried to turn my head away and Tommy lifted his mouth from mine just long enough to slap me across the face. I was too stunned to shout.

"I'm gonna count me some freckles now," he said. He yanked at my jeans. I squirmed to the side and my nine clattered out onto the floor and slid beneath a table.

"What was that?" He loosened his grip on me for a split second and I dove under the table. I hit the gun with my elbow and it flew across the floor and landed under a booth. *Fuck!*

Then Tommy was back on me. He pulled my head back by my hair and twisted my right arm up behind my back. He was kneeling on me; I felt like I was pinned under a horse. I screamed but I knew it wouldn't do any good. ("Louder, Sam!" yelled Dad.)

A second later there was a loud thud and Tommy collapsed on me, dead weight. Then he was lifted off of me and I heard another loud thud.

I rolled over. Milo was standing there, breathing hard and rubbing his knuckles. He'd thrown Tommy up against the wall.

Without a word Milo reached down and eased me up. I was trembling so hard I could barely stand. He helped me to a bar stool and I sank into it.

Milo walked over to the booth and got my gun out from under it. He came back to the bar and placed it in front of me. I put both of my hands on it. Neither of us said anything for a few minutes.

Finally, Milo said, "You want me to shoot him?"

I giggled a little.

He smiled. "Or do you want to do the honors?"

"I want to do the honors." I took my gun, stood up and once I was sure I was steady on my feet, I walked over to Tommy and kicked him in the knee. When he didn't move, I kicked him in the ribs.

He groaned. "Fuck, what the fuck—" He opened his eyes and looked up into the barrel of my gun.

"You don't work here anymore, Tommy," I said.

"Jeesus Christ, that a gun?" He scrambled down the wall like a shit-scared crab.

"Get up," I said.

He stared at me. Blood was running down his cheek. Milo's punch split the skin near his eye.

"Get up!" I shouted.

He grabbed a table, pulled himself up and stood there swaying.

"Now get your things and leave. And don't ever come back here again."

"But—"

I aimed the gun a little to his left and fired into the wall.

"*Move!*"

He ran behind the bar, grabbed some keys and hobbled out the front door. An engine turned and I heard wheels spinning. Gravel spattered the door as Tommy pulled up and yelled, "Crazy bitch!" The wheels spun some more in the gravel and he squealed out onto the pavement.

Milo locked the door, walked behind the bar and grabbed the Dewars. He poured us each a drink and we sat there sipping for a while.

Eventually I looked up and said, "Thank you." I took another sip. "But why were you still here?"

"I was waiting for you. You left your backpack."

Thank God.

"Do you have it?"

"Yeah, it's in my truck. I came outside right after you left because you forgot it. I tried to catch you. Then I saw your car was still here, so I figured you'd be back. When you didn't show up by closing time, I decided to wait, and then when you got here, you ran inside so fast….I *told* Tommy to let you know I had it, so I figured you'd be right back out. When you seemed to be taking too long I came over and looked in the window. You know the rest."

"Your timing was good." I shook my head. "He was shitfaced."

"Another proud graduate of the 'one for you, two for me' school of bartending," said Milo. "You were pretty good with the gun." He grinned.

I blushed.

Milo brushed his fingers over my left cheek. "But I think you're going to have a shiner, Tough Stuff."

There was that electric shock again. I felt my blush deepen.

"Yeah, well," I mumbled. "Would've been a lot worse if it

weren't for you."

Milo must have sensed my discomfort. He pulled his hand back and laid it on my manila envelope. It was right where I'd put it before beginning my search under the bar.

"Oh, that's...um...."

"You're helping Dennis on the Plimoth Plantation murder."

Shit.

Chapter 6

Milo followed me back to my house and walked me inside. I told him that me and my 9 mm would be just fine even if Tommy did have the balls to show up, though I was pretty sure he didn't, but Milo wouldn't take no for an answer. Secretly, I was relieved.

"Got any frozen veggies in your freezer?"

I looked at him blankly.

"You want vegetables at one in the morning?"

"No. For your *face*. That eye's swelling up."

Oh.

"Um, no. Don't eat vegetables much."

"Vegetables are good for you."

"Corn chips have corn in them."

"Corn chips won't keep your eye from swelling shut."

He had a point.

I opened the freezer. There was a pound of hamburger with freezer burn and an empty ice cube tray. Hamburger it was. I pulled it out and pressed it against my face, walked over to my chair and sank down.

"Thanks again, Milo. I owe you."

"Got a blanket?"

I blinked and then the light bulb came on.

"Oh, no, no, you don't need to—"

He flopped down on the couch and put his feet up.

"I'm staying."

I stared at him for a minute.

"Well, at least get your shoes off my sofa. You're getting lobster juice all over it."

He laughed and I went to find him a blanket.

Sun was streaming through my window when I woke up the next morning. I could smell coffee, which was confusing because I usually went to Dunkin' Donuts for coffee in the morning. Pepper rode shotgun; it was our daily outing.

Then I felt the ache in my face and remembered. Milo was here. *Shit.*

I pulled on some jogging pants and my dad's hoodie and looked in the mirror. Bed head is not a good look for me, especially when paired with a nearly shut black eye. I grabbed my Boston Red Sox cap and mashed the frizz underneath, but that was even worse. The red hat clashed with the green and purple around my eye. I pulled the hat back off and found a scrunchy and pulled the frizz back in a ponytail. I ran into the bathroom and applied makeup to my good eye. When I leaned back and looked I saw a she-Cylops with too much eyeliner. I groaned and washed the makeup off, then added back some mascara. I went downstairs.

When I came into the living room, Milo was sitting at my desk with the contents of Dennis' envelope spread out over my desk. He had a mug of coffee and his longish hair was perfect. I rushed over.

"What do you think you're doing? That's confidential police stuff."

"That you shouldn't even have. I want to help. I've been studying—"

"Dennis will kill me if he finds out you've seen this stuff. *I* haven't even seen this stuff yet."

"Yeah, well, I have and I have some thoughts. I've been reading since six. Lobstermen get up early." He smirked. "Apparently private investigators don't."

I glanced at the clock on the wall. It was nine-thirty. *Damn.*

"I'm up at six most mornings too, I'll have you know." Sometimes seven, if I were being honest, and occasionally it was closer to eight, but Milo didn't need to know that. I stacked up the paperwork.

"Hey, don't! I've sorted out all the info. Stuff on the victim, stuff on her husband, stuff on the crime scene."

I kept shoving the documents back into the envelope.

"I will make my own piles, Milo. Dennis told me I could help him on this. He also told me not to fuck up his pension."

Milo's raised eyebrows formed a question mark.

"If the Chief finds out I have this stuff, he'll have Dennis' ass."

"Well then, we won't tell the Chief." He grabbed the envelope. "Just hear me out, Sam."

I glared at him. He glared right back.

Finally I said, "I need coffee." I turned and went into the kitchen. I could hear Milo putting his piles back in order. I gave

43

Pepper some kibbles and fresh water, poured my coffee and added cream. I took my time about it, but I couldn't think of a single way to get rid of Milo. He'd already seen the stuff; I couldn't put the genie back in the bottle. And the genie *was* awfully good looking.

I grabbed the refrozen hamburger and put it against my face and carried my coffee back to the living room.

Milo started in before I was even seated.

"Anna Fuller, age twenty-eight, was the victim. Dennis and Turk interviewed her husband yesterday. They also went through her condo, which is down on Water Street. Pretty nice digs. She was working in Boston. Husband's name is Alan Perkins. Looks like they met in the city; he works downtown too. They'd been together for nearly two years, got married in September."

I sipped my coffee and moved the hamburger package around my eye.

"Nothing remarkable about either of them in the initial interviews, frankly. I've looked over all of your stuff here too, and I like the connection with Elizabeth Smit's husband and the message left with the body, but I also think we should check out the actor who found her. Your notes say he was about to be fired."

"*I* think it's too early to say anything and I have a lot of work to do. I *also* think you should be off pulling lobster traps somewhere. Dennis will have my hide if he finds out you've seen all this stuff."

We stared at each other again for a full minute. I was trying to look severe, but the black eye/hamburger combination was working against me. And he was so damn cute.

He sighed.

"Look, you heard my dad last night. He doesn't want me on the boat. And I'm not...ready to go work in the city. *And,* as I proved last night, you could use a man around. You might be good with a gun, Sam, but hand-to-hand you suck." After a few more seconds, he added, "And I don't like the idea of you doing this all alone."

Flip. My heart was doing somersaults again. I felt my face turning red and was thankful I could hide behind the hamburger.

"But Milo," I said, "most of my work for Dennis will be done online. You *know* what I do. Dennis agreed to let me help. *Me,* not you or anyone else."

"Sam, I won't do anything you don't okay, all right? Just think of me as your sidekick...your Robin. And if we go out to do a little reconnaissance, I've got your back." He grinned. "Maybe if I play my cards right, I can have a little of your back*side* as well."

I got up and took my coffee and ground meat and stared out the slider at the ocean. My blood pressure was up; I felt giddy, like I was blissfully skating on very thin ice. I'm not sure what scared me more—the threat of Dennis' wrath or the idea of letting Milo have a little of my backside. But after my run-in with Tommy, I felt vulnerable.

I spoke to the sliding glass door. "You agree to stick with me and not run off playing Sam Spade on your own? We have to be discreet, Milo. It's no joke; it's Dennis' job....Not to mention a murderer."

"Cross my heart and hope not to die."

He rose from my desk as I turned around to face him.

"You got any eggs?"

Chapter 7

Milo worked my kitchen like Emeril Lagasse, though thankfully, without the *Bam!*'s. He made an omelet that was shockingly good given the meager contents of my refrigerator. He found some bread heels and toasted and buttered them, then sliced up my one overripe tomato and sprinkled it with salt.

As he seated himself at the counter, Milo said, "If we're going to be holed up in here investigating, we're going to need food."

"I have food."

"You do *not* have food. You have granola bars and cheese doodles. And three eggs, which we are now consuming. The cheese was green on the edges; I had to trim a quarter inch off the sides. And the only meat in the house has been thawed twice now in the service of your shiner." He pointed with his elbow at the hamburger package lying on the counter next to me.

"*That* needs to go in the garbage." He shoveled a big bite of cheese omelet into his mouth.

"I know that!" The 'use or freeze by' date was back in 2010 anyway. "You're here to be Robin, not critique my pantry. Talk to me more about the case."

I kind of liked the whole Batgirl thing.

Milo chewed thoughtfully.

"What we need to figure out is *motive*. Dennis and Turk are on the forensics, the lab stuff, and they can go interview people officially. Where we want to go is *inside* the killer's head."

That sounded a little less fun than Club Med.

Milo continued. "Why *hang* her? Why Anna Fuller? What does AD mean…Anna's Dead?"

"Wait, what's AD?" This was new to me.

"She had a cloth band around her upper arm, with the letters AD printed in red on it."

I pondered this without comment. I had some catching up to do.

Milo continued with his litany. "Was it random? And how significant is the crime scene? Is Plimoth Plantation part of the message, or is it just a good, creepy, isolated spot to do the deed?"

Milo forked a bit of toast, a slice of tomato, his last bit of omelet and added another bit of toast. Sandwich by fork.

"Was she sexually assaulted?" he continued. "Did the husband get pissed and then try to make it look random? Was she an heiress and now he's got the ring? *Why* did this guy do this?"

We both chewed.

"That's the sixty-four thousand dollar question, I guess," I said finally.

I tossed my plate in the sink, ran some water on it, refilled my coffee and headed back toward the living room. Milo raised a lot of good questions, the answers to which might be scary. Not to mention dangerous. But this was what I'd been itching to do.

("Time to put up or shut up, Sam," said Dad.)
"You're not going to do your dishes?"
I turned and looked back at Milo.
"Batgirl doesn't do dishes. *Robin* does dishes."
"So, Robin cooks *and* does the dishes?"
"And anything else Batgirl doesn't have the desire or skills to do. That's why Batgirl *has* a sidekick in the first place."
"I can think of some desires Robin might fulfill for Batgirl." Milo put his lips to the back of my neck. *Joinggg!* I was *not* ready for this. I lurched away from Milo, turned around and glared at him. I raised my arm and pointed at the sink.
"Dishes!"

While Milo finished the washing up, I sorted through the paperwork and studied Dennis' findings. The crime scene photos were particularly awful. Anna Fuller was about my age. She'd been an attractive blond, had a good job, was recently married. I felt tears swelling under my eyelids. *Dammit, Batgirl doesn't cry; she nails the bastard who did it.* Milo came in and was staring at the photos with me when my front door opened. Panicked, I jumped up.
"Mrs. Trimble!" I hissed.
"Sam," she called in her screechy voice. "Put your gun away, it's me…"
Milo grinned. "You pulled your gun on her?" he whispered.
"Quick! She can't see all this. Go charm her. Take her in the kitchen. *Something.*"
Milo hurried into the foyer; I was piling up papers and

turning them upside down.

"Hi, Mrs. Trimble, how are you? I haven't seen you in *ages*...Can I get you a cup of coffee? Right in here."

I grabbed my bulletin board off the wall, ran to the couch and shoved the board underneath. I did the same with the white board, then rushed back to my desk.

"Sam, Mrs. Trimble brought over some homemade coffee cake," Milo yelled. He entered the room slowly and raised his eyebrows at me. I nodded. Mrs. Trimble was crowding at his heels. At least she was dressed and wearing undergarments today.

"Good morning, Mrs. Trimble. It was so nice of you to bring coffee cake." I smiled broadly.

She looked at me and frowned.

"What happened to your face, Sam?"

Shit. I'd actually forgotten my black eye.

"I, uh, well, I guess I had a few too many last night...I banged it on the door leaving the Trap." I shrugged.

"Hmm...What's Milo doing here? He spent the night here?"

"I drove Sam home last night, Mrs. Trimble...like she said, she had a few too many. But I slept on the couch."

She stared at both of us, lips pursed.

Finally, she said, "Sam's car is out there. *And* it was out there at four-thirty this morning when I started on my coffee cake."

She waited. She looked around. She stared at my desk. I was getting ready to throw myself across it if she tried to pick up my papers.

Mrs. Trimble looked at me hard. "I don't think you drank

too much, although Lord knows your father always did, God rest his soul, and I *don't* think Milo slept on the couch."

("Always was a nosy witch," muttered Dad.)

She looked from Milo to me and back again, but neither of us said a word. "Well, I guess an old woman should just mind her own business." ("That's right!") Dad, again.

She set her coffee mug down on the end table and went out the back door.

"Thanks again for the coffee cake," I called after her. She didn't look back.

"Sheesh," I said. "The fricking devil brings baked goods."

"Wish she were right about the couch," Milo mumbled. Then he looked at me with a twinkle in his eye. "So, you pulled your gun on Mrs. Trimble?"

"Yeah, twice now."

Milo laughed. Eventually I giggled too, and Milo laughed even harder. The mental image of me pulling my nine on little old ninety pound Mrs. Trimble was hysterical, I had to admit. I turned around and through the window I could see her back in her kitchen window again, shaking her head. I jerked my head back around.

"Big Brother has blue hair," Milo choked.

After another minute, I exclaimed, "Okay, enough. We've got work to do."

Still smirking, Milo pulled a chair over and sat down next to me. My core temperature shot up by several degrees, but I ignored it. Batgirl wouldn't hook up with Robin I told myself, and anyway, I wasn't ready to hook up with anyone, especially not Milo. I repeated this to myself a few times mentally, daring Dad to comment. For once he kept his trap shut.

Milo was giving me a funny look.

"You good?" he said.

"Yep. I'm good. Let's see if there's anything up yet on the autopsy. After that we'll get an inside look at Anna and Alan's lives."

Milo raised his eyebrows again. "And how do we do that?"

"Elementary, my dear Milo. We hack their Facebook accounts."

Chapter 8

The autopsy results were in, and Milo and I paged through the scanned report. Cause of death was cerebral ischemia, or insufficient blood flow to the brain. No surprise there. There'd been no skin under her nails, and no bruises apart from around her neck. There was some chafing around her wrists where she'd been bound, and broken nails, but the medical examiner concluded there wasn't much of a struggle. She wasn't sexually assaulted.

"She knew him?" Milo said.

"Maybe....or not."

"She'd have fought if a stranger grabbed her."

"Probably, unless he drugged or stunned her," I replied. "Tox screen isn't in yet. Or maybe he just pointed a gun at her. That would be pretty convincing too."

"Would the autopsy show it if she was tasered?"

"I'm not sure; I'll ask Dennis."

Milo thought for a moment. "She was seen leaving work around six. Her car came out of the parking garage at six-twenty. Time of death is estimated at one in the morning. If it took her an hour to get back to Plymouth, then we have a gap from seven-twenty 'til one or thereabouts."

"No, Alan Perkins said she called him just before eight. He was working late; she was already home. Dennis and Turk found her work clothes on her bed. She was hanged in a jogging suit."

"So she goes jogging and the killer grabs her?"

"Maybe."

"Do the phone records rule out Perkins as a suspect?"

"Well, no. He could have made it to Plymouth from Boston before the time of death. And if it were Perkins, that might explain the lack of a struggle. *And* he doesn't have an alibi after that phone call. So, no. We can't rule him out. Not yet."

Milo leaned back. I leaned forward. It was still warm in there.

"Let's see what Anna Fuller and Alan Perkins post about on Facebook."

Anna Fuller had been a bubbly Facebook chatterer. At least once a day she posted something. There were photos of her dog, of the beach, of Alan. Some funny political shares indicated she was a liberal.

She and Alan made a handsome couple. She'd changed her relationship status on Facebook to "engaged" on the fifth of July in 2012; he must have proposed on the Fourth. She had photos of the two of them out on the Boston Harbor for the big Fourth of July celebration. The *U.S.S. Constitution*, the oldest commissioned battleship in the U.S., was brought out that year in celebration of the bicentennial of its victory in the War of 1812. Thousands attended; I remembered reading about it online.

This year she'd talked a lot about the wedding, playfully

moaning about things like her dress dilemma: strapless or halter top. In late September she uploaded a new collection with at least a hundred wedding photos. She named the album "Officially a Ball & Chain."

Anna's posts drew lots of comments and "Likes"; she was a popular woman. She had nearly four hundred Facebook friends. I think I have around thirty. Again I felt the pain of her senseless death. ("Rule #1: You can't become emotionally attached to the victim, Sam," said Dad.)

"Easier said than done," I muttered to the computer monitor.

"What's easier said than done?" asked Milo. He obviously wasn't tuned in to the Dad channel. I blushed.

"Nothing, nothing, just thinking out loud. Let's switch over to Perkins."

I tapped around a bit, but Perkins didn't even use Facebook's privacy settings. No hacking required in order to see his profile. I'd noticed in various hacking forays that a lot more women than men hid their profiles from lurkers, for obvious reasons. Too bad Anna Fuller's caution hadn't kept her safe.

Alan Perkins wasn't much of a FB talker. He had a few photos, most the same as Anna's, and he occasionally shared a political joke. He liked *Mad Men* and *Weeds*.

"Good taste in TV," said Milo.

"If you say so," I said. I usually read a book out on the deck in the evening. Austerity measures had forced me to cancel cable a year ago.

"I'm not getting the sense that this couple had problems," said Milo.

I leaned back and sighed heavily. "Well, we can't rule

Perkins out, but, it does seem as if they were disgustingly happy."

I hacked into Anna Fuller's Microsoft Outlook program at her work and we studied her emails and calendar. Her emails were mostly work related, with a few to her mother thrown into the mix. In her calendar, in addition to work-related meetings, she'd noted 'Drinks with Zeke' two weeks ago, 'dentist appointment' in a week, and 'family reunion' in late November. Not one mention of an appointment with a hangman.

"You think this could be work related?" Milo said.

"I don't know," I said slowly. "Probably not, but let's look some more at the company and the co-workers she spent the most time with."

We spent another hour on it.

Finally, I'd had enough. I stood up and stretched.

"Time to digest," I said. "Let's take a break and then look into John Clarkson and the Smits. Anna Fuller looks more and more like a random victim to me."

"A break sounds good to me," Milo said. "Maybe we can take a break up in your room?" He put his finger on my chin and tilted my head up. *Oh shit.*

"Milo, what the hell? Since when are you so interested in me?" I stepped back and glared up at him. I couldn't solve a murder *and* resist my attraction to Milo at the same time. I was only Batgirl, I wasn't super human.

"Since 1999."

I stared at him. "Yeah, right, Milo."

That was low. I'd barely seen him over the past decade and now he was trying to suggest that he'd been thinking about me all this time? I wasn't falling for it. I stormed out on the deck and then swung around, nearly crashing in to him.

"You know, Milo, it's one thing to come on to me, to flirt, to talk about sex. That's what guys do. But for you to suggest that you've been thinking about me for all these years is just insincere, manipulative bullshit. You want it that bad, go work on someone else; I won't let you fuck with my emotions, Milo Cooke." I was breathing hard and a fire was spreading through my belly. "You know what? We're done here for today."

I avoided his eyes. He reached for me and I shrugged him off and ran down the steps to the beach.

"Just go!" I yelled without looking back.

A minute later I looked back. Milo was gone.

Pepper was trailing me down the beach as I huffed along. He took off running ahead and then stopped, scratched around in the sand and raised his tail.

"Pepper, no!" I yelled, but it was too late. White Horse Beach, in Pepper's opinion, makes one dandy litter box. Now I'd have to get a plastic bag and come back before some toddler stuck his shovel in it. Or mistook it for a chocolate-covered pretzel.

"Christ, Pep," I said as he scampered up and did his sideways jump-run thing past me. Taking a dump always gave him a surge of energy.

"We've had this talk before. I didn't *want* a dog when I got you."

But despite his quirks—the occasional dump on the beach, the occasional dead mouse on the kitchen floor—Pepper was my best bud. Lately there had been whole weeks where he was the only one I talked too.

"What do you think, Pep? Was I crazy to go off on Milo like that? I mean, he did save me from that moron Tommy last night....but still."

Pepper ran ahead after some gulls.

"Hey! Are you listening to me?"

He came trotting back.

"I thought Milo was just, you know, flirting. That's what guys do, they flirt. They think about sex like eight times a minute. How could he say what he said, like he's been pining away for me since high school?"

("You're still mad he didn't try harder after Mom died," said Dad. "You secretly wish he'd stuck by you, even when you were a bitch and pushed him away.") Fucking Dad. He'd nailed it.

I picked up a small stone and tossed it up the beach. Pepper ran after it and then stood perplexed among the thousands of pebbles.

"Come on Pep," I yelled. I turned around and headed back toward home. I needed to call Milo; I owed him an apology. And I had an appointment with a cat turd.

Chapter 9

I got a plastic bag, returned to the offending spot and did my duty with the doodie. Pepper sniffed around like he'd never been there before and couldn't imagine where that little pile came from.

"You know *exactly* how that got there," I said to him. He just stared back at me with his round, yellow eyes, long black tail straight and high. He was the picture of a clear feline conscience.

"Oy vey," I muttered.

We wandered back up the beach. I wasn't sure what to say to Milo. I wanted to atone for my freak-out without making him think that he could keep hitting on me. My emotional stability was questionable; part of me was desperate to think that he and I might get together again, and the other part was scared shitless that he was just looking for a fuck-buddy. I wouldn't be able to handle that.

I was mumbling out loud, practicing what I would say when we got back to the house.

"I got food," Milo called from the kitchen.

Jeeesus! Who else wanted to let themselves into my house when the mood struck?

I stormed into the kitchen, all notions of atonement and calm adult-like behavior forgotten.

"Just what the hell—"

Milo turned from the counter and put his hands on my shoulders and looked down at me.

"Sam. Stop. I'm sorry."

I stared up into his liquid brown eyes and Goddammit, tears stung my eyelids.

"I'll stop with the come-ons, okay? I like you Sam. I've always liked you. But I shouldn't have been so pushy. Let's work together and see what else develops."

I turned my head and sniffled.

"Batgirl and Robin, right?"

I was quiet for another few seconds. Finally, I looked back at him and said, "Did Robin bring something good for lunch?"

He grinned. "Holy tuna salad, Batgirl!"

I was drying the last of our lunch dishes—I figured I could only push the sidekick thing so far—when Milo said, "Why don't we go talk to John Clarkson? In person."

"And say what? We're not official, Milo."

"We'll tell him we're freelance writers. This thing's all over the news. He won't know the difference."

I thought it over.

"I guess that could work...but I'm more interested in Charles Smit and his so-called church."

"Right, I know, but the best way for us to talk to him is to go to his church on Sunday. Which we should do. But in the meantime, let's talk to the actor."

He was right. Which bothered me a little. I wanted to drive, so to speak. But...he was right. I shrugged. "I guess so."

We reviewed Clarkson's statement on finding the body and Dennis and Turk's interview notes and Clarkson's rap sheet. He'd been arrested for assault in 1997 and his ex-wife put a restraining order on him in 1999. In 2004 he'd been arrested for DUI. Clarkson wasn't on Facebook and we didn't have a photo, so I hacked the DMV and found his driver's license.

He was forty-five and decent looking, with longish grey hair, pale blue eyes and rosy cheeks and nose. He was five ten and weighed one eighty according to his license—which put him around two hundred pounds. There's a ten percent decline in body mass whenever a person walks through the door at the Department of Motor Vehicles. It's a well-documented phenomenon.

"He says he was at the Galway Pub the night of the hanging," said Milo.

"And Liz Smit thinks he's got a drinking problem. DUI seems to confirm that."

"Would ye like a pint of bitter then?" Milo said in a terrible Irish accent.

I laughed and said, "Let me change and try to do something with this eye."

An hour later we parked along Court Street in Plymouth and headed for the Galway Pub. It was nestled among the brick shops and bars that lined the main commercial drag through town. Shamrocks dotted the sign and an Irish flag hung above the door.

A skinny woman with long, dark dyed hair and too much makeup stood out front talking on her phone. She was somewhere between thirty and sixty—it's hard to tell with sun worshipers. She wore a short pink sun dress covered by a tatty cardigan and accessorized with stilettos and an extra-long cigarette. Not exactly the image Virginia Slims had in mind.

She smiled up at Milo as we walked by, paying me no attention whatsoever. I stifled a giggle as we took our seats at the bar. He rolled his eyes, but before he could speak, Ms. Slims pushed into the bar and perched on the stool next to Milo.

"Work it," I said under my breath. I rose and went to the ladies room.

The Galway Pub was a cramped watering hole with a bar down one wall and a few small tables along the other side. The décor consisted mostly of funny Irish signs, like "When Irish Eyes are Smiling, They're Usually Up to Something" and "God Created Liquor to Keep the Irish from Conquering the World." There was no dinner menu, but a nice display of lottery tickets hung behind the bar. I wondered how often the patrons got lucky with those. Probably the bar owner was luckier.

When I came back, Virginia had removed her cardigan and her dress strap had 'slipped' down off her shoulder. Her hand rested on Milo's arm and she had her face close to his, regaling him with some story from her Miss Plymouth days. *Seriously?*

I sat, smiled, and waited for Milo to bring me into their conversation. She narrowed her eyes at me and then pulled her hand away from Milo.

"Did *he* do that to you, honey?" she asked in a husky voice. Two packs a day for sure.

61

"Oh, no! I was in a minor car accident."

"Well good. Can't stand a man who beats on his woman."

"Oh, I'm not Milo's—"

"Margie, this is Sam Warren," Milo said smoothly. "She's my…assistant. Sam, this is Margie Cooper."

I kicked Milo's shin but smiled sweetly at Margie, who, once reassured that Milo wasn't a hitter, returned her hand to his arm.

"Margie was telling me about how a bunch of the Plimoth Plantation crew drinks here. When you were in the bathroom. She knows John Clarkson, too; she says he's here most days by six."

I smiled and nodded. That meant Margie was here most days by six too. It was only four.

"I was telling her how I'm writing an article on the Plimoth Plantation murder and would like to interview some of the actors," he added.

He's writing an article?

"Well, I guess we got lucky," I simpered.

"So, like I was telling him," Margie said, "John and some of the Plantation crew was here that night. But John and Melissa—that's his latest squeeze—got into it and he stormed off early."

"Do you remember what time that was, Margie?" Milo smiled.

Margie wrinkled up her forehead and took a sip of her drink. "Well, I was outside talking on the phone when he left. Let me check my calls." She took a new iPhone off the bar and tapped expertly through the screens with inch-long blue fingernails.

Could someone please explain to me why this raggedy woman in a K-Mart dress has an iPhone and I don't? It's like the body mass phenomenon at the DMV. Indisputable. The lower a person's economic status appears to be, the higher the probability that they will own the best cell phone available. I looked at my old flip phone and sighed.

"Right, here it is. I was talking with my daughter, Terry. She called at 11:15 and we talked for ten minutes. John stormed by just as I was saying goodnight to Terry. So, around 11:25."

"Wow, thanks, Margie. I guess I owe you a drink for that." Milo called to the bartender, who was seated at the other end watching television.

"Can we have another for the lady, please? On me."

Margie beamed. I had a feeling she didn't pay for many drinks. Maybe that explained the iPhone.

"Was John here last night, Margie?" I asked.

She glanced at me then replied to Milo.

"Hell, yes, he was here last night, bragging up a storm just cuz he found that body over there. Like that makes him some kind of celebrity. He sat up here telling the story over and over again. Didn't he, Sherry?"

The bartender rolled her eyes.

"I got it memorized." In a deep, exaggerated British accent Margie said, "Got in to work at nine-fifteen like always, opened up the house and walked in as usual. Went to stow my keys and my phone in the corner and I walked right into her!" Margie snickered. "John still thinks he should have gone to work for the Royal Shakespeare Company, 'if only family obligations didn't hold me back,'" she added in the accent. We all chuckled.

My mind wandered as Margie and Milo continued talking. If John Clarkson left the pub around eleven-thirty he would have had enough time to get to Plimoth Plantation well before the estimated time of death. But that only worked if he grabbed Anna Fuller *before* going to the bar—unless he didn't come in at six that night. Anna Fuller called her husband from their condo around eight and he arrived home to an empty condo at ten-thirty.

I leaned around Milo. Margie's strap had fallen even lower and a lacy pink bra was peeking out from under her sun dress. Her cleavage was deep and brown and lined with a thousand little wrinkles. Note to self: Sunscreen!

"Margie, do you remember what time John came in two nights ago? Was he here at six like usual? Did he come in with Melissa?"

Margie gave me an irritated look but then wrinkled up her brow again. Finally, she smiled at Milo. "Actually, he got here around nine that night. His gang came in earlier, but he got here later. He was with Melissa. I just figured he and Melissa were doing the nasty."

She said this with no hint of embarrassment while looking right into Milo's eyes. Plymouth, Massachusetts, America's Home Town, otherwise known as Cougar Town USA. I still couldn't figure out Margie's age, but her blatant flirting with Milo was getting on my nerves.

I hopped off my bar stool.

"Milo, don't forget you've got that…thing. We'll have to come back later to speak with John Clarkson and the other actors." I smiled at Margie. "It was sooo nice to meet you," I added, before marching out the door.

Milo thanked Margie, gave her a peck on the cheek, threw some money on the bar and sauntered after me.

Milo had an amused look on his face all the way back to

my house, but despite his maddening smirk, I refused to take the bait. Maybe it bothered me a *little* to see Margie all over him, but I wasn't about to admit that to Milo. Not after my performance that morning. And anyway, he already knew it. We both knew it. We just weren't going to discuss it.

"So, what do you think?" I asked. "Clarkson had time to do it, unless he *was* doing the nasty with Melissa between eight and nine." I made finger quotes when I said the word 'nasty.'

"Maybe he found out he was going to get the boot. Wanted to ruin the Thanksgiving season for the Plantation. Get back at Mrs. Smit."

I twisted this around in my head.

"But if he really has a drinking problem, wouldn't he have been too shitfaced to do such a clean job? So far, forensics isn't coming up with squat. Not a single fiber or hair. We should see if the bartender remembers what he drank that night. Maybe he ran a tab."

"True," Milo said. "Or maybe it wasn't a one-man job?"

"Interesting." I said. "I've been working under the assumption it's just one guy. But you're right. Maybe there's more. Maybe it's not even a guy."

"Well, the ME said she wasn't raped, so it got me thinking again about motive."

I nodded. "Right."

No brilliant deductions came to me. Why *would* someone hang a young woman at Plimoth Plantation? And what the hell was "In the name of God, Amen" supposed to mean? We rode in silence the rest of the way home.

Chapter 10

I went out to my deck with some cheese doodles. Milo might know how to cook, but cheese doodles were a staple in my diet and that wasn't about to change just because he put some vegetables in my fridge. I sat munching and studying the waves for a couple of minutes, then brushed the neon orange powder from my fingers and called Dennis.

"Whatchya got, Nance?" he answered. I could hear Turk chortling in the background; they were in the car somewhere. He was using a hands-free device.

"John Clarkson was out drinking the night of the murder at the Galway Pub, but he didn't get there 'til nine and he left at eleven-thirty. And Elizabeth Smit is planning to fire him. I'm going to go back there tonight and mingle with the actors. Seems a bunch of them are regulars."

"Sam!"

"Don't worry, Dennis, I'm going to pretend I'm writing an article. I'll be casual, I'll ask lots of questions everybody already knows the answers to, and then see what comes up when they've had a few drinks. I'm told they're quite a bunch of drinkers."

"Hmph."

"It'll be fine, Dennis! I can do this, no problem. Whereas *you* would never be able to pull it off—they'd know you're a cop in a heartbeat."

"She be right 'bout that," said Turk. "They got yo face under 'homicide dick' on Wikipedia."

Dennis snorted. "Like you use Wikipedia."

"I be a modern detective," said Turk.

"I'll call you if I get anything good. What'd you guys get today?"

I wanted to turn the conversation away from my undercover plan before Dennis officially nixed it. As for Milo…well, I could always say we just ran into each other at the bar if it came up.

"We spent half the day up in Boston talking to her parents, co-workers and bosses. Everyone loved her; she did a good job…" Dennis sighed heavily. "Big fat goose egg is what we got today."

"Anything new on lab stuff? What about the tox screen?"

"Clean."

"And the patch on her sleeve?"

"Standard white cotton, used in sheets sold at Wal-Marts across the country. Same with the ink, any red Sharpie. The Feebs got their analysts on the 'AD.'"

"Okay, well…oh, wait. What if she got hit with a stun gun? It looked like not much of a struggle, so maybe she knew the guy. What if she were tasered?"

"Tasers leave marks and confetti all over the place. But a low voltage stun gun applied to her clothing might knock her out with no mark. We talked about it, but he could have just taken her at gunpoint."

"Okay, thanks Dennis. I'll call you." I hit 'end.'

Well that sucked. We had no way of knowing if Anna Fuller knew her killer or not.

After downing a big bowl of Trix, I scoured my closet for something that might look attractive, but wouldn't look like I was *trying* to look attractive. After living in my dad's hoodies for several years, I didn't want to be too obvious.

I stood staring into the closet for nearly five minutes.

"As Dennis would say, a big fat goose egg is what I got, Pep," I said. He opened one eye, yawned and then went back to sleep on my bed. Lotta help he was.

I settled on jeans and a collared white shirt, with a wide black belt and platform sandals. You can wear those when your date is tall. Not that this was a date. This wasn't a date; Milo and I were working. But still, he was tall.

I spent some time working the frizz, but in the end I put it back up in a clip. Humidity sucks. The eye was still partly closed, but I used some extra cover-up and hid most of the purple. I put mascara and eyeliner on both eyes. Still not great, but at least I didn't look like a Cyclops any more. I put my nine in my backpack and headed out.

I walked into the Galway Pub at five after eight. I didn't see Milo, but I did see John Clarkson and a few of the other actors I'd taken photos of yesterday morning. I took a seat at the bar and ordered a Scotch.

"So I was rushing a tad, running a bit late ya see, and I walked right into the 'ouse. Couldn't see, ya know, eyes weren't adjusted yet, and Bang! I bloody walked into 'er! Thought it was a joke, ya know, but shite, when I saw 'er eyes...And the smell!"

Margie was on the opposite end of the bar and I saw her roll her eyes. I smiled at her and she smiled back. She'd gotten Clarkson's story exactly right. She picked up her drink and walked around Clarkson's group and sidled up to me.

"Honey, you sure that boss of yours didn't slap you around none? I know a place..."

I laughed.

"I'm sure. Trust me, Milo wouldn't hurt a fly. In fact, Milo's life partner says *he's* the one who always has to kill the spiders at their place out in P-Town." Ha! *That* ought to keep Margie from baring her breasts when Milo arrived.

"Oh," she said. She took a drink. "Shame. S'always the lookers." She glanced past me and smiled. "Speak of the devil."

Milo squeezed in next to me. He was wearing a white collared shirt and jeans. *Great.* Now we looked more like the Bobbsey Twins than Batgirl and Robin.

"Ladies," he said and then ordered a beer.

Margie picked up her drink and said, "Good luck with your article," and headed over to talk with a pot-bellied, balding guy at the juke box.

Milo seemed confused as he stared after her. I giggled but kept my mouth shut. Finally he shook his head and looked down at me. "You ready to do this?"

"Yep."

He picked up his beer and approached Clarkson.

"Mr. Clarkson?"

The actor turned on his stool and studied Milo.

"Yes?"

"Milo Cooke. I'm a freelance writer doing a story on the

murder at Plimoth Plantation. I understand you found the body; I wondered if we could talk for a few minutes."

I stood and positioned myself between them.

"This is Sam Warren, my assistant," Milo added.

"Well, sure, I guess I can answer your questions. Bloody awful experience it was." He lowered his voice and leaned closer. "You can pay me for the story I presume?" The accent had morphed. Now he sounded like Frazier. Or was it Niles? Whichever one was the snootier one.

I put my hand on Clarkson's arm and smiled. Maybe the Margie Method would work here. "John…it's John right? Can we buy you a drink? I just can't wait to hear your story. And all about your work as an actor, I'm a *huge* theater fan. What can we get you?"

Clarkson looked me up and down and smiled. "Vodka tonic," he said.

I ordered his drink and said, "Why don't we sit over here at the table, then maybe after you've told us all about it, we can talk to your colleagues some. For background."

I smiled at the four others in the group. Two plump thirty-something women with pale hair and eyes looked back at me with suspicion; the two men, one about forty with greying hair and the other maybe thirty, tall and blond, smiled back with more enthusiasm.

"Would you be willing to talk to us about your work at the Plantation?"

They all nodded.

"Buy that lot a drink and they'll yammer 'til closing time," John said loudly in his British accent as he stood. The three of us moved over to a table in the corner.

Milo pulled a pen and a reporter's notebook out of his back pocket. *Nice touch, Milo.* He took a sip of his beer and leaned over the table.

"So, John, tell us everything you can. About your job, your character, and give us as much detail as possible about what happened yesterday morning."

John recited the lines he no doubt delivered dozens of times a day at the Plantation.

"My name is John Billington. I came to New Plymouth on the Mayflower in November, year of our Lord one thousand six hundred and twenty. I'm what they call a Stranger, don't have much use for the ways of the Saints—the bunch that sailed here from Leiden. They're a religious lot, always after me for my sharp tongue. But I say we came here to be rid of the strictures of government and I aim to say my mind!" Clarkson pounded the table with his fist.

"Now, that William Bradford, lives across the way from me, he can't abide my ways. He's a pious Saint and 'e's been governor of Plymouth these last six years. We quarrel frequently. Put me in the stocks, 'e did, a few times. But I say my piece, nonetheless."

I touched Clarkson's arm again. "Tell us about working at the Plantation. You don't have to do it in character, though I must say, your interpretation is genius."

He smiled broadly. "I *am* one of the finer thespians in the bunch, truth be told. Most of the others have no formal training at all. But yes, I suppose it will go faster if I just tell you what happened. Could I get another drink?"

"Of course!" I jumped up and added another vodka tonic to our tab. If Milo's wallet was as anorexic as mine, we might have an issue—but I'd worry about that later. I brought the drink back to Clarkson and sat back down.

"I've been at the Plantation for nearly ten years and I've been playing John Billington the entire time. It's been a nice job, at least until..." He shook his head. "Forgive me. Anyway, I'm on five days a week; I've been speaking my piece in that cottage for so long I can do it in my sleep. Sometimes I think I do." He laughed.

"A nice job until what?" I asked.

"Oh, nothing. I just haven't gotten on with Elizabeth Smit recently. I often don't get there early; we open at nine, but it takes the tourists some time to watch the movie at the welcome center and make their way over to the village. Usually I'm in position by nine-fifteen, nine-thirty at the latest. Yesterday I arrived at about nine-fifteen and strolled out to the village. I let myself into the cottage—"

"Do they lock them at night?" Milo asked.

"The cottages? No, we just close them up like the Pilgrims would have. So Wednesday morning, I let myself in and headed toward the corner where I put my personal things. It was a bright sunny morning, and I couldn't really see yet when I entered the dark room, but as I say, I can do this in my sleep. I'm heading to the corner, thinking something smells off, when something whacks me in the side of the head. I yelled a little and jumped back. Nothing should be hanging there; it's a low ceiling to begin with. When my eyes focus I see this woman, tied up. Her legs bent up behind her and tied to her wrists. And the face—Dear Lord, I will never forget that face. Blue skin, eyes wide open, red where they should have been white. For a split-second I thought someone was playing a joke on me, but then with the smell, and the face....I knew it was real. I ran out of there and yelled for the others. Thank God there weren't any tourists down there yet. Then I got my phone out and called Liz. Marty and I, he plays Bradford, we went back in and looked again. That's when I saw...er..."

"Saw what?" I asked with another smile.

"Oh, nothing, just the body, we could see the body better, that's all."

Dennis must have instructed him to keep the note and the patch a secret.

"So anyway, Liz showed up just a few minutes later and she sent us all up by the parking lots. She went to call the police. I gave them my statement a little while later. That's really all I can tell you; the place has been closed since. We're all hoping they'll reopen in a week or so. Thanksgiving's prime time for the Plantation and most of us need the income."

"Tell us more about Mrs. Smit," said Milo. He'd been taking diligent notes, even though we already knew most of the story. I'd been studying Clarkson. So far, he seemed believable—but then, he was an actor. He spoke like a Harvard boy but he had a troubled past. It was eight years since the DUI and closer to fifteen since the assault charge. But had he really changed? Or was he just a very good actor?

Clarkson hesitated. "You will keep your sources confidential? It might not be a good career move to speak out of turn about the boss."

Little late for that, John.

"Oh, yes, John," said Milo. "I may not even use it; the story is about the murder, after all. But I can name you as the person who found the body, right?"

"Oh yes, the papers already did. This morning I spoke with a television reporter as well."

"So, Mrs. Smit?" I prompted.

Clarkson took a big swig of his drink.

"You see, I liked her very much at first. She took the position...oh, nearly two years ago. She was enthusiastic and eager to get our—the actors'—opinions on things. She seemed to appreciate our knowledge and experience. Unlike her predecessor." He grinned at Milo. "She's quite a looker too. But over the last six months or so, she's gotten...uptight. I felt— rather, we felt—that she'd been playing us in order to learn her job. Once she knew what she was doing, she became very tiresome. I was actually written up for being late." He shook his head; his eyes were sad. "She changed."

"Do you know her husband?" I asked.

"Charles? Yes, we're acquainted. A bit of a stuffed shirt. *Terribly* religious. But I can't say I really *know* him. We've met at a few functions."

"Right, well, thank you so much for your time, John," said Milo. He closed up his notebook and put it back in his pocket.

"Might I have another drink?"

We moved together back to the group at the bar and I tried not to cringe as I put another $8 vodka tonic on our tab. I was still nursing my first Scotch.

For another forty-five minutes Milo and I chatted with the group of actors and actresses. Melissa Hopper, one of the pale, plump women, was hanging on Clarkson and threw a few nasty looks my way. The other woman, Susan Porter, was very touchy feely and hanging on Milo's every word.

It seemed every female in the free world wanted Milo.

And I spent the morning pushing him away. What the hell was wrong with me? ("Nothing wrong with taking it slow, Sam," said Dad.)

David Colter was the tall blond guy. He tried to cozy up to me, but I couldn't get too worked up about Colter's band. The NumChucks. After listening to him for five minutes, I decided the Numb Nuts would have been a better name.

The older guy introduced himself as Daniel Wakefield. He played William Brewster at Plimoth Plantation, but he said little while the rest of the group worked their moves and played their roles. When I asked about Marty, the William Bradford actor, Clarkson said Marty went out of town for the weekend, since they were, after all, on a bit of a vacation.

The group got louder and less interesting as more drinks were consumed. Finally, Milo and I excused ourselves, thanked them all and made our escape.

As we walked out the door I turned back and saw Margie speaking with Susan Porter and gesturing in our direction. Porter exclaimed loudly "You're shitting me!" and looked our way. I suppressed a giggle.

"What?" said Milo.

"Oh, nothing."

for the glorie of God, and advancemente of the Christian faith

"You know, Reggie—you don't mind if I call you Reggie, do you? No, I suppose that's the least of your concerns. Reggie, I want you to know that I have the utmost respect for academic professionals. I do. I understand that it may be difficult for you to believe me, given our present circumstances, but let me assure you, I am sincere."

Tears were streaming down Reggie's face and she moaned beneath the duct tape that was wrapped around her mouth and head. She shook her head frantically up and down, to show him that she believed him.

"There is, however, a problem that has arisen over the years. The system has taken God out of our schools. Do you go to church, Ms. Cummins?"

She hesitated only slightly, then nodded her head up and down slowly. Her eyes were wide, staring at the man in the black mask. In the dim light of the moon, his eyes appeared to glow.

"Tut, tut, Reggie. You see? Insincerity and hypocrisy are just two of the many serious problems we face in our society today. Surely, as an educator, you must acknowledge this. And yet, you hold a position where you have influence over our *innocent youth. Where your faithless choices may impact their development."*

She clawed at the ropes binding her wrists. Beneath her the bench she was seated on rose and fell gently. He'd crouched down and was lighting a fire in a metal bucket. The flames flared and then died down as a small chunk of fire starter began to burn. He added a few small pieces of wood. Then he rose and went back to his duffel bag. From it, he pulled out a two-foot long metal rod, with a wooden handle at one end and a dark metal circle at the other end. There was a solid flat triangle centered in the circle. He returned and propped the end of the branding iron in the flames and stood back.

"You are no doubt aware, Ms. Cummins, as a teacher and a local, that this nation was founded by two types of people. The Saints, whose reverence for God prompted them to seek a new land where they could establish a community founded in Christianity, unburdened by the whims of an egotistical monarch. But alas, for financial reasons, the Saints were forced to accept the Strangers amongst them. Many of these were greedy, lawless people. Godless people. As a result, today we live in a nation angrily divided. A nation where the Saints' faith and goodness has been diluted by the evil of the faithless. Where laws are made by men—and women—who make a show of loving God and then commit sin after mortal sin."

He stood silently for five more minutes. The wind blew Reggie's hair in her eyes and she closed them. When she opened them again, he was pulling the branding iron out of the fire. The end glowed a white orange.

"Ms. Cummins, these conditions are no longer tolerable. You have not only turned your back on the Lord, you have sinned

in a most base fashion. For these crimes, tonight, I fear you must die. For the glory of God, and advancement of the Christian faith."

Chapter 11

The sharp scent of the ocean wafted into my room through the open window; all was still dark on the horizon. I sat up, puzzled. I was generally an early riser, but not *this* early. Pepper lay heavy across my shins, but I was used to that.

The sound came again; my cell phone was ringing. At five o'clock in the morning? I slid my feet out from under the cat and ran downstairs, following the ringtone. Where'd I leave the damn phone? I hit the lights in the kitchen and grabbed it off the counter in time to see the call end. I checked the log. Two missed calls from Dennis.

Not good. Nervously I dialed him back.

"Sam," he said, "we got another one."

After a moment I said, "Shit."

"Yeah, no shit, *shit*. We're at the Mayflower II. A fisherman saw the body on his way out this morning. Hung her right from the mast. If you stay in the background, you can come down here and observe. From your car, Sam, *not* officially. I just wanted to let you know. You probably don't need to come down really, but—"

He sounded tired and discouraged.

"No, no, I will. I'll just put on my running clothes and jog by. See what I can see from the periphery. See who else is about in the neighborhood."

"Good, yeah. That works. I'll call ya later. Oh, and Sam?"

"Yeah?"

"Make sure you've got your gun." He hung up.

The sky was clear and the air was still warm for October. Apart from the occasional cry of a gull, my breathing and footsteps were all I could hear as I ran along Water Street around Plymouth Harbor.

The flashing blue and red lights of the squad cars near the ship were jarring against the grey backdrop of the peaceful waterfront. A few hints of light could be seen in the east over the ocean, but sunrise was still an hour away. I squinted in the dim light as I ran by, but I couldn't see anything hanging from the masts. They'd already taken the body down.

The Mayflower II is a full-scale replica of the original Mayflower. Built in Devon, England in 1957, she then sailed across the Atlantic to Plymouth in a recreation of the original Pilgrim voyage. Today the Mayflower II rests in the harbor near Plymouth Rock and, as part of the Plimoth Plantation operation, separates tourists from their money in exchange for a hands-on educational experience. Here too, costumed actors play their roles, sharing with tourists what life on board the ship was like during the Pilgrims' sixty-six-day journey nearly four hundred years ago. Occasionally, the Mayflower II still sets sail.

An ambulance was parked up on the pavement near the ticket booth and I could see a group of people huddled behind it.

I thought I recognized Turk's tall figure but it was hard to be sure. Anyway, I was here to see if anyone else was watching, not to huddle with the boys in blue.

    I had my 9 mm in the front pocket of my hoodie and I clutched it tightly. It was still dark, and there was, it was now obvious, a serial killer on the loose in Plymouth. I'd resisted the urge to call Milo; I took shooting and self-defense courses for exactly this type of work. I couldn't just call in a man every time things got sketchy. ("Well, you *could*," said Dad.) No, this was my gig, Dennis called Batgirl. Not Robin. Actually, Dennis didn't even *know* about Robin, but that was beside the point.

    I kept my face angled down but watched out from under the brim of my Red Sox cap for occupied cars or people as I ran up Water Street. I didn't see a soul until I neared the entrance to the public boat ramp, where a few fishermen and lobstermen were pulling in. I jogged in place for a couple of minutes, then turned around and ran back up the sidewalk across the road from the water. I knew *real* fisherman when I saw them.

    Water Street was lined with T-shirt shops and restaurants, bars and ice-cream parlors. On a summer afternoon this place was packed, but in early October at six in the morning it was eerily empty. I slowed to a walk when I got back to Plymouth Rock and climbed the steep steps up to where a giant bronze statue of Massasoit stood looking out over the harbor.

    What would *he* think of all this? Probably the same thing as Injun Bob. Another white guy gone crazy. I bet if he had it to do again, Massasoit wouldn't be so nice to the Pilgrims that first year.

    As I approached Carver Street, where I was parked, I heard an engine turn. I crouched down and swung around.

Below me on Water Street, a car pulled out of the semi-circular parking area behind Plymouth Rock. The car headed south on Water Street, back toward Route 3A. I was too far away to make out the plate, but it was an oldish sedan. An oldish, darkish sedan with two doors. Or maybe four. That was the extent of my knowledge of car body styles. I turned around and sprinted toward my Mini.

I pulled onto Carver Street and floored it around the sharp curves and up the hill to where Carver merged with Leydon Street. At 3A I ran the red light and turned left. I floored it again, slowing when I reached the next intersection. I looked down Water Street. No one. I hit the gas again and continued down 3A out of downtown. By the time I reached Bradford's Liquors, the light of the sun was appearing and a few more cars had joined me on the road. I slowed from eighty down to a snail-like sixty. But none of the vehicles I saw were darkish or oldish or even sedanish. I slowed down to the speed limit and continued home.

Milo was leaning on the bumper of his truck and holding a large cup of Dunkin' Donuts coffee when I pulled into my driveway. *Shit.*

"Good morning," I said cheerfully as I got out of the car. "You're bright and early today."

"Don't give me that shit, Sam." He sounded angry.

I looked up into his eyes. Yep. He was angry. I stared down at my feet.

"I guess you heard…"

"Yeah, I heard. Dad runs the police scanner every morning before he goes out. And what did *I* do when I heard there was another murder? I rushed over *here*, to get my *partner*, so we could check it out. *Together.* So we could have each other's backs. Except, this is the funny thing, Sam. You know what *my* partner did? My partner took off without me."

I stared at my sneakers. "Look, Milo, I'm sorry. Dennis called me at five this morning. I wasn't going to call you when it wasn't even daylight yet."

"Why not?" Milo wasn't angry. He was furious. "Why the hell *not,* Sam? I would have called you if the tables were turned."

His self-righteousness was getting to me. I looked up at him.

"Look, I didn't have a lot of time to think it through, okay? I threw on some clothes, grabbed my gun and went. This is, after all, *my* job, *my* career. What *I* trained to do, not you. I don't even know why you're doing this with me. Why aren't you wearing a fancy suit down on Wall Street somewhere? Having martini lunches?"

Milo's face was white. Not red. White.

"Okay, Sam. Fine. I see how it is." He shoved the coffee in my face. "Here. This was for you."

He walked around to the side of his truck, climbed in and slammed the door shut. He spun his wheels on my gravel driveway as he backed out, and then he was gone.

I walked slowly into my house and went into the living room. The room, with its paper-strewn desk and murder board and lobster-juiced sofa felt big and empty. Through my window I saw Mrs. Trimble in her kitchen. She was shaking her head at me. How the hell does she know *everything?* I locked my doors, went upstairs, lay down on my bed and cried.

Chapter 12

When I woke up, it was nearly ten o'clock. *Shit.* I grabbed my phone off the nightstand. No missed calls. None from Dennis. None from Milo either. Pepper had been curled up along my side but now he stretched. I swear that cat's more than three feet long when he stretches. Four with his tail.

I rubbed his long belly and murmured, "Back to me and you, Pep. That's all right. We were just fine before *he* came along anyway. Weren't we?"

Pepper yawned and patted my arm with his paw. I took that to mean he agreed. Or was he just humoring me?

I shuffled into the bathroom, peed and then stood in front of the sink and looked in the mirror. *Yikes!* Hat head/bed head/no makeup/puffy red crying eyes combined with one still greenish black eye is definitely not a good look for me. I started the shower.

A half hour later I was at my desk, working hard at pretending I was working hard. I kept thinking about Milo and how hurt he'd been. I'd done my hair and put on makeup. Just in case. I wondered if he was sitting home, looking his best and waiting for me to come grovel. I didn't think so. He had a Y chromosome. He wouldn't give a shit what he looked like.

I'd had a couple of thoughts I wanted to explore since I last surfed the Ether. First, I'd gotten a funny feeling about John Clarkson and "Liz" Smit, as he called her. I wanted to go back further into their emails and check His and Hers home accounts as well. And phone records. Maybe they had a thing. And maybe they didn't anymore, and maybe Clarkson was an unstable sociopath gone over the edge.

Why was he so hell bent on working this case with me, anyway? I couldn't believe that he'd really harbored feelings for me all those years. Or rather, I could believe it a *little*—I'd certainly thought about him from time to time since we broke up. But why would he pursue me now?

I wanted to see if any of my persons of interest had a darkish sedan registered with the DMV. I wanted to check out Marty, aka Martin Atherton. I also wanted to dig in on Charles Smit some more, before attending his church on Sunday. And I *would go*, with or without Milo.

I spent some time perusing the Sight Ministries web site, but a half an hour later I realized I had no idea what I'd been reading.

"Holy hell, Batgirl," I said aloud. "You're useless. Really? *Really?!*"

I stood up and stomped around the room. I went out on the deck and closed my eyes, but the smells and the sounds of the waves weren't working their usual magic. I opened my eyes and surveyed the beach. A couple stood kissing, their bare feet in the surf. *Seriously?* I hurried back inside.

Pull yourself together, Sam. I grabbed my cell phone and

tried Dennis. Maybe he could tell me about this morning's victim. No answer. *Shit. Shit. Shit.*

After another minute, I ran upstairs, put on my favorite Dad hoodie, grabbed my backpack and yelled for Pepper.

I called on the way over to make sure it was a good time. Laura sounded chipper on the phone.

"Come on up. We'd love to see you."

"You sure you feel up to it?"

"Absolutely, Sam. I've been having a pretty good week." She sounded sincere.

"I'm on my way."

Twenty minutes later we bumped down the Cooke's rutted driveway. Grady and Laura and Milo lived on the water in Duxbury, in a small, faded Cape Codder surrounded by big, shiny new McMansions that didn't even try to look Olde. The Cooke family had owned the property for generations, refusing to sell out even as the value of waterfront property skyrocketed. Grady had his own dock, and mountains of lobster traps littered the yard down by the boathouse. A few retired lobster boats teetered on cement blocks. I figured the neighbors called it "local color" when their guests commented.

I pulled up next to the house. Pepper jumped out ahead of me and trotted to the door. I knocked on the screen door, yelled "Hello" and let myself in. Pepper ran over to the Cooke's ancient Chihuahua, Lady, and licked her forehead. Lady opened one eye and lifted an eyebrow but otherwise didn't budge. She'd endured Pepper's ministrations before.

Milo looked up at me from the kitchen table. He had the

newspaper open in front of him. I walked slowly toward the table, but before I could say anything, Grady came in through the back door.

"Samantha! So nice to see you." He smiled at me and walked to the stairwell by the door and yelled. "Laura, Samantha's here." He sat down at the table. "You want a cup of coffee?"

Milo snorted. "She already had hers this morning." He looked back down at the paper.

"I'd love a coffee, Grady, thank you."

Laura came down the stairs in a bright red turtleneck and jeans. Her head was covered in a pretty, colorful scarf and I guessed she'd been up there arranging it over her still mostly-bald head. Her large brown eyes were as lovely as ever, and though she was thin, she looked a lot better than the last time I'd seen her.

I stood and hugged her. "Laura, you're looking really good."

"You mean for a bald, emaciated cancer patient? Thanks." She laughed. No, she guffawed. Laura had the biggest, loudest laugh of any woman I'd ever met. I loved that laugh. I was feeling better already.

"Well, yeah, that's exactly what I mean. But seriously, Grady says your doctor is optimistic."

Laura smiled and looked down at the table, like she was embarrassed. Or afraid to jinx it.

"Yes, the last screen was very encouraging, Sam. Dr. Hamlin thinks one more round of chemo and I'll be in the clear."

Tears welled up in my eyes. I'd been afraid to even *think* how I would react if another important grown up in my life died.

I don't actually think of myself as a grown up. Maybe by the time I'm forty.

"You have no idea how good that is to hear, Laura." I sat back down and lifted the coffee Grady'd set down in front of me. "Here's to you."

Milo was looking at Laura with a faint smile.

"I'll drink to that," he said, and raised his mug. Grady and Laura followed suit and we all clinked mugs and sat there looking pleased for a minute.

After we'd all basked in Laura's glow, she turned to me and asked, "So, what's new with you, Sam? And what happened to your eye?"

From the Cooke's dock in Duxbury I could see White Horse Beach. I tried to make out my house, but from here they all looked the same. Little grey dots. Milo and I had taken our coffee outside after I explained to Laura that I needed Milo's advice on a project. I wasn't sure she bought the story about the kitchen cabinet door colliding with my eye, but she and Grady had shooed us outside like flies.

"Look, Milo, I'm sorry about this morning. Really. I just. I need—"

"Don't worry about it, Sam. I'm sorry too. Can we get back to work now?"

Men. Always wanting to talk about their feelings and overanalyze things.

I turned to him and grinned. "Let's go."

Chapter 13

I had a mile-wide smile on my face all the way from Duxbury back to Plymouth. After just two days, I realized, it *mattered* what Milo thought and how he felt. About me. *Especially* about me.

"Shit, Pep," I muttered. "Who am I and what have I done with *Sam?*" I shook my head, but the grin stayed in place. Pepper just looked at me and yawned.

I was approaching the entrance to Plimoth Plantation. As I glanced right, I pulled my foot off the accelerator, hit the brakes and swung sharply into the driveway. Milo had said he would be about half an hour behind me; he needed to help Grady with some equipment on the boat. I might as well see if I could have a look around. I drove slowly down the shady driveway.

The yellow crime scene tape was tangled on the ground at the side of the parking lot entrance and there were a handful of cars in the lot. A uniform was sitting on the wooden steps that led into the museum; he jumped to his feet when he saw my car pull in. I pulled up next to the other cars and stepped out.

"I'm sorry, Ma'am, the Plantation's closed."

Ma'am?

"Oh, but I...I left my backpack here when...you know, Wednesday." I cleared my throat and squared my shoulders. "I work here. But my medicine is in the backpack and I need it; I can't get a refill for another week. I'll only be a few minutes." I smiled sweetly.

"I'm not supposed to let anyone in but the Director and a couple of other—"

"Look, see that building right over there?" I pointed to a random building on my left. I didn't know what it was, but I knew it wasn't part of the exhibits. "I just have to go in there; it won't take very long at all."

The uniform sighed. "Fine, just make it snappy please."

I scooted past him and up the stairs before he could change his mind. I walked quickly down the paved sidewalk, wondering how snappily I could get all the way to the Billington House. I wanted to read the crime scene, maybe try to get into the head of the killer the way my favorite fictional PIs did. I glanced over my shoulder and saw the cop watching me. I smiled and waved. Swearing under my breath, I headed toward the unknown building. With my luck it would house the HVAC system.

The heavy door closed silently behind me and the corridor grew dark. What *was* this place? It wasn't a heating system facility or a storage building, but neither did it look like administrative offices. Since it seemed snooping around the Billington House was out of the question, I'd hoped maybe I could get a look at some of Liz Smit's colleagues. See if any of them looked like serial killers.

I stood for a moment and then edged forward. About thirty feet ahead yellow light spilled from an open door on the left. I approached it, wondering just what I would say if someone should appear. In the lighted room I heard at least two people speaking in low tones. I stopped a few feet before the opening and pressed myself up against the wall. I listened for a moment but I couldn't make out the words. I leaned my head forward and stole a glance inside.

Injun Bob was standing facing away from me, speaking to someone seated at a table. The walls of the room were lined with shelves of books; it was some kind of library. Bob's substantial girth was blocking the upper half of the seated person, but there were papers and oversized tomes spread all over the table. The large feet and shoes under the table definitely belonged to a man.

I pulled my head back to the wall and tried desperately to figure out what to do next. I listened some more but the voices were too faint—until I heard Injun Bob clearly. "No problem, dude," I heard him say. "Ciao." He was approaching the door.

I rushed along the wall back toward the entrance. There was a closed door on the other side of the hall and I threw a look over my shoulder. I could see Injun Bob in the door; he'd turned back with more parting words for his friend.

I lunged across the hall. If the door was locked, I was busted. I grabbed the knob and it turned. I opened it, slid inside and pushed it closed without latching it. As I stood there shaking, both hands clutching the doorknob, I saw Injun Bob's large shadow lumber past the frosted window. I held my breath. If he even glanced to his left for a *second*, he would see my silhouette. The shadow stopped for a moment, just past the door, then continued on at its unhurried pace.

I waited a full minute and then exhaled. One millimeter at a time, I pulled the door toward me and slid my eye to the crack.

The light was still on in the room down the hall. Who was in there doing research? I pulled the door open further, thinking I'd risk one more look in the library. Just as I was about to step back out into the hallway, the light down the hall went dark and the door was pulled loudly closed. *Shit.*

Once again I lunged into my hidey-hole and pushed the door nearly shut. A few seconds later, a tall figure walked quickly by; whoever it was didn't glance my way. Once again I waited a full minute before I dared peek out. All was dark.

I crept down the corridor to the library door and tried it, but it was locked. Dejected, I wandered back toward the outside door. At least fifteen minutes had passed; by now the uniform's panties were definitely in a twist.

I'd been so close to something—or some*one*—that might be important to the case. Maybe. But instead of finding a vital clue, I was coming away with nothing. Sighing, I grabbed the doorknob and yanked. The knob didn't turn. I was locked in.

"Really?" I said out loud. This was the proverbial icing on the cake. I rushed back down the hall. Entering the room where I'd hidden, I race-walked around a conference table and looked at the windows. They were the kind you find in a high school classroom; the ones that pull in at an angle. Holding my breath, I grabbed a handle, turned and pulled. It opened. *Thank God.* But the opening was only about ten inches and the drop into the bushes below looked to be about five feet. This was going to be interesting.

I pulled a chair over to the opening and stood on it. I couldn't decide if I should try to slide out on my back or on my belly. I finally decided belly would be better. I turned around on the chair and faced away from the window. Slowly, I balanced on one foot as I slid the other through the opening. I reached behind me and grabbed the top of the window opening with one hand and the open pane with the other. Praying that the angled window pane would bear my weight, I lifted my second foot off the chair and wrangled it into the opening.

Now I was hanging by the window ledge, feet out the window and belly on the open pane. I eased myself down. My fingers were slipping; I was going into the bushes. A second later my grip released and I slid down the slanted window pane. My nose hit the trim and I saw stars. Then I was falling. Twigs and branches and sharp leaves grabbed my midriff, which was exposed now, since my shirt, like my nose, had caught on the window frame. My head and chest fell down and I caught myself with my arms just before my head bashed into the wall. I was hanging upside down between the bush and the building, the bush clutching my legs and my arms supporting me from the ground. I looked down; my nose stung as the blood rushed to my head. Carefully, I pulled each of my legs out of the bush and slid into the dirt. *Smooth, Sam.*

I sat there for about thirty seconds and then gingerly stood. I pulled my shirt down, wiped my nose on my sleeve and picked some leaves out of the frizz. I reached up and pushed the window closed, then squeezed through the bushes to the sidewalk and walked quickly back toward the entrance.

Climbing the stairs and looking down into the parking lot, I couldn't see the cop. I scanned the entire lot. No one. I turned around and jogged toward the visitor center.

The Henry Hornblower Visitor Center (Henry being

Hattie's son) was a large, modern building with a shop, a theater and a café. I figured the admin offices were in there somewhere too, and since the uniform was MIA, I had a bit more time. I skirted the entrance and headed right. About twenty feet past the doors I wiggled through the large shrubs that surrounded the building. There were three windows along the wall, just low enough that I might be able to see in.

Back to the wall, I scooted as quietly as possible toward the first. I stopped and strained to listen, but I didn't hear any voices. I turned my head and raised one eye to the corner. Fluorescent lighting shone down on a paper-strewn desk and a computer monitor that had gone into sleep mode. There was no one in there.

Ducking, I tiptoed under it and approached the second window. Now I could hear muffled voices. I froze and listened, but I couldn't make out any of the words. It sounded like a man and a woman; the woman's voice was raised at times. Must be *Missus* Smit.

I risked a quick glance. A slim woman in slacks and a professional blouse was standing in front of another desk, her hands on her hips. She had highlighted hair; her face was turned away, but it was certainly Liz Smit.

Seated at the desk was a man with greying brown hair; I recognized Aaron Stevens, the chief financial officer. He had a bit more silver around the temples than in his staff photo, but he was a handsome man, probably in his forties. He wore a chambray shirt with the cuffs rolled up.

Stevens shook his head and shuffled through a pile of papers as Smit railed about something. He pulled one out, slapped it down on the desk and pointed angrily. Stevens lifted his eyes back to Smit and I pulled back sharply. Heart pounding, I stood there for a couple more minutes, but I simply couldn't hear any of the argument. Both were obviously angry, but I had no idea why. I would have to check for new emails to see if I could find the cause of the disagreement. It probably had nothing to do with the murder anyway.

Meanwhile, the uniform down in the parking lot had no doubt issued a BOLO by now. Be On the Lookout for a suspicious looking, frizzy-haired woman running amok at Plimoth Plantation.

I slipped away from the wall, through the shrubs and rushed back to the parking lot. As I came down the steps, I still didn't see the police officer. Odd, but hey, it worked for me. I hurried over to the Mini, started it and was shifting into reverse when I heard him yell, "Hey!"

I dropped my head, closed my eyes and shook my head. Then I looked toward the woods off to the right, from where his voice had come. At first I couldn't see anything; then I saw the uniform walk out of the forest. He was carrying Pepper and his face was bright red.

"Been chasing your fucking cat for the past fifteen minutes," he said with disgust. "Might want to close the windows next time you park somewhere with a cat in the car!" He glared at me and thrust Pepper through my open window.

"I am so sorry, officer! I can't believe I did that."

"Yeah, well you did. Now get outta here." When I didn't move immediately, he shouted, "Now!"

Gulping, I said, "Thank you so much." I shifted into reverse and pulled out. Pepper curled up on the passenger seat, obviously tuckered out by his stint on the lam. As I pulled out onto the highway, I laughed out loud.

"Well done, Pepper!"

I giggled the rest of the way home.

Chapter 14

Milo was sitting in his truck in my driveway when Pepper and I pulled in. We got out and headed toward the front door.

"Were you waiting long?" I asked. I ran my hand self-consciously through the frizz, but I seemed to have gotten all the foliage out.

"Nah, stacking the traps took a little longer than I expected. I just got here."

We walked up to the door and I opened it.

"So, check this out," I said as we entered. "I stopped at Plimoth Plantation on my way home, and I wound up—"

"Well, well, well." Dennis' voice boomed from the living room. "I guess Nancy Drew decided to call in Joe Hardy? Or is this Frank? Or have you enlisted the help of both of the Hardy Boys?" Dennis leaned forward and rose from my sofa, glaring at Milo. "Who else do we have on the team?"

Pepper strolled in.

"Ah, yes."

Apparently Dennis was the newest member of the Sam's House is My House Club.

"You want to explain to me exactly what you think you're

doing, Sam?"

"Dennis!" I said it a bit too loudly. "Hi! Where's your car?"

He sat back down, crossed his arms and frowned at me.

"Dennis, let me explain," Milo began.

"No. I want *Sam* to explain. I want to know why she's chatting like some co-ed with *you* about confidential police business. I really want to hear this."

I sighed heavily. "Look, Dennis, it just happened. Milo helped me out the other night, and then he saw the paperwork—"

"Helped you out with what?"

"That prick Tommy at the Trap jumped her, that's what! If I hadn't been there, he probably would have raped her. After you drove off and left." Now Milo was angry too.

"*What?*" Dennis stood up and turned to me. "You didn't report this?"

"No, she just scared the bejeezus out of him with her gun. After I threw him off her. Then I saw the paperwork she had and… I've been helping her." Milo stared defiantly at Dennis.

I turned my head back toward Dennis. It felt a little like watching a tennis match.

"JeesusHChrist," Dennis said and sank back into the couch again. He looked at me.

"You weren't planning to tell me?"

I flushed. Since Dad died, I knew Dennis thought of me like a daughter. But I wanted to be thought of as a colleague. Maybe someday, an *esteemed* colleague. ("Gotta earn them stripes Sam," said Dad. "Can't ride my coattails.") Like I didn't know that.

"Dennis, nothing happened. Nothing much. Milo stopped

him and then I pointed my nine at him and told him to take off. I told him not to show his face there again." I shrugged. "It's done." Dennis didn't need to know about the round I'd fired off either.

"That what happened to your eye?"

"Uh...yeah. He smacked me before I could get to my gun."

Dennis shook his head. "S'a blessing your father's dead or I'd be locking him up right about now. This was a bad idea. I never should have—"

"Dennis, it wasn't a bad idea; it doesn't have anything to do with the case! And Milo and I have some good ideas. What have you and Turk got so far?"

Dennis sighed. "We got some leads, but nothing to hang our hats on yet. I brought the pictures and info on this morning's victim." He lifted an envelope off the couch and waved it at me. "Turk dropped me off and went to Dunkin' Donuts. I thought we would pow wow when he got back."

He looked at Milo. "You understand this is highly irregular and could cost me my job?"

"I understand that you involved Sam and, like it or not, I'm going to do this with her. And yes, I understand that both discretion and caution are required. I'm not particularly interested in getting killed."

Dennis stared at Milo. Milo stared at Dennis. I stared at the floor.

Just then Turk ambled in. How long would it be before Mrs. Trimble joined us?

Turk looked from Dennis to Milo to me, then back to Milo and finally to Dennis. He raised a large white bag with pink and brown lettering.

"Daaamn niggas. Ida known this was a tea party, Ida brought crumpets instead."

Dennis, Turk, Milo and I sat around my coffee table and pow-wowed. The woman hanged on the Mayflower II that morning was named Regina, aka Reggie, Cummins. The air was still cool between Dennis and Milo, but as we ate donuts and discussed details, the dialogue began to flow.

I described what I'd seen at Plimoth Plantation earlier, but no one seemed impressed, even though I left out the part about hanging from the bushes. "Whoever it was, he was in there doing research. Probably on the Pilgrims," I said with just a hint of a whine.

"That's what people *do* at the Plimoth Plantation research room, Sam," said Dennis.

"Right, but it's closed right now, so that means it was someone who works there."

"That's what people who *work* at Plimoth Plantation do," he said.

"But Liz Smit and Aaron Stevens were arguing about something."

Dennis just shook his head. "In case you forgot, there was a murder over there two days ago. The place is closed and I'm sure management is under a lot of stress. Unless they were arguing over where to hang the next body, you ain't got squat. You're lucky that uniform didn't put you in cuffs." I'd left out the part about Pepper creating a well-timed diversion.

Miffed, I let Dennis and Turk share their latest. They'd interviewed both Mr. and Mrs. Smit at length the day before. The

Smits both had alibis for the night of Anna Fuller's murder, and neither Dennis nor Turk got the feeling they were hiding anything. Milo and I planned to attend services at Sight Ministries on Sunday just the same.

"How good's the alibi?" Milo asked.

"Good enough for now," replied Dennis. "We got nothing on these people."

"There might be a partner."

"Serial whack jobs generally work alone."

"It might be the exception that makes the rule."

"It *might* be a waste of time."

"Yeah, well, it's not like we're *official*." Milo made finger quotes.

"Meanwhile, another young woman gets the noose. And actually, the Board of Selectmen decided today to offer a reward for information leading to the arrest of the Pilgrim Slayer."

"The Pilgrim Slayer?" Milo and I said together.

"This morning's paper. Fucking reporters."

I didn't want to sound shallow, but... "How much is the reward?"

"Ten thousand dollars."

"Wow."

Dennis looked at me.

"I know, I know. Don't fuck up your pension for a lousy ten thousand dollars."

Ten thousand dollars would be a *fortune* for me.

"What we *need*, Sam, is a link between the victims. There's nothing obvious. They don't look alike, work alike, know any of the same people..." He sighed. "What can you tell me about the note? 'For the glory of God and advancement of the Christian faith.'"

"That's easy, Dennis. It's in the Mayflower Compact. Along with 'In the name of God, Amen.' 'In the name of God, Amen.' is used lots of other places, *including* in the connection I found to Charles Smit." I looked at him meaningfully. "But I'd say the second message confirms it. The killer is quoting from the Mayflower Compact." I showed him my printout and explained the historical significance of the document.

"Show them the picture of the brand, Turk," said Dennis. Turk pulled a photo out of the pile on the coffee table and laid it in front of me and Milo. It showed Reggie Cummins' shoulder; the fabric of her sleeve had been cut away. On her shoulder was an angry red burn. She'd been branded with an upside down triangle inside of a circle. My stomach clenched.

"What's it stand for?" I asked.

Dennis stood. "The analysts are working on it. What I need you to figure out, Sam, is how these women were picked. We got no prints or DNA, no motive that makes any sense, and so far, no link between the vics. *That's* what I need you to find. On the *computer*, preferably. I only agreed to this in the first place because of your…"

"Understood, Dennis. We'll find the link."

Dennis looked at Milo. "*Your* job is to make sure Nancy Drew here doesn't do something stupid."

He turned back to me. "We've got extra patrols all over town and guards twenty-four seven around the Mayflower II, Plimoth Plantation, the Forefather's Monument and Plymouth Rock. But if we can't figure out the pattern soon…" He shook his head and said to Turk, "Let's go. Autopsy's in a half an hour."

For once I was glad I was unofficial.

"Find the link, Sam," he yelled, before slamming the door shut.

Milo was on the floor with papers scattered about as he read, sorted and made piles. I was at the computer, digging deeper into Reggie Cummins' life. She was thirty-two, single, and worked as a kindergarten teacher in Duxbury. She was a little overweight with short, dark, feathered hair. Kind of plain. No criminal record, not even a speeding ticket. She played a lot of Café World on Facebook and seemed rather…nerdy. Not nice to say about the dead, I know, but it takes one to know one. Café World was probably more fun than the Proctor & Gamble intranet. I cross-checked her fifty-five FB friends with Anna Fuller's three hundred and eighty-seven friends. No matches. I turned to her Wall posts.

"Sam."

"Yeah?"

"Reggie Cummins had a note in her class planner. On the fifteenth. It says, 'Zeke, 7:00.' On the thirteenth, Anna Fuller's Outlook calendar said, 'Drinks with Zeke, Wine Cellar, 7:00.'"

Our eyes met. Zeke's not exactly a common name. And The Wine Cellar was right up the road. I nodded at Milo. "I think I fancy a fine rouge this evening."

"It's a date," he said with a wink.

I flushed and turned back to my computer.

I spent the rest of the afternoon following up on loose ends. When Reggie Cummins' online presence failed to reveal anything remotely connected to Anna Fuller—or to anyone named Zeke—I turned back to the Plimoth Plantation staff for a deeper dive.

First I checked the email server for any new messages between Liz Smit and Aaron Stevens, the CFO. There were many related to the shutdown, the economic impact, and how to spin it in the media. There were some snarky interchanges—these two really didn't see eye to eye—but there was nothing that extended beyond the operational and financial effects of the hanging.

I went back further and reread several weeks of messages hoping that, now that I had new insights, maybe something I'd missed before would catch my eye. I didn't find anything untoward between Smit and Clarkson; in fact Clarkson seemed to only check his messages about once a week, if that. I still needed to find personal email addresses for each.

There were a handful of messages sent to Aaron Stevens from someone outside of the organization. The emails stopped about three weeks ago, but someone named PlymouthRocks@yahoo.com had messaged him regularly throughout the summer. The emails were sent from an Android device and said little: "Call me please?" "Hey, give me a call when you have a sec." "Talk later?". Sounded like a girlfriend. It seemed they'd broken up.

I pondered whether or not I could get the mobile phone number through the Yahoo mail server and then hack Stevens' calls for a match. It could probably be done, but it would take several steps, and breaking into the mobile carrier's system was certainly a felony. Not worth it at this point. I made a note to ask Dennis if they or the FBI had requested call logs for Smit, Stevens or Clarkson.

I went back to Sight Ministries and reread Charles Smit's

electronic correspondence for the past three months. The man was hard-core. He'd recently kicked one long-time female member out of the church after she questioned certain church precepts related to higher education for women—or lack thereof. Apparently college was a no-no for young women, although it looked to me like disagreeing with Charles was the real faux pas. After another half hour, I couldn't take anymore. I shut down my computer and leaned back.

"I'm going to hit the shower," I said to Milo.

"Nothing good?"

"Nothing as good as that Zeke connection you found."

I shuffled up the stairs. None of *my* leads were leading anywhere; Robin was starting to outshine BatGirl. And he still had perfect hair. I sighed. At least there was wine on the horizon.

Chapter 15

The Wine Cellar was, appropriately, located in the basement of a newer building on Route 3A. I jogged past it on those days when I actually did the things on my To-Do list. Dim, romantic lighting reflected off the stone walls; racks of wine bottles stood between the dining tables. A stone archway and wooden barrels completed the feeling of a French wine cellar. The menu was comprised of tapas and fancy desserts; at seven o'clock on a Friday, the trendy spot was filling up. Milo and I took a seat at the bar.

We'd brought along photos of both Anna Fuller and Reggie Cummins. Reggie's note hadn't specified a location for her meeting, but we were hoping Zeke was a creature of habit or that someone would at least recognize Anna's photo and remember her companion. I'd already searched the phone companies and DMV for Zekes or Ezekiels living in and around Plymouth, but came up empty.

I ordered a glass of Malbec and Milo had an imported beer. The bartender wasn't that busy, but he seemed to have only one gear: slow. The restaurant owner, on the other hand, was flitting about, taking orders, making drinks, running credit cards and helping the chef, who also worked behind the bar, with the food orders. This guy wasn't just hands on; he was full-body on.

"Maybe we should come back when it isn't so busy," I said, taking a sip of my wine.

"Or maybe we could just enjoy ourselves, eat some nice food, and see if something develops," said Milo.

With the case or with us? My face grew warm.

"Relax, Sam. It's Friday night. We worked all day, and we're here to work too. No reason we can't have a meal and a drink while we're at it."

"Milo, this glass of wine costs more than I have in my checking account right now. I really can't afford this." It was humiliating to admit it.

"I've got money."

"Your dad pays you that well on the boat?"

Milo snorted. "Hardly. I made some money when I was at school. I have savings and some investments. I'll buy."

Milo has savings? Investments? When did he become a grownup? We were only thirty for God's sake.

"I…uh. Okay." The wine was divine. The last time I bought wine it came in a box. If he wanted to buy it, I could force myself to drink it. "And anyway," I added, "we're going to earn that ten thousand dollar reward. I'll pay you back."

"If you insist."

Milo waited for the bartender to glance our way. A couple of minutes passed. I looked at Milo, who was politely watching the bartender watch TV. Finally, I couldn't take it.

I turned to the owner who was right in front of us putting a scrumptious looking dessert together. "Excuse me," I smiled. "Could we see some menus?"

Five seconds later, we had the menus.

"It's all about who you know," I said.

"You know him?"

"No, but I know *types.*" I swiveled my stool sideways and leaned toward Milo and spoke in a low voice. "As a private investigator, *I* am a student of human nature. And he—" I pointed my chin toward the owner, who was now on the floor taking an order. "*He* cares. He wants us to come back and tell all our friends about how great this place is.

"*That* guy—" I nodded back toward the bartender. "He's standing there drying the same glass for the last five minutes wishing he'd gone to college or won last week's Powerball or had a terminally-ill rich aunt." I took another swig of my wine.

"He *knows* we'll tip him fifteen percent on the tab whether he hustles or not. Probably twenty percent; it's just bad *form* to tip any less than that in a place like this. And since we wouldn't want to look like cheapskates, he figures we'll tip him well even if we pass out from hunger and fall off our bar stools before he takes our order." I emptied my wine glass and set it on the bar. "And you know what? He's right." I leaned back, smiled and raised my hands palms up. "Human nature."

Milo threw his head back and laughed loudly. His laugh was like Laura's, only deeper. I felt all warm inside, although that might have been the wine. The bartender turned around and looked at us for a second, then went back to drying his glass and staring at the tube. We exploded with more laughter.

While we were still giggling, the owner came over and asked, "Do you know what you'd like to have?" We both cracked up again and he gave us a funny look, but waited patiently while we sputtered out our order. I got another glass of wine. I wished

Mrs. Trimble could see me now. It seemed the two-year date hiatus was over. Or maybe I was just getting buzzed. Whatever it was, it was fun.

We enjoyed our tapas and dessert and I enjoyed a third glass of wine. All thoughts of serial killers and Pilgrims and hanged women were forgotten. We listened to the live music and when the singer said that this would be his last song, I couldn't figure out where the time had gone. I looked around. The bar was nearly empty and there were only a couple of tables still occupied in the dining room.

Milo stood. "I'll show these pictures to the owner now. Seems like he basically lives here. Maybe he'll remember something."

I smiled and nodded. I was all fuzzy inside and not anxious to think about the case. Milo wanted to work, let him work. And anyways, I wasn't sure I could balance on my heels anymore.

Milo approached the owner at the computer terminal at the other end of the bar. They talked for a few minutes and Milo took out the pictures and showed him. They talked for a few more minutes. I thought about throwing spitballs at the bartender until he offered me another drink, but decided that would be unwise considering my lips were numb. Finally, Milo came back over. He shook his head. *Shit.*

He pulled his jacket off the back of his stool and slid his arm into a sleeve. The bartender, sensing it was tip time, was right there in front of us with the tab. He laid it down and picked up the printouts Milo had laid on the bar.

"Hey, I know her," he said.

We both looked at him.

"Reggie Cummins. We went to high school together in Duxbury. She was in just a couple of weeks ago."

We grilled him for the next ten minutes. When we left, Milo tipped him twenty percent.

See?

When we got to my house—Milo drove the Mini after I mentioned my numb lips—I flopped into my chair and pulled off the high heels. I was on the down side of my buzz. Not as much fun as the ride up.

"I just wish one of them recognized Anna Fuller, but how many Zekes can there be that go to that little bar?" Milo said.

"I didn't find *any* Zekes with phones or drivers licenses around here," I reminded him.

"Well, we'll just have to extend the search to Boston. Anna worked in Boston. The killer is obviously hung up on something related to Plymouth's history. It doesn't mean he lives here." Milo was making notes on a legal pad and putting individual pages into his various piles.

"Mid-forties, maybe, salt and pepper hair. Couldn't tell his height; they were sitting on the couch. Not fat, not thin. The guy paid in cash. That's not helpful either. I shouldn't have tipped so much."

"Right," I raised my finger. "but it might mean he's the guy," I mumbled. "Hiding his tracks and all."

"*I* paid in cash, Sam. Does that make me guilty of something?"

I looked at him. "I'm quite sure you're guilty of something." I closed my eyes.

Milo didn't say anything for a second. I opened my eyes. He had a funny expression on his face, but then he smiled. "*You're* guilty of intoxication. Let's get you upstairs."

He walked over to me and took my hand. "Come on, Batgirl. Bed time." He pulled me up. I smiled at him. I reached up and put my hand on his cheek.

He shook his head. "No, no, no. Not like this, Sam. Not when you're half in the bag. Come on, let's go out on the deck for a few. You need fresh air and a big drink of water so you're not hung over in the morning."

He walked me out to the deck and propped me against the railing. The moon was nearly full and the reflections on the water rippled with the waves. I took in a deep breath of salty air through my nose and felt my head clear some.

I turned around, leaned my back against the railing and watched Milo in my kitchen. He looked good in there. He looked good *everywhere*. He filled a glass of water and then went to the freezer. I could have told him there weren't any ice cubes, but when he opened the door, he dropped the glass. It shattered and then he yelled for me. He was reaching into the freezer as I rushed back inside. He pulled something long and black out of the freezer. Last time I looked, there was nothing in my freezer, not even ice cubes.

Then it hit me. *Pepper!*

Chapter 16

"OmigodOmigodOmigod!" I was sobbing as Milo laid Pepper in my lap. I folded myself over him and rocked back and forth. He wasn't moving. Pepper was my *family!* "No, no, no, no…"

I pulled up my sweater and folded him against my skin. I could feel his ribs expand and contract, he was still breathing! I wrapped my arms around him under my sweater and stroked him.

"Pepper," I said. "Pepper, wake up. Call the vet, Milo!"

He grabbed his phone and then looked at me. "What vet?"

"I don't know, any vet! The phone book's over there."

"Oh, Pepper, what happened?" Tears were still streaming down my face. I rubbed his sides and head. "Pepper…"

He jerked. I felt his claws in my belly button and then he was out from under my sweater, shaking himself in the middle of the kitchen floor. I lunged for him.

"Pepper! Oh, Pepper, thank God. Are you okay?" I pulled him back up on my lap and he sat down. I rubbed my hands up and down his sides and back and stroked him under his chin.

"Are you getting warmer?" He lay down and curled up in a ball with his nose tucked under his tail. I continued to rub his back and sides with both hands.

"You still want me to call the vet? I found an emergency number." Milo was holding his phone and the phonebook.

"Um, I think he's okay," I said. I stroked him under his chin. He was purring.

"Milo, how could this happen? I locked the doors, right? I know I locked the doors. Who would do such a thing?"

He shook his head. "I watched you lock the doors, Sam. Where's your gun? I want to check the rest of the house."

I nodded toward my backpack on the breakfast bar. Milo dug around for a while.

"What the hell *is* all this shit? You sure there's a gun in here?"

"It's there!" I continued to stroke Pepper. His breathing seemed steady and strong.

Finally, Milo pulled my nine out of the backpack, checked the cartridge, and moved toward the stairs.

"Stay here, Sam."

I wasn't going anywhere as long as Pepper was curled up on my lap and breathing. I nodded.

Milo went up the stairs slowly, the gun down at his side. I heard the floor upstairs creak and the lights flicked on in the hallway. I heard him in the two bedrooms.

"It's clear up here," he called and then came down the stairs.

He moved back into the living room. I watched him over the breakfast bar. He checked the windows. One was open, but the screen was in place. Then he went and examined the slider.

"Whoever it was came in here. Now that I think about it, I

didn't have to unlock it when I took you outside. And I can see marks. Someone jimmied it open." He looked at me.

The one time I needed Mrs. Trimble and I was sure she was asleep.

I stared back at Milo, still stroking Pepper. "What does this mean?"

"It means I'm staying here."

At three in the morning, the swollen moon had moved toward the west, but the bright light still seeped into my bedroom. I tossed and turned. Pepper was sprawled out next to me, his paws twitching in his dreams. He seemed none the worse for his stint as a catcicle.

Somebody knew I was investigating the murders. The message was clear. *Cool it.* Cool it or someone might get dead. The only suspects we'd spoken with were the actors from Plimoth Plantation—everything else Milo and I had done was from the safety of the Ether. Unless the killer was as good at hacking as I was—highly unlikely—no one should be the wiser. Could Dennis' phone be tapped? That was also pretty unlikely, though possible. Maybe someone had followed Dennis to my house and spied. But Dennis was no rookie; he'd have noticed a tail. Mrs. Trimble would have noticed someone lurking in the bushes.

Injun Bob? He'd struck me as a little different, but not menacing. Still, he might have followed me home Wednesday. I'd been so excited, I probably wouldn't have noticed. And then there was the dark sedan I'd attempted to follow yesterday. Maybe the reason I never caught up with it was because he'd hidden and then got behind me.

I rolled onto my back and stared at the ceiling. At this point, short of checking for fingerprints on the door, there was really no way of knowing who'd broken in. And if I mentioned this to Dennis he'd send me to Disney World for a week. Or a month. Or forever. I wasn't going to tell Dennis.

Chapter 17

"You need to tell Dennis," said Milo.

I was sitting at the breakfast bar wishing I could just mainline the caffeine. I'd slept for maybe an hour. Milo was doing something that involved flour and eggs. And a pan. There was a lot of rapid movement around the kitchen. I watched in a daze. Then he pulled a bottle of syrup out of the fridge. Ah ha! Pancakes. Sam Warren, Private Sleuth Extraordinaire.

"If I tell Dennis about the break-in, about Pepper in the freezer, he'll put me on a slow boat to China. You won't see me again for a year."

"Sam." Milo looked at me severely. "This was obviously a threat. Worse, whoever did it probably didn't expect you to go in the freezer last night, since there's nothing *in* your freezer. They really wanted to kill Pepper." He set a stack of fluffy pancakes in front of me.

I pushed it back. "I can't eat right now. You have these." I stood and refilled my coffee and went to my desk.

"We have a lot of loose ends we haven't explored," I said. "One of them will tie this case up in a bow." I sat down and fired up my laptop. Then I stood and looked at the white board. I went into the kitchen, grabbed some paper towels and window cleaner, and went back to the white board. I spritzed the cleaner all over and wiped it clean.

"Let's start from the top," I said.

Milo carried his pancakes and coffee into the living room and sat down on the couch.

"We have two young women hanged in historically relevant locations."

I wrote Anna Fuller on the top left and Reggie Cummins on the top right. Under Anna Fuller I wrote Plimoth Plantation. Under Reggie Cummins I added Mayflower II. Then I wrote the two phrases from the Mayflower Compact under each. Below that I drew two little squares and filled in 'AD' in red in one and created the circle with the triangle inside the other.

"The only link we've found so far is some guy named Zeke." I wrote that in the middle of the board and drew arrows to each name above.

"We think Anna Fuller had drinks with Zeke, though we can't be one hundred percent sure since no one remembers seeing her. We know Reggie Cummins had some kind of meeting with a Zeke as well. And we know she was at the Wine Cellar two weeks ago with some average looking guy. Fuller was married, but Reggie was single, so maybe it was a date? Where does an introverted kindergarten teacher meet a date?"

I drew another arrow from the name Zeke back to the right hand column.

"She worked at the elementary school in Duxbury," said Milo.

I wrote Chandler School.

"I'm going to read the walls of all of her Facebook friends and see if I can find anything. Maybe someone set her up with

Zeke."

"Online dating," said Milo with a mouth full of pancake.

I looked at him.

"She didn't go out a lot, seemed kind of nerdy…maybe she signed up for an online dating site."

I pointed my marker at him. "Excellent thinking, Robin."

I wrote 'online dating?' beneath Chandler School.

I drew another arrow from Zeke to the white space below Anna Fuller's column.

After thinking for a minute, I drew a question mark. We didn't know what the connection between Anna Fuller and Zeke might be. She wasn't dating, and she didn't work with any Zekes or Ezekiels. This was a question for her friends, her parents or her husband. I wrote Alan Perkins/parents/friends under the question mark. I looked at Milo.

"Maybe we should attend Anna Fuller's funeral."

"I don't think Dennis would like that idea."

"I don't think we'll tell Dennis about that idea."

Milo shook his head and sighed. "You realize what all of this means?"

Did Milo just have an epiphany? Find the missing connection and figure out who the killer was?

"What?"

"You're stuck with me. Twenty-four seven. Until somebody catches this guy."

I could live with that.

Evidently, I wasn't quite as pathetic as I thought. It may have taken two years, but at least I sort of had a date last night, without the assistance of an online dating service. But then, maybe if I *had* used a service, it wouldn't have taken two years. I decided that if another year went by without a date, I would definitely try an online service. Every other single person in America, it seemed, was already signed up. I looked up at Milo, who was browsing the Chandler School web site on his laptop.

"Have you ever used an online dating service?" I asked.

He raised an eyebrow at me.

Right. Stupid question.

"Why?"

"I just had no idea how *many* services there are. Millions of people use these sites."

I pulled the sheet from my printer tray and read. "Match.com, eHarmony.com, AdultFriendFinder, Zoosk, chemistry.com, ChristianMingle.com, Seniorpeoplemeet.com, perfectmatch.com, date.com, matchmaker.com, OKCupid.com, datehookup.com, Singlesnet.com, PlentyofFish.com.

"Tastebuds.fm is for people who want to date people with similar taste in music. Ashley Madison is for *married* people who want hook-ups on the side. Compatible Partners is for same sex relationships, so are Gaydar and GayRomeo. Ourtime.com is for people who are over fifty but still too young for Seniorpeoplemeet. True.com screens its members to make sure they aren't felons."

I looked back at Milo. "Does anyone just meet in a bar anymore?"

"Every single night."

I shook my head. "This might take a while."

A half an hour later, I was trolling ChristianMingle.com's database when my phone rang. It was Dennis.

"Got something I want you to check out, Sam," he said without introduction.

"Shoot."

"Anna Fuller's mother, Charlotte Fuller, maiden name Thornton, is a member of the Mayflower Society. So she's descended from one of the original Mayflower passengers. Reggie Cummins' grandmother on her father's side was apparently *also* a member, but her mother didn't know anything about it and her dad is dead. The grandmother's maiden name was Warren, same as you. Margaret Warren. Turk called over there yesterday, but the Historian General at the library was a pain in the ass and wants a warrant before he gives us anything. I figured you might be faster than a warrant, especially since I don't got a lot to give a judge and it's Saturday."

I grinned. "You got it, Dennis; I'll call you if I find anything. Oh, Dennis?"

"Yeah?"

"Do you have bank or credit card statements for Reggie Cummins? I'm looking for charges from a dating service."

"Turk has the financials. Meet us later at the Trap."

"'Kay." I flipped my phone shut.

"What's up?" asked Milo.

"Both Anna and Reggie may have been descended from original Mayflower passengers." I didn't know why that would make someone want to kill them—there had to be millions of people in America descended from the Pilgrims—but at least it was something to sink our teeth into.

I cracked my knuckles and went to work.

Milo stood and stretched. I tried not to stare as his flexed muscles. I failed. He smiled down at me.

I felt a flush creeping up my neck and turned back to the computer. I pretended to study the screen. I was *still* trying to get into the Mayflower Society database. I'd worked in NSA sites that were easier to hack.

"I didn't ask the owner of the Wine Cellar if he has security cameras," said Milo.

I looked up at him. "Shit. He probably *does* too; he seemed like the anal type."

"And you know *types*."

I grinned. "I think we've established that. You should take a ride up there and check."

"You need to come with me."

"Milo, don't be ridiculous. It's two o'clock on a Saturday afternoon. There are people all over the beach. All over Taylor Ave. Nothing's going to happen here now."

He frowned.

"Milo, *you're* not going to get a lot off the computer, not like I can. Let me do my thing and you go do yours. You can't just sit here babysitting." I picked up my gun off my desk. "I've got my gun. And The Wine Cellar's only five minutes up the road."

"Bat Man hates guns, by the way."

"Yeah, well Batgirl likes hers just fine."

He shook his head. "Someone tried to send you a very clear warning last night, Sam."

"And if anyone walks through that door that isn't you or Dennis or Turk or Mrs. Trimble, I'll send them a clear reply. It'll sound like Bang."

121

"Tough talk."

"I'm a tough girl." Except when I'm bawling over my half frozen cat.

"Hmm."

I exhaled loudly. "It'll take you what? Twenty minutes? Just find out if they have cameras. If they do, Dennis can officially ask for the recordings."

"I can just call and ask."

"Just go look. Have a beer. I'll be right here when you get back."

Milo seemed uneasy, but finally he said, "Fine. I won't be more than thirty minutes."

He went into the kitchen and then came back into the living room with my broom. He studied the sliding door and then broke my broom over his knee.

"Hey!"

"I'll buy you another broom."

He took the broken-off handle and fit it into the runner for the sliding glass door so that it couldn't be opened.

He turned and headed toward the front door.

"I'm locking you in," he called. The front door opened and then slammed shut.

I heard the key in the lock and the deadbolt turned. I smiled to myself. It felt good to have someone worry about me. Especially when that someone was Milo. I turned back to my computer and went back to work.

Fifteen minutes later I still wasn't in. These fricking Pilgrim progeny took their privacy seriously. Why belong to a society if you didn't want to show off about it? I sighed and leaned back in my chair, mentally debating alternate workarounds.

My front door knob rattled and the hair on the back of my neck rose. I grabbed my gun. It was too soon for Milo to be back and anyway, he had the key. I rose and walked around the couch in a crouch and checked to make sure Pepper was in his climbing tree. He was curled up and sleeping in the top bunk.

I moved quickly through the kitchen into the foyer and stood pressed against the wall behind my front door. I hadn't heard the door knob rattle again after the first try. After another thirty seconds, I leaned over and looked through the peep hole. No one. I turned back toward the living room and walked slowly through the foyer with my gun raised in front of me with both hands, like they taught us in shooting school. I stopped short of going into the living room, pressed myself against the wall and then angled my head around the corner.

Mrs. Trimble was standing at the back door with her forehead pressed to the glass and her hands cupped around her coke bottle glasses. *Really?* She didn't even have any baked goods with her.

Exhaling, I slid my nine into the waist of my jeans, pulled my hoodie down over it and walked into the room. She smiled and waved.

I glanced around the room at all my murder stuff. *Shit.*
I walked over to the door and yelled through the glass.
"Sorry Mrs. Trimble, my door's broken."
"I'll just go back around front," she screeched.
Crap.
As she hobbled down the deck stairs, I grabbed my white

board and bulletin board down off the walls and slid them under the couch. I took Milo's piles and turned them all upside down. This was getting to be routine. Then I hurried to get the door.

"Hi, Mrs. Trimble."

She walked past me and headed straight for the living room.

"Sam, did you know there was somebody out on your deck here last night? After you and Milo left?"

She really does know everything.

"Did you see who it was? Someone broke in last night. That's why the back door's not working."

"You know, we never used to even lock our doors around here." Her eyes were darting around the room; I could see the mental inventory being catalogued.

"Did you see who was on my deck?"

"Well, I'd been in bed for a couple of hours, but I got up to go. That happens when you get older you know; I haven't slept for more than two hours at a time since my seventies."

"But what did you *see?*"

"Well, it must have been around eleven. I was just flushing and I looked out and I saw someone walk across your deck and go around front. It was dark, though. You really should leave your back porch light on."

"What did he *look* like?"

"I hurried into the front bedroom, but Roger was sleeping in there, so I had to climb over him. It took me a minute to get to the window. I make Roger go in the spare bedroom when he snores. Sleep apnea."

I waited. She was staring at my desk. I glanced over. *Shit.* The Mayflower Society page was still up on my monitor.

"Are you a member of the Society too, Sam?"

"Mrs. Trimble, who did you *see* here last night?"

She looked back at me. "Well, I didn't see anyone, Sam, not clearly. I'm not even sure if it was a man or a woman. By the time I climbed over Roger, whoever it was had gotten into their car and was pulling away."

I figured it was hopeless, but I asked anyway.

"I don't suppose you got a license plate."

"Oh, no, I didn't have my glasses on. I couldn't see those little numbers."

I sighed.

"But it was a white Honda Civic Coupe. The LX, either 2004 or 2005. I couldn't swear to it, but my money's on the 2004."

My jaw dropped and I stared at her. "You couldn't see the person who was walking around on my deck, which is just below your bathroom window, but you can identify their car, down to the make, model and year?"

Mrs. Trimble giggled. "I guess that's about right, Sam. Roger's always been a car fanatic; he's been taking me to shows for more than sixty years. We get Automobile Magazine, Car and Driver, European Car Magazine, Hot Rod Magazine, Luxury Auto, Motor Trend…about six more I guess, but you get the idea."

"And you *read* them?"

"Well sure. Believe it or not, Sam, I don't sit around baking coffee cake *all* day long." She had a rather smug look on her face, and I couldn't deny it—I was impressed. If only she'd been with me the other morning when I was chasing that darkish, maybe sedan.

"Could I borrow some of those magazines sometime? I should learn more about cars, too. For my work."

She looked at me shrewdly and nodded. "That would probably be wise, Sam." She stared around the sanitized room. "Well, I suppose I should be going. I just wanted to tell you what I saw." She glanced back at my computer monitor.

I had to throw her a bone. "So, are *you* a member of the Mayflower Society, Mrs. Trimble?"

"Oh yes, lifelong. I'm descended from the Howlands. You must be a Mayflower descendent too. Name like Warren and all."

I'd never really thought about it before, but her comment provided an opportunity. "You know, I'm pretty sure I am, and now that it's just me, I was thinking maybe I should establish my family's lineage. Just in case, you know, I never have any heirs…"

"Tut tut, Sam." Mrs. Trimble patted my arm. "Just because it's been two years since your last date doesn't mean you have to start thinking like an old maid. You're still a pretty girl, although I really can't understand why you insist on wearing those nasty old sweatshirts all the time."

I was tempted to tell her about my evening at the Wine Cellar with Milo, just so she'd get past that whole two-year dry spell thing, but she didn't give me a chance.

"Girls don't get married at seventeen anymore like they did in my day. I'd say you still have a year, maybe even two, to try and find Mr. Right."

Was she joking? Or did she really believe that I needed to marry by thirty-two or I'd be doomed to spend the rest of my days with a dozen or so cats? The old bird was tough to read, but I would worry about my marriage prospects some other day.

"Tell me, Mrs. Trimble, what exactly do you get as a member of the Society? I wanted to look at the web site, but I can't log in until I become accepted as a member. Could you log in and show me a little?"

"Oh sure, Sam. I have a look once a month or so, just to see who's died and whatnot."

About ten minutes later I heard Milo put the key in the front door. I jumped up, a little too quickly. "Well, Mrs. Trimble, thank you so much for showing me the site. I think I'll head over to the Mayflower Society next week and get the ball rolling."

"Is someone coming in your front door?" She looked up at me. Those sharp blue eyes looked tiny behind her thick lenses, but obviously they didn't miss a trick. "I thought you locked it."

"That's, uh, that's Milo. I gave him a key, we're…uh. Well, I'm helping him with a surprise for his mother. You know she's been ill." Nice save, Sam.

"Isn't that nice." She looked at me with a smirk, leaned over and whispered, "Hope it's not a surprise that'll need its diaper changed nine months from now." She stood to go and shook her head at me. "Hook-ups do not count as dates, Sam."

"Mrs. Trimble!"

Milo walked in, saving me from further punishment. She winked at me and said, "One or two years, Sam, remember that. Oh, and I really hope you decide to join the Society. Everyone who's a Mayflower descendant really should, you know." She smiled at Milo as she shuffled past and let herself out the front door.

"One or two years for what?" Milo had a bewildered look

on his face.

"Oh, never mind her," I said. "Woman thinks she's Betty White, that's all. What'd you find out?"

It turned out The Wine Cellar did have security cameras. Milo had ordered an import at the bar and chatted with the same slow-moving bartender who'd recognized Reggie Cummins. Not only were there cameras, but Milo also learned that recently the staff was checking the footage every time the owner wasn't around. Seemed the boss had been flirting a lot with one of the regulars and there was a running bet among the staff as to whether or not he'd get caught on tape some night after close with his proverbial pants down. The bartender had fifty bucks riding on an indiscretion before Thanksgiving.

"Did you ask him any more about Reggie and Zeke?"

"Nah, dude was way more interested in his wager. It was very 'wink, wink, nudge, nudge' if you know what I mean. I didn't want to say too much."

"Okay, I'll let Dennis know. They can get a warrant and pull the video Monday."

"Just let him know they only have about four more days to get it. The disk rerecords after three weeks. That's why the staff makes sure to check the footage often."

I explained to Milo how Mrs. Trimble had given me access to her Mayflower Society account, and sat down at my computer. I had to laugh as I logged back in. Her password was Porsche911. I had a feeling Mrs. Trimble was quite the spitfire in her day. *Hell, she still is.*

Chapter 18

Dennis and Turk were seated in a corner booth when Milo and I got to The Trap. The pool tables were busy and the gulls were in position around the bar. A cover band played in the corner and a few dancers swayed nearby. As we waited to order, the band launched into a truly awful version of The Proclaimers song, 'I Would Walk 500 Miles.'

Milo and I stared in horror as the band members marched their legs up and down in unison and belted out the lyrics in an overdone Scottish accent. Several dancers joined in the march and sang loudly along. It was an absolute train wreck. Milo and I looked at each other and cracked up.

A woman named Eileen was slinging drinks; I'd seen her there a time or two back before Tommy took over the Wednesday shift. Eileen was fiftyish with her long grey hair in a braid and an ample bosom. She had cheerful brown eyes. She leaned on the bar, placing her impressive cleavage front and center. "Evenin', folks, what's your poison?"

I tried not to stare as Milo ordered. I glanced up at him, but he was keeping his eyes firmly on Eileen's face. *Impressive self-control.* She served us and we carried our drinks over to the booth.

We shared our latest. I still hadn't cracked the Mayflower Society database, but I was close. Milo told Dennis about the video at the Wine Bar and Dennis said he'd get a copy.

"We spent the day at Plimoth Plantation, interviewing employees," said Dennis.

"Dat be one funny crew," said Turk.

"Well, Liz Smit is wound pretty tight, and some of the actors are a little nutty, but I'd be nutty too if I had to wear a Pilgrim suit all day and talk to tourists in *Ye Olde English*." Dennis chuckled and took a swig of his beer.

"Anyone stand out?" I asked.

"Not sure," said Dennis. "There's definitely something about Smit. I think half the men who work there have a crush on her. But as far as her being involved in the murders?" He shook his head. "Can't really see it. Aaron Stevens was a smooth character, but I..."

"The CFO?" I said. "His sheet's clean."

"We'll be checking alibis tomorrow," Dennis said. "They all tell a good story, but then half of them are actors."

Just then a woman in fancy designer jeans and an excess of gold jewelry came over and slid into the booth next to Dennis. "Hi, Dennis," she said, putting her manicured hand on his arm. She had a sleek brown bob and her lipstick was flawless. I guessed she was in her late forties.

Dennis smiled at her, but he looked uncomfortable. Turk was staring into his lap and his shoulders were shaking. Laughing on the inside.

"I'm Sam," I said. "And this is Milo."

"Well, hi, Sam and Milo. I'm Barbie. I'm a friend of

Dennis.'" *Barbie?* Corporate Barbie with the pantsuit maybe. "We met each other down at the courthouse."

I raised my eyebrows.

"I'm a judge," said Barbie.

Just then Eileen appeared at our table. "Can I get anyone a refill? Dennis, would you like another?" She leaned over on the table and put her girls right in front of Dennis' face. I had the distinct feeling she wasn't asking about his beer.

"*Excuse* me," said Barbie. Eileen's boobs were practically touching Barbie's nose.

Slowly, Eileen stood straight. "Sorry," she said to Barbie in a very un-sorry tone of voice.

Barbie's cheeks were red now. "I'd like a glass of white wine please. Do you have a Pinot Grigio? A 2008 if you have it."

Eileen looked at her. "We got a white and we got a red. You want the white, I take it?"

"Yes. Whatever," Barbie said and turned back to Dennis. "Dennis?"

"Sure, Eileen. Bring another round for the table if you would," he replied. "Thanks, hon," he added.

"Vulgar woman," Barbie said after Eileen left.

"Be nice, Barbie. Eileen's a friend of mine."

"What's that song? Oh, I know. 'I got friends in low places....'" she sang and then laughed. None of us joined in; we were, after all, regulars at the Trap. "Sorry," she said. "I'm just *kidding.*" She turned back to Dennis. "So how's the case? It's all anyone talks about at work now."

"It's a bitch, Barbie. That's really all I can say. A real bitch."

"Well, you know you can call me any time. Stop by for a

drink..."

Just then Eileen came back with our drinks on a tray. She put the tray down heavily and one of the beers fell over. It spilled into Barbie's lap.

Barbie jumped up. "You did that on purpose!"

"I'm just *so* sorry," Eileen said. A dark wet spot was spreading across Barbie's crotch. "Let me get you some napkins."

I grabbed my Scotch from the tray and took a gulp. This was getting good.

Eileen turned to go to the bar for the napkins and Barbie stuck her foot out. Eileen tripped and went sprawling onto another table, where more drinks were spilled. An old gull was staring down Eileen's sweater as she pulled herself up out of the mess. She came back at Barbie and pushed her. "You bitch!"

"Slut!" Barbie said and pushed her back.

"Whore!"

Dennis was out of the booth now and pulled Eileen away. "Calm down ladies. Let's just calm down here."

Barbie glared at Eileen, then she grabbed her coat. "I'll be calling your boss in the morning." She turned to Dennis. "Call me if you'd like to meet for a drink in a *respectable* establishment, Dennis." With that she stormed out the door.

The bar had grown quiet during the ruckus; now everyone laughed. I felt a little sorry for Barbie, but then, she was rather undiplomatic, especially for a judge.

Eileen shrugged out of Dennis' grasp. "Sorry, Dennis, but I can't *stand* women like that. Thinks she's so much better...I didn't really *mean* to spill the beer, you know."

Dennis looked at her with a smirk. "Not sure I believe you, darlin', but if you'll bring us another, we'll be square."

She looked down at her wet sweater. "Guess I'll go stand in front of the hand dryer," she said. She brought Turk another beer and disappeared into the ladies room. Dennis sat back down and we all laughed some more.

"Aren't you the ladies' man," I said to Dennis. "What's up with Barbie?"

"She slummin' after her divorce," said Turk. "She be tired of men in suits. Now she after a rough 'un."

Dennis shook his head. "Woman's stalking me. Yesterday she showed up where we always eat lunch. I'm gonna have to mix up my routine."

"And Eileen?" I asked. I never knew Dennis had such an active social life.

He shrugged. "We've been friends for a while."

Interesting. This was a side of Dennis I'd never seen before, but I was encouraged to learn that there was still hope for romance later in life. At this rate, I might be fifty before I figured out what I wanted. I looked at Milo out of the corner of my eye. Or rather, before I *trusted* what I wanted.

Guilty of willful murder, by plaine & notorious evidence

"It might surprise you to learn, Ms. Bishop, that abortion was commonly practiced in Plymouth Colony. Here, as in England at that time, women ended unwanted pregnancies with black root, cedar root or other common herbs. In fact, abortion drugs were widely peddled across America until the time of the Civil War; it was a very large and lucrative business."

The man shook his head and sighed heavily. He looped a length of rope around his shoulder and placed his foot on the massive tree. He wore spurs over his tall boots and he ascended the wide trunk quickly.

"You see, even the great men who founded our nation were in some matters…ill-advised. It was commonly held at that time that until the quickening—until the child could be felt moving—that the fetus was merely part of the mother, rather than a unique and blessed life."

Carolyn watched with wide eyes as the man reached the first large branch and easily scooted out. He sat comfortably astride the foot-wide arm of the giant oak about a dozen feet off the ground. He took his rope from his shoulder and looped it around the branch.

"As a matter of fact, Ms. Bishop, moral outrage with this murderous practice didn't really emerge in America until the 20th Century. Why, even the anti-abortion laws that were passed in the late 19th Century had no basis in morality."

He finished fashioning the noose and dropped it. As the rope bounced, Carolyn tried to shuffle backwards into the dense brush, but he'd bound her hands and feet securely and tied them together, wrists to ankles. She fell over and the dry leaves that carpeted the ground scratched her cheeks and filled her nostrils. Still, she tried to scoot along.

Seconds later, strong hands grabbed her and pulled her roughly upright. She tried to scream again, but her mouth was gagged with duct tape and the muted sound faded quickly in the shroud of fog that blanketed the hill.

He crouched before her, his cold, flat eyes staring into hers. "I haven't finished your lesson in morality, Carolyn. It's important to me that you understand why you're here tonight."

He stood and dragged her by her armpits under the waiting noose, then moved in front of her. He reached into a pocket and pulled out a small scrap of cloth.

"No, the doctors that championed the illegalization of abortion in the 1800's didn't care about murder or God's children. They were more concerned that midwives and charlatans were taking business away from their practices. And, because the so-called Female Monthly Pills were often highly poisonous, even fatal, the medical profession and the AMA succeeded in its campaign to illegalize abortion throughout the states."

"Eighty years later this same Godless group of men supported the legalization of abortion. But they were wrong.

Murder is a mortal sin...and abortion is murder."

The man dug in his front pocket and pulled out a safety pin. He attached the scrap of cloth to Carolyn's shoulder, and then reached for the noose that hung above her head.

"Carolyn Bishop, you are guilty of willful murder, by plaine & notorious evidence. And so tonight you will die."

Chapter 19

"*He's* scary," Milo whispered in my ear.

I turned to reply, but the angry glare of a man seated in the pew in front of us stopped me short. I looked down and studied the program in my hands. Milo reached for my hand and gave it a squeeze and I felt at once thankful for his presence and flushed with heat. That electric shock thing wasn't getting any weaker.

The Sight Ministries congregation gathered in a large, traditional white clapboard structure with a tall narrow steeple. The building was large,—I'd stopped counting at two hundred people occupying the highly polished pews—hidden by dense forest on both sides, and it backed up to Little Island Pond.

According to town records, the church owned a twenty-five acre plot with a lot of frontage on the pond. A lot of water frontage means a lot of money in Plymouth. The Ministries' books and toys and conferences—all hawked shamelessly on its web site—apparently sold well. Charles and Liz Smit lived in the "parsonage," which was on the water as well. We'd passed the large, impressive home on our way to the church. Milo's Duxbury neighbors would approve.

"Our nation is *gripped* by fear," Smit was saying. He was a tall, well-built, distinguished looking man with thick salt and pepper hair, pale blue eyes and unnaturally white teeth. He wore navy blue slacks and an Oxford shirt with a tie, but no robe, no white collar. His sleeves were rolled up. His voice was deep, at times melodic, but he raised it often with booming emotion. There'd be no napping during a Sight Ministries service.

"We feel fear over the elections. Fear over the economy. Fear over the environment and fear of terrorism." He clutched the pulpit and leaned into his microphone. Almost as one, the congregants straightened their backs and pressed forward. In a loud whisper he said, "But we no longer fear the Lord."

Leaning back, he bellowed, "Proverbs 8:13. The fear of the Lord is to hate evil." He gazed out over his audience. People were nodding and whispering Amens to themselves. He waited a moment to give the passage its full weight.

"Instead of hating evil, Americans toy with it. We toy with holidays like Halloween…"

My mind wandered as I studied the faces in the congregation. Young couples and families with a lot of children filled the pews. Some older men and women came dressed in their Sunday finest, blue hair set and comb-overs rigid with gel. There were more men than women; in fact, there weren't *any* women seated alone. Where were all the widows? I always thought church was big with widows.

I didn't see anyone that I recognized but I tried to commit faces to memory, particularly the younger men. I figured it would take someone strong to hang a woman and leave no sign of struggle behind—although Smit himself appeared quite fit for his age. I put him at about fifty.

All of the women wore somber, conservative clothing; I felt conspicuous in my stylish red dress with matching heels. I'd worn it for college graduation; it was one of only two dresses in my closet. Now I realized I should have worn my black, Dad's funeral dress.

Smit was building up to a furor again.

"Do not make light of evil! Halloween was conceived in evil. It's a celebration that uses children to promote fascination with darkness and..."

I stretched my neck and tried to get a look at the faces behind me. Immediately several angry eyes caught mine. I turned quickly forward. These people took Charles Smit very seriously.

"Halloween makes light of the very things that the Bible defines as evil. Stand against such things and the world will find you very scary indeed. But do not be afraid, friends. God *wants* you to do what is morally right. Trust him completely and never be gripped by an ungodly spirit of fear."

Smit had lowered his voice again and I sensed the thrilling climax was coming. He started in a low voice but got louder as he progressed.

"The scariest thing you can do this Halloween, my friends, is to get on your knees as parents and pray that the Lord will send you many children. Children who will fear *God*, not man. Children who will shun the glorification of witchcraft. Cultures that toy with evil end up being cultures of *death*." He gazed solemnly around the room.

"The Christian response is to be a people of *life*," he continued. "That means babies."

Babies?

"It means fearing God by honoring His command to be fruitful and multiply. It means remembering that the Scripture describes children as a blessing and a reward. Raise children that fear God more than man, and that will be answer enough to our Halloween-and-darkness-obsessed culture; for if you trust God over your womb and commit your children to a holy education, you will be very scary to the modern world."

A glaze of sweat sparkled on Smit's brow. His eyes roamed the aisles; they seemed to connect with each and every parishioner. I stifled a shudder and looked at my lap before his gaze could meet mine.

In a thundering voice, he concluded, "Come, my children, listen to me; I will teach you the fear of the Lord." He lowered his eyes, clutching his podium. "Amen."

The men parroted Smit, their Amens echoing loudly throughout the nave, but when I chimed in I got another sharp look from the man in front of me. I raised my eyebrows at Milo and glanced around the room. Only the men were responding; the women were looking at their laps or mouthing their Amens silently with their eyes closed.

Apparently Charles Smit expected the fairer sex to shut up and make babies. But those babies shouldn't go Trick or Treating; Halloween was a no-no.

My mother always took me trick-or-treating when I was young. One time in particular, when I was maybe five or six years old, stood out sharply in my memories. I'd worn layers of long underwear and two turtleneck sweaters under a cheap, cotton candy-pink *My Little Pony* costume. Mom walked me up and down Taylor Ave, making sure I said 'thank you' and chatting easily with the neighbors and the other parents out in the cold night.

We collected a pillowcase full of candy and cookies, finally returning home with rosy cheeks and burning ears. She inspected the loot and then Dad and I were allowed to eat some. I got to stay up past my bedtime. Mom and Dad had a couple of beers and there'd been a lot of laughter. I treasured that memory; there was nothing evil about it.

And even if you believed the origins of Halloween were evil, how did you make the leap from that to an obligation to procreate? It was creative, if nothing else. I watched Charles Smit some more. He was intense; his eyes darted about the room as if daring someone to challenge his word. But was Charles Smit a murderer?

Some hymns were sung—by the men—and a collection plate was passed. Milo put five dollars in the plate, for which I was grateful, although the wrinkled bill looked small next to the dozens of crisp twenties that lined the shiny brass plate by the time it reached our row.

Smit closed by reminding his flock to see a recently released Christian film in which a small town mayor valiantly takes on the ever-widening war on Christmas. *There's a war on Christmas?* I'd heard about Iraq and Afghanistan; I guess I didn't get the memo about this latest conflict.

Smit marched down the aisle purposefully, smiling and nodding to the gentlemen as he passed. When he reached our row, Smit stopped and leaned in. He spoke to Milo. "Good morning and welcome to Sight Ministries. I don't believe I've seen you here before."

"Yes, it's our first time, sir. Your sermon was very—" Milo hesitated for only a fraction of a second, but I saw Smit's eyes narrow. "—very stimulating, sir. Food for thought indeed." He paused. "This is my fiancé, Sharon...Stone. We've just moved to Plymouth."

I extended my hand but Smit stopped me with a raised hand. Still speaking directly to Milo, he said, "Women must be silent in the church, sir. You can introduce your fiancé outside, before fellowship." With that he nodded at Milo, backed out of the pew and continued out of the chapel.

After a moment, we followed. I shrugged on my long, black coat and buttoned it as we walked, avoiding the parishioners' curious glances. When we got outside Milo and I walked a little ways from the crowd, which was becoming loud and now included the voices of women as well as men.

When we were far enough away from the others for privacy, I looked up at Milo.

"Seriously? Sharon Stone? *Really?*"

Chapter 20

Milo threw his head back and laughed that great laugh. I whacked him on the shoulder.

"You know *exactly* what went through his mind the second you told him my name is Sharon Stone. What were you thinking?"

Milo's laughter finally sputtered to a stop. I stood glaring at him, waiting.

"The guy caught me off guard, Sam; it just popped into my mind." He shook his head sheepishly. "Sorry."

"That's just great, Milo. I was already the Jezebel in a red dress in there and now you've got him thinking I don't wear panties."

He smiled and raised his eyebrows. "Do you?"

I smacked his arm again, then glanced nervously toward Smit. He probably wouldn't approve of women beating on their fiancés either, although I figured Margie at the Galway Pub would be proud.

Luckily, Smit was facing away from us. Liz Smit stood beside him, along with another couple. She smiled broadly at her husband as he entertained them with wild hand gestures and, presumably, a funny story. The couple soon burst out laughing. Liz Smit chuckled and linked her arm through his, then grasped her husband's arm with both hands. She'd insisted that the emergency dispatch operator call her *Missus* Smit. Possessive? Insecure? *Both?*

But how did that fit with my theory about her and John Clarkson? Maybe it didn't. Maybe my theory was hogwash. I hadn't yet hacked into their personal email accounts to check for any personal communication, but I had no doubt that John Clarkson had spoken of Liz with a high level of familiarity.

As I stood there pondering, Milo took my hands and leaned over. "How do you want to play this, Sharon? Should we go speak to David Koresh now?"

I squinted at him but nodded. "So what's *your* name?"

Milo didn't hesitate. "Hanibal. Hanibal Fechter."

I giggled. "Seriously, Milo, we can't be obvious frauds. You can be Brian. Brian Kinney. We're from Colorado."

Holding hands, Milo and I approached the first couple of Sight Ministries. We waited politely off to the side while the minister shook hands and clapped shoulders with the other men. Milo's large hand was warm and dry, but my palm was sweating. I really couldn't put my finger on *why*, but Smit made me nervous. Maybe it was that whole possible serial killer thing, but really, it went beyond that. It was just *him*. I noticed that Smit still had little to say to any of the women who passed through his orbit. Liz Smit did a lot of smiling and nodding, basking in her husband's aura.

Finally Smit noticed us waiting and turned to face us.

Again, he addressed Milo. "So, you two are new to Plymouth. What brings you to the cradle of the nation?"

"Oh, the usual," Milo said easily. Now he'd had time to think. He put his arm around me and pulled me closer. "Sharon just got offered a great job in Boston, but we didn't want to live in the city." He laughed. "Really, we can't *afford* to live in the city, at least not until I can find a job, too. But with this economy…"

Smit frowned. "And you are…?"

"Brian Kinney, sir." He extended his hand and they shook. "It's a great pleasure; I've read a fair bit about your ministry. It's one of the things that brought us to Plymouth." Milo smiled down at me and I was surprised he didn't add, "isn't that right, dear?" I had to physically stop myself from rolling my eyes.

"Well, Brian, if you've read a great deal about Sight Ministries, then surely you understand our views, and yet…" Smit paused, a grave look on his handsome face. "I suppose you have time to find work, but you should know that we prefer to see our wives *home* with the children. Once you're married, your wife's first duty will be to serve her husband—*you*—*not* an outside employer."

Liz Smit was still clinging to her husband's arm. I wondered why *she* got to work outside the home. *Missus* Smit was tall, nearly as tall as her husband, with sleek highlighted light brown hair. She had large, round blue eyes and a long, narrow nose and neck. She was pretty, although there was a jittery, bird-like quality to her darting eyes and pinched smile. She was studying Milo. I wondered what he would say next.

He chuckled nervously. "Well, yes, of course I've read your tenets of Biblical Partriarchy, but—"

"Ah, but you see, there *are* no buts." Smit's voice was

145

excited.

He *lives* for this shit, I thought. For the fight, for the chance to demonstrate his moral superiority.

"That's *exactly* the kind of thinking that has led our society astray. God's covenants may *not* be bent for your convenience, Brian. Biblical patriarchy is a scriptural doctrine. Faithfulness to Christ requires that it be believed, taught, and lived. Not 'once you find a job' Brian. But *each and every day.*"

He turned toward me. "Ms. Stone, what is your profession?"

I felt the red creeping up my neck again. "I'm a...I work in finance." I was channeling Anna Fuller now.

"And what about your father? Do you serve him well? *This* is your duty until the day he gives you in holy matrimony to Brian."

"Oh, well, sadly, my father passed away a few years ago." The best lies often have some element of truth.

Smit nodded thoughtfully. "I see. Yes, well then, you must devote yourself to your future husband."

I smiled and gushed. "Oh, yes, I do, Mr. Smit." I leaned against Milo. "I'm completely devoted to Brian." I looked up into Milo's amused eyes. "He's my *world.* Er...along with my Lord of course."

Smit looked us both up and down for a long moment, his hooded eyelids raised with what I took to be skepticism. He wasn't convinced that we weren't black sheep. Really dark, black-as-night sheep. As we waited for Smit's response, I noticed that behind him most of the parishioners were now moving down a brick path toward a cluster of smaller buildings. The women split off toward one building while the men continued on farther.

Time for fellowship.

I wondered if we'd be invited to stay. Smit was still studying us, absorbing every detail of Sharon and Brian. I felt like I was inside one of the new airport scanners, the ones that show everything. Even panties (or lack thereof).

Out of the corner of my eye, I saw a white car pulling out onto the road from the far end of the parking area. I glanced back at the crowd moving into the fellowship halls. No one else was leaving just yet.

The day before, Mrs. Trimble had returned bearing a stack of car magazines and an Internet printout of the Honda Coupe she'd seen outside my house. It was a little bit too far away for me to be sure, but the white car heading down the church driveway was definitely maybe a Honda Coupe.

Just as Smit opened his mouth, I grabbed Milo's arm. "Honey, I nearly for*got*. We have to go visit your grandfather; he's expecting us." I looked back at Charles Smit and smiled. "Thank you for your hospitality and the wonderful sermon." I turned to Liz Smit as well. "It was lovely to meet you both. Come on, Brian." I dragged Milo away and hurried toward the parking lot.

"Well, *that* wasn't very subservient," Milo muttered as I pulled him toward the car.

"Milo, I just saw a white car leaving here that looked like a Honda Coupe. Like the car Mrs. Trimble saw Friday night. Come *on.*"

We hurried to my car. Milo went to the driver's side.

"No way, I'm driving," I said and grabbed the door handle.

"Sam..."

"Milo, move! Remember? Batgirl? Robin?"

He sighed and ran around to the passenger side and jumped in. "Charles Smit is *not* going to let you join his congregation," he said as I backed out.

"Charles Smit is a misogynistic whack job and you couldn't *pay* me enough to join his congregation. He's basically preaching that women have to stay home, wait on their husbands and make babies. We can't even *talk* in his church, for God's sake. No pun intended."

"Why don't you tell me how you *really* feel?" Milo said and laughed, but he fell quickly quiet and when I glanced over I could see no amusement in his eyes. We were silent as I pulled the Mini up to the entrance. There was nothing remotely funny about the hanging of two young women. I spun the tires pulling out of the gravel parking area and accelerated down the driveway.

Two minutes later we were still alone on the road.

Milo blew out his breath loudly. "So where's this Honda?"

"Well, there's only one way out of this place." I hit the gas and shifted into fifth. "We're going to catch up and get the plate."

We rounded the final bend in the long, curving Sight Ministries driveway a few minutes later. No white Honda. I skidded to a stop at the end of the driveway and leaned forward looking both ways down the road. Nothing white and nothing Honda Coupe-ish.

"*Dammit,*" I said, slapping the dashboard.

Chapter 21

"I'm getting into the DMV database right now," I was saying as we walked through my front door. "and looking up every single—"

"Sam." Dennis was standing in my kitchen. His thin hair was mussed and the whites of his eyes were streaked with red. I hadn't thought it possible, but the baggy pouches under his eyes were even larger. His shirt was rumpled and his khaki pants had dirt stains on them. Turk was seated at the breakfast bar and staring at an array of eight by ten photos. Crime scene photos.

I walked slowly past Dennis and stared at the pictures. In the photos, a young woman was hanging by her neck from a thick branch of a huge oak tree. Only about half of the brown leaves remained on the tree and the photo, taken shortly after sunrise I guessed, was a study in contrasts; the dark lines of the tree and the branches and the body against a light sky. The shot was artistic; pretty, in a grotesque way. Like Anna Fuller, the woman's bound hands and feet were tied together behind her back, arching her body into a reverse fetal position. Her hair was long, dark and curly and probably had been very pretty. It hung down to where her feet met her wrists, and I was reminded of a circus trapeze artist. But the bulging eyes, the protruding tongue, the blue face—that was far more horrifying than anything the makers of Charles Smit's dreaded Halloween icons could imagine. I backed away, forcing down the bile that rose in my throat. Milo put his hands on my shoulders.

"This morning?" I asked.

Dennis nodded.

"Where?"

"This is behind the Mayflower Society House, near their library. By the parking lot off Winslow Street," said Dennis. "We had extra patrols on all the major tourist spots, but this place is closed on the weekends in the fall and..." He sighed heavily. "We fucked up. We didn't have anyone there."

I touched his arm. "Dennis, there aren't enough cops in Plymouth to cover every single historic site. This whole town is historic, for God's sake."

He brushed off my arm. "I should have known. This guy's messages have to do with the Pilgrims. The Mayflower. I don't understand it yet, but we should have been covering this place."

Dennis wasn't going to stop berating himself any time soon so I changed the subject.

"What was the message this time? Was there a patch? And who is—who was she? Do you know yet?"

"Patch had a blotch of what looks like blood on it." Turk handed me a photo and then picked his notebook up off the counter and read. "The message was 'Guilty of willful murder, by plaine & notorious evidence.' 'Plaine' spelled p-l-a-i-n-e."

"But that's not—"

"It's not in the Mayflower Compact," Turk said. "Muthah

fuckah's diversifyin.'"

I hurried to my desk and fired up Google. I typed in "Guilty of willful murder, by plaine & notorious evidence." I was afraid nothing relevant would come up, but as I read the very first page a shiver ran down my spine.

Dennis, Turk and Milo had all come into the living room after me and were staring at me, waiting. They'd seen me shudder.

"It's in a page called www.mayflowerfamilies.com," I said. I read aloud. "John Billington the elder, one that came over with the first..."

I paused and lifted my eyebrows. Here was a Billington connection. "Billington 'was arraigned, and both by grand and petty jury found guilty of wilful murder, by plain and notorious evidence. And was for the same accordingly executed...'" I typed around some more.

"It's from an account of the early Plymouth Colony written by William Bradford," I said. "*Of Plimoth Plantation.* Billington was hanged on September 30th, 1630." I leaned back and looked back up at Dennis. "He was the first person executed for murder in the Plymouth Colony."

"What *is* that?" I stared at the glass in Milo's hand.

Dennis and Turk had left hours ago; for the past ten minutes Milo had been making a racket in the kitchen.

"Taste it."

"Uh... I'll pass."

"It's good for you."

I stared at the thick purple froth skeptically. "What *is* it?"

151

"It's a fruit and veggie smoothie. I brought my Nutribullet back with me when I went home to get more clothes."

"Fruit *and* veggies? In the same shake?"

"Yeah, it's got spinach, grapes, blueberries, banana, grape juice and ground sesame seeds." He took a big gulp and a purple mustache appeared on his upper lip. "Yum." He licked his lip.

I stared up at him. "That sounds gross." I grabbed a slice of the cold pepperoni pizza still lying in a grease-stained cardboard box on the coffee table. I folded it in half and shoved a third of it in my mouth. "*That's* yum," I said, chewing.

Milo shook his head with a smile. "You say so." He continued to stare down into my eyes as I chewed, and once again, a flush crept up my neck. The pizza tasted like cardboard with marinara sauce and the cold, solidified cheese wasn't breaking down. I chewed harder. I put the rest of the slice back in the box and finally managed to choke down what was in my mouth. I took a long draw on my beer, but still I didn't look away from Milo's eyes. The heat in my face was spreading down through my body. I had a mental flash of reaching up to him, putting my arms around his neck and kissing him. In the next scene he was picking me up and carrying me up to my room, romance novel style. Rhett Butler style. I shook my head. He was still gazing down at me.

"*What?* Come on, we've got a lot more to do here." I took my beer around to my desk chair and sat back down in front of the computer. "Now that Dennis is gone I can look for that Honda." I still hadn't told Dennis about the break-in Friday night.

Milo sighed, flopped down onto the couch and stared at the piles of paper and photographs surrounding the pizza box. "It's nearly midnight, Sam. I'm beat and I know you are too." He took another big sip of the purple gunk. "Let's get some sleep and start fresh in the morning. Based on the pattern, he isn't going to kill anyone tonight. Tomorrow, Dennis and Turk will be able to tell us what the autopsy showed."

Milo was right. So far, the killer had struck every other day, so with any luck, there wouldn't be another victim waiting for us in the morning. But that only gave us another twenty-four hours before he would kill again. That afternoon we'd made a lot of progress in terms of understanding the messages and who John Billington was, but we still had no good leads on the killer.

I stared at my computer screen for a moment but the DMV site's small print was swimming before my eyes.

"All right," I said to Milo finally. "You're right. Let's get some sleep." I brought Milo the pillow and blankets for his makeshift bed on the couch. As he made up his bed, I shut down my computer, organized my desk and threw away the rest of the cardboard pizza.

As I did this, I waged a mental battle. I *could* let him sleep in my bed. That couch wasn't even long enough for his six foot four frame; meanwhile, upstairs, I had my parents old king size bed. It wasn't really fair; me in that huge, comfy bed while Milo was wedged into my couch. We didn't have to *do* anything. It could be innocent. I glanced over at him, the offer on the tip of my tongue.

Pepper was in the middle of the fleece blanket on the couch and was kneading as if his life depended on it. Milo looked up at me, saw that I was watching and said, "Look. Sam's pussy *does* want to sleep with me." He laughed and disappeared into the bathroom off the kitchen.

Furious, I stomped up the stairs. Milo had just reminded

153

me why I pushed him away in the first place. He was a *man*, and men are crude and immature and have one track minds. "Just remember, Milo, Pepper's a *boy*," I yelled down the stairs.

In bed, I tossed and turned. Thoughts galloped around in my head like a herd of spooked mustangs. The sky was bright and I rose and stood for a while at my window, watching the waves advance and retreat over the glowing sand. I opened the window. I needed to breathe the air, to inhale its briny scent. At first I couldn't get Milo's stupid comment and my traitorous feline out of my mind. Pepper *always* sleeps with me.

Then I thought about Milo's lovely dark chocolate eyes and the way he'd watched me chew that pizza. The amusement in his expression. His comforting hand that morning at church. I thought about him carrying me up the stairs and the ensuing events in my Harlequin Romance fantasy. About the heat I felt every time he was near.

A wonderful, cool breeze gusted in off the sea. I lowered my face and let it blow down the neck of my t-shirt. My attraction to Milo needed to be tamped down for a number of reasons. We had work to do. He was a man. A really *hot* man— he could do better than a freckled-faced, frizz-haired hacker with next to no income. He hurt me once before. And now I could add the purple gunk to my list of reasons to stay away from him. *Spinach and grapes and sesame seeds?* I would stick with my cheese doodles, thank you very much.

Finally, I closed the window and returned to bed. Rather than drift off, however, I lay awake, rethinking everything we'd uncovered that afternoon. We now knew that the Billington house wasn't a random choice at Plimoth Plantation. Somehow the killer was equating these women to America's first murderer—and punishing them in the same manner.

John Billington came to Plymouth on the Mayflower with his wife Elinor and two sons, John and Francis. He signed the Mayflower Compact. Ironically, the Billingtons were one of few Mayflower families to survive intact that first winter in Plymouth. While only one passenger died during the Mayflower's two month journey to "Northern Virginia," by the spring of 1621 more than half of the original settlers had perished due to illness.

But the entire Billington family lived to become a frequent source of strife in the settlement. Even Elinor was whipped and put in the stocks once, on charges of slander. Governor Bradford and Billington clashed frequently in those early years, as Billington railed against the Leiden Church and its influence in the new colony. In a letter Bradford sent to England in 1625 the governor called Billington a 'knave.'

When Billington was found guilty of shooting and killing John Newcomen after a fight in a tavern five years later, Bradford consulted with the leaders of the neighboring Massachusetts Bay Colony before ordering Billington hanged. According to Bradford's lengthy hand-written record of the colony's early years, *Of Plimoth Plantation*, he was advised that Billington 'ought to dye, and the land be purged of blood.' To this day, Billington's descendants proclaimed his innocence and cited Governor Bradford's animosity as the reason behind his wrongful execution. By most historians, however, Billington was considered the United States' first murderer.

Chapter 22

"Sam, get your ass down here; we got something." Dennis' voice entered my mind from a distance. "Sam!"

I sat up in bed. The sun was bright outside my window and Dennis' voice was loud at the bottom of the stairs. Both were jarring.

"Sam, get up! I ain't got all day."

"Coming," I called, scrambling out of bed and heading to the bathroom. The case was screwing with my sleep patterns. It was nearly two when I fell asleep this morning; normally I'd be out by eleven and back up around seven. It was going on nine.

I brushed my teeth and threw the frizz into a ponytail. My shiner had nearly faded; just a hint of yellow and green remained around my eye. I washed my face and put on mascara. Redheads need mascara no matter *what* the occasion; skimpy blond eyelashes are just not a good look for anyone. I threw on a Dad hoodie and some jeans and scurried down the stairs.

Dennis, Turk and Milo were in the kitchen. Self-consciously, I made my way between the three men and poured myself a cup of coffee. I had always been a morning person, but a morning *people* person? Not so much. I stirred in cream and sugar, turned around and leaned against the counter, blowing into the steaming liquid. Dennis was pulling some paperwork out of his briefcase. Turk was leaning against the sink and Milo had taken a seat in one of the stools at the breakfast bar. Once again, Milo's hair was perfect. How did he *do* that?

Finally I said, "Well? I'm up. What you got?"

"This is the autopsy report on Carolyn Bishop," said Dennis. He handed me the paperwork. "She was twenty-seven, lived over in Manomet. She was a paralegal in town.

"How'd—"

"Wait," Dennis interrupted. "This is the important part. She had an abortion recently. Probably within the past month."

He waited for me to react. I took a sip of coffee and turned this around in my mind.

"Okaaay. I guess that explains the blood on the patch. But how does that tie to John Billington?"

"Some people think abortion *is* murder, Sam. Maybe these women are being punished, like John Billington, for murder. We found the paperwork in her desk; we know what clinic she used. We're heading over there now to see if we can find anything. See who works there. See if Fuller or Cummins were ever patients. Then we'll talk to the families; try to find out if either of them ever had an abortion."

"The ME didn't put anything about abortion in his reports on Fuller or Cummins," I said. I had those reports memorized.

"No, but the doc says it wouldn't be something they would see unless it happened within the past few weeks. The body would be back to normal by about a month afterwards."

"So the killer's going to hang every woman in Plymouth who's had an abortion?" I said incredulously. "That's crazy. It's impossible. And their families may not know if they did have an abortion. That's not something everyone shares with Mom and Dad."

Dennis shook his head and sighed. "It's all we've got right now."

I thought about the religious angle. "*If* you're right, it still brings us back to Charles Smit—"

"Not necessarily, Sam. A *lot* of religious folks are opposed to abortion. Remember Brookline?" I'd been a kid at the time, but I remembered. A religious, anti-abortion extremist had shot and killed the receptionists at two different clinics on Beacon Street.

"Yeah, but Dennis, most pro-lifers aren't crazy enough to kill over it. And what about Fuller's patch? And Cummins's brand. If the blood on Bishop's patch means abortion, or murder, then the other two must stand for different crimes. Or *sins*. Smit is an extremist; just yesterday he was preaching about how women should make lots of babies. He told me *my* duty is to stay home and serve my husband. Not to have a career. Maybe *that's* why Anna Fuller was targeted."

We were all quiet for a minute.

"Sheet," said Turk. "Ma woman don stay home an serve me. They any sisters in that church?"

I glared at him.

He shrugged. "Just axin.'"

I knew for a fact that Turk had a lovely, intelligent girlfriend; an impressive woman who was doing her surgical residency. But his sarcastic humor was ill-timed.

"It fits," I insisted. I looked at Milo. "Back me up here, would you?" I was getting frustrated; it seemed so obvious to me. I looked back at Dennis. "Smit, or his so-called church, has *got* to be in the middle of this."

"Sam, we told you, Smit's clean. He—"

"Then someone else in that church. One of his followers has gone off the deep end. *Something.* There has to be a link."

Finally, Milo spoke up. "They're definitely an extreme group. If it's not Smit, it could be someone else in the church."

Thank you. I turned back to Dennis. "It makes sense. It fits."

He shook his head. "Smit has followers all over the country, and it *could* be anyone within a hundred mile radius, for all we know at this point," said Dennis, snapping his briefcase closed. "Bastard's careful too. We got one rogue hair off Carolyn Bishop during the autopsy. That's it, from all three vics, and it probably came from someone she worked with." He stared down at his scuffed loafers for a moment. "You two keep at it. Until we know for sure what the connection between these three women is, we haven't got a prayer of catching this guy. And he's due to strike again. Tonight." He pulled his briefcase off the bar, turned and headed for the door.

Turk set his coffee mug in the sink and looked at me. "Sorry," he said. "I say some dumbass shit sometimes. I don't mean it."

I smiled half-heartedly and rubbed his arm. "I know, Turk. And I get bitchy sometimes." I shrugged. "It happens." *It's just how we deal with crisis.* Milo shuts down, Turk spews stupid ghetto shit and I turn into a raving bitch. Dennis just gets more intense, which is saying something.

"Happens when there's a murderin' muthah fuckah in our town," said Turk. "We gonna nail his ass, Sam."

I looked up into Turk's eyes, so serious for once.

"Damn straight, Turk."

He nodded, turned and followed Dennis out the door.

"We need to find Zeke. If we can find a Zeke linked to Carolyn Bishop, he's our guy. We need that video and we need a Sight Ministries membership list." I downshifted and slowed for a group of seniors shuffling across the road with their tote bags and chairs. After a chilly weekend, the early October air had grown warm again and the retirees were headed for one last day on the beach with their newspapers and paperbacks and thermoses of coffee. Or martinis, for all I knew.

I studied them as they passed. Their faces were light; their demeanor, carefree. They had done their time. Made their money, paid for their homes, raised their kids. Their skin was saggy and their hair—what there was of it—was white. But they looked happy. *Relaxed.* I wondered if I'd ever reach a point in life where I didn't worry over when the next payday would come. Over how to pay the property taxes. I wondered how saggy my skin would be by the time I got there. Assuming I did get there. Lost in my private pity party, it took a moment for Milo's next words to register.

"You need to get into the Mayflower Society database, Sam. See if Carolyn Bishop was also a descendent. See if *any* of them were descended from John Billington," Milo said quietly. "Or all of them."

I looked over at him. Milo was in the passenger seat; Pepper was standing on Milo's thigh with his front paws on the window, watching the parade of seniors. A couple of them saw Pepper and smiled and pointed. Dogs rode shotgun all the time, but a cat staring out a car window was a novelty.

"Milo, that's it!"

"Maybe, maybe not. There are thirty million Americans descended from the Pilgrims. That's nearly ten percent of the entire *U.S.* And it doesn't explain the badges or the brand."

Milo smiled and gave the laughing seniors a salute. Pepper was staring down suspiciously at a scruffy little grey dog trotting alongside the group.

"I guess it doesn't really tie in with Dennis' abortion theory. *Or* Charles Smit," I said and sighed audibly. "Or maybe it does. I just don't know anymore."

There were simply too many loose ends in this case. So much more to coax out of the Ether—from the white Honda to John Clarkson and Liz Smit's communications, to finding Reggie Cummins on a dating site. We needed to figure out the AD and the triangle. I wanted to hack into local abortion clinics now too, to see if Anna or Reggie showed up in any of the records. But we'd decided to attend Anna Fuller's funeral this afternoon in Boston, which meant I only had a couple of hours before I needed to shower and dress. Impatiently, I watched as the last of the blue hairs entered the crosswalk. I was *decades* away from leading their leisurely life.

I was cranky. I reached into the waxy white bag beside me, pulled out two donut holes and shoved them into my mouth. We'd been to Dunkin' Donuts. After Dennis left, I threw a mini-tantrum when Milo wouldn't let me take Pepper for our morning ride. He'd finally acquiesced, but insisted on coming along. He was still in bodyguard mode. Then, all Milo ordered was an egg white flatbread, which made me even crankier. I grabbed another Munchkin. He would probably whip up another disgusting smoothie when we got home. There was something called kale in my refrigerator. What the hell was kale anyway? It looked like spinach on steroids.

Finally, I accelerated on down Taylor Avenue; the seniors were now holding up progress on the stairs down to the beach. A minute later we were approaching my house and I gasped.
Mrs. Trimble was standing at the end of my driveway wielding an aluminum baseball bat.

Chapter 23

"He just left, Sam! The white Honda guy. I chased him off your deck." Mrs. Trimble was panting and her stance was downright scary. The bat was resting on her shoulder but she looked ready to knock one out of the park. I stared at her in shock.

"Don't just stand there, Sam, go get 'im!" she screeched. Milo, Pepper and I had all jumped out of the car when I pulled up to the curb.

"Take Pepper inside, Milo. I'll be right back." I dove back into the car and took off before he could stop me.

I floored it around the corner at the end of Taylor Ave, praying there weren't any octogenarians or mothers with strollers in the crossing ahead. I flew past the post office and the general store and rounded the next bend. I caught a glimpse of brake lights just before they disappeared, about a quarter mile in front of me. I didn't even have my backpack, meaning I didn't have my gun, but I wanted that plate number, pedestrians be damned. I was pushing sixty mph now.

A few beachgoers on the sidewalk yelled at me as I flew by, but I kept it floored. The bicycle cops stopped covering the beach in September; as long as I didn't hit someone, it would be fine. I continued up the hill, rapidly scanning both in front of me as well as passing driveways. I hadn't seen a white car yet. As the road leveled off, I pulled myself up by the steering wheel, praying for the Honda to be there ahead of me. It wasn't. I slowed a little, but by now I could see nearly all the way to the light at 3-A.

When I got to the light, I cut a slow turn in the ice cream shop parking lot and studied the cars. Then I crossed the road and checked out 7-11 and Walgreens. *Nothing.* It was like the guy had an invisibility cloak. Maybe *he* was Batman.

Finally, I headed slowly back down White Horse Road. I turned onto each side street and trolled the cul-de-sacs as I worked my way back down the hill. Only one street off White Horse Road continued out of the neighborhood; apparently, White Honda Dude had taken it. I spent another twenty minutes riding through the quiet back streets in search of the elusive Honda, but it was no good. He'd gotten away again.

Dejected, I pulled back onto White Horse Road and headed down toward Taylor Ave. As I was turning onto my street, my phone rang. Milo.

"Thank God." Milo exhaled loudly. "What happened? Where are you?"

"I'm almost there, Milo. I'll see you in a minute." I hung up and threw the phone into the passenger seat. Who was I kidding? I sucked at this. Maybe I should consider beauty school. But I sucked at beauty, too.

Milo and Mrs. Trimble were sitting on the back deck. Milo stood when I opened the door. I shook my head at him and sank into a deck chair.

Out on the beach, happy people were tossing Frisbees.

Collecting seashells. Seeing them made me even more depressed. Tears welled in my eyes.

Milo sat back down and said, "Tell her what you got, Mrs. Trimble."

The old woman looked at me. "Well, I'm sorry I didn't get more, Sam, but I did see part of the license plate before he got away," she said. "I was wearing my glasses this time."

I sat up. "You did? What was it? Was it a Massachusetts plate?"

"Yes, Massachusetts. First three were 828. I think. Or maybe it was 82B. But then, I guess it could have been B28. But that's what I saw, hopefully that helps." Mrs. Trimble was remarkably calm for a ninety year-old who'd just chased someone with a baseball bat.

"That *definitely* helps," I said. I jumped up and ran inside for a notebook and pen. I snagged the Dunkin' bag off the counter and rushed back outside. Quickly, I unwrapped my sausage, egg and cheese bagel and shoved a quarter of it in my mouth. Chewing hard, I wrote down the various combinations Mrs. Trimble had given me. Now I had him. That mother fucking, cat freezing bastard was *mine*.

I swallowed and said, "Okay, start at the beginning for me. Tell me exactly what you saw. Everything that happened. *Every detail.*"

An hour later I was standing wrapped in a towel in front of my closet. It was pushing noon and Anna Fuller's funeral was at one thirty. I figured we needed an hour to get to Boston and another half hour to find the cemetery. Driving in Boston was always a crap shoot.

I looked at my Dad's funeral dress. It was a very classy, simple black dress and I had a great pair of black heels that I could just about walk in to wear with it. But the thought of putting it on again bothered me a little. It brought back memories I didn't want to revisit. ("Get over it Sam, I'm still with you in spirit," said Dad.)

"Yeah," I whispered, "and you're still a pain in the ass." I smiled as a few tears spilled down my cheeks. He was right, of course. It was just a dress. I pulled it out of the closet, scavenged in my drawer for pantyhose, and got dressed.

A few minutes later I had myself pulled together. I'd even broken out the makeup bag and added some smoky grey eyeliner, a hint of blush and lipstick to go with my standard mascara. The face in the mirror looked a little strange to me; I vaguely recognized her from my NSA days. I couldn't decide if she was cute or clownish. ("Cute," said Dad). He was probably biased, but I went with it. I hobbled down the stairs.

Milo was working on his laptop on the couch. He was wearing a charcoal grey suit with a lighter grey shirt and a maroon and black paisley tie. His hair was combed and his chin was freshly shaved. He looked amazing. I stood in the doorway staring at him. When he turned and looked up at me, that familiar flush worked its way up my neck.

"What?" I finally said.

"You look nice."

"Thanks," I mumbled and went to my desk. "You, too." I grabbed my backpack. I didn't own a cute little bag to go with the dress, but I figured I could leave the backpack in the car at the cemetery. "You ready?"

"Yeah. But I was thinking. Maybe we should take Pepper somewhere in case White Honda Dude comes back when we're not here."

I looked at Pepper. He was lounging in the middle bunk of his tree, his paw casually slung over the side. He stared at me with his placid yellow eyes.

"Excellent idea, Robin. But where?"

"We could take him to my house, but I'm not sure we have time before the funeral."

I looked through the window at Mrs. Trimble's house. "We can take him to your place later this evening. I'll call Mrs. Trimble for now." She was turning out to be a valuable team member after all.

A few minutes later we stood waiting for Mrs. Trimble to answer her door. I was holding Pepper away from my dress and he was squirming. Milo carried a bowl of kibble and an improvised litter box. I knew there was a reason I kept that aluminum roasting pan after Thanksgiving three years ago.

Mrs. Trimble opened the door and squinted at the cat through her coke bottle lenses. She didn't look thrilled.

"I, uh, I really appreciate you letting me leave him here," I said, following her inside. "We'll pick him up around four or four-thirty." I set Pepper down. He strolled over to the kitchen cabinets and worked his paw behind the door. Pepper loves to spend time in the cabinets; sometimes he sleeps curled up in my frying pan.

In about five seconds, he had a cabinet door open and was halfway in. Mrs. Trimble grabbed him and, holding him far away from her chest, carried him out to the living room. There she had a plastic toddler corral set up, probably something she kept for her grandchildren (great-grandchildren?). She put Pepper inside the pen, which was about three feet high. He looked up at her quizzically, then gracefully jumped out and proceeded to use the leather couch as a scratching post.

"No, Pepper!" I cried. I crouched down and carefully removed his claws from the leather. I picked him up and turned back to Mrs. Trimble. "Maybe this wasn't such a good idea." I took in her expensive furniture.

"Do you have an office or a guest bedroom?" asked Milo. "We can just shut him in; it's only for a few hours."

She nodded. "Follow me."

We went through the dining room and came to a closed door. She opened it and the pungent scent of cigars wafted out. Mr. Trimble was lying in a recliner in a blue velour track suit. He was puffing on a stogie and watching a soap opera on television. *The Young and the Restless.* I knew because Victor looked the same as he did twenty years ago, when I was ten and tuned in all summer long.

Mr. Trimble took the cigar out of his mouth and looked us over.

"Roger, Sam's cat is visiting for the afternoon. I want him to stay in here with you," said Mrs. Trimble.

Milo set the roasting pan litter box in the corner and the kibble a few feet away. I put Pepper down. He stood motionless for a moment, then jumped up on Mr. Trimble and kneaded his substantial belly. Pepper can spot a soft belly a mile away. Mr. Trimble stared down at him for a few seconds and then tentatively scratched Pepper's chin with his free hand. The cigar was still spewing toxins from his other hand but I figured now would be a bad time to mention the dangers of second-hand smoke.

"Are you sure this is all right?" I asked.

"What's his name?" asked Mr. Trimble.

"Pepper," I said.

"Well, as long as Pepper doesn't mind watching my stories, he can stay. But I'm in charge of the remote," he said to the cat. "Understood?" Pepper continued to knead. Soon, I knew from personal experience, Pepper would probably start drooling. At least Mr. Trimble didn't have boobs. It really hurts when Pepper kneads your boobs.

Mr. Trimble looked up at us. "We'll be fine," he said. "Now scram, I'm trying to find out whether or not Phyllis is going to leave Nick for Ronan." Mrs. Trimble rolled her eyes and we filed out of the den, leaving Mr. Trimble and Pepper to their soaps.

Ten minutes later Milo and I were cruising up Route 3. It was a beautiful, warm fall day and I was enjoying the moderate traffic, weaving in and out of other cars and trucks. As I drove, I made a mental list of questions I wanted to ask if we got a chance to talk with Alan Perkins. Number one was whether or not he knew Zeke or how Anna knew someone named Zeke.

"Don't do anything crazy, Sam," said Milo. "But there's a white Honda that's been behind us since we hit the highway."

Chapter 24

I looked in the rear view mirror and then checked my side mirror. "Where?" I asked. My heart was pounding.

"He just pulled into the right lane behind the red pickup. Four cars back," Milo replied. "I noticed it about a mile after we got on the highway. He's been staying back, but following your moves."

My knuckles were white on the steering wheel and my palms were growing damp. I pulled into the left lane to pass again and sped up a little. We were doing about seventy down the two-lane highway. The speed limit was sixty-five. As I accelerated around a service van, I saw the white car pull out.

"I see it," I said. "Can you see the plate? Does it start with 828?"

"It hasn't gotten close enough for me to see. I'll watch; *you* keep your eyes on the road," said Milo.

The highway opened up and I gave it more gas. I wanted to force the guy to have to catch up, to test whether or not he was actually following us. It wasn't like white Hondas were uncommon; it could easily be a coincidence. I was pushing eighty now. I got past the last car in the right lane and pulled in front of it.

"Should I take the next exit?" I asked. I looked in the mirror again. The white Honda was passing now, still a couple of cars back.

"Not yet," said Milo.

"Can you see what the driver looks like?" I glanced in my side mirror again, but the Honda had returned to the right lane; there was an SUV between us now. The gap between the Mini and the SUV lengthened.

"He's wearing sunglasses and a hat."

"Get my gun out of my backpack," I said. Milo leaned between the seats and pulled my backpack into his lap. He dug around for a moment and pulled out my nine.

"It's loaded?"

"Always," I replied. "Safety's on. Leave it on for now," I added. I didn't know how much experience Milo had with guns, but my experience was limited to the firing range. I didn't want to put our combined lack of skill to the test unless necessary.

The distance between my Mini and the SUV behind me was now about one hundred feet. The white Honda was still behind it.

"The North Pembroke exit is next," I said. "I'm going to take it. If he follows, I'll pull into the shopping mall and we'll nail him."

"I really don't think the killer would follow us in broad daylight," said Milo, glancing over his shoulder. The Honda was still behind the SUV.

"I don't give a shit *who* it is," I said. "He put Pepper in the fucking freezer!" My anger, fueled by adrenaline, was boiling up. I was coming up fast on a mini-van. I cut into the left lane.

The speedometer read eighty-five. Now I could see several cars in front of the mini-van, and the exit was only half a mile away.

"Watch this," I said, and stepped harder on the gas. I pulled past the van. Five seconds later, I was passing a big delivery truck. "Is he trying to follow?"

"Not ye—yes. He just pulled into the left lane. He's gaining on us."

There was one last car in front of the delivery truck, a red Mazda Miata. The exit was a quarter mile away. I floored it, pushing the Mini up to ninety. I passed the Miata just as we got to the exit. I yanked the steering wheel hard to the right and we cut across in front of the little car and careened onto the exit ramp.

"Did he follow?" I asked breathlessly as I downshifted and fought to keep the Mini from flying off the long curved exit ramp. I looked quickly at Milo. He was clutching the 'oh shit bar' in one hand and still had my nine in the other. He looked like he was holding his breath.

Finally Milo exhaled and looked back through the seats. "Yeah, I don't know how he got through those cars, but he's coming round the bend now. Plate looks—*shit*."

"What?" I yelped. "He have a gun?" I was getting ready to floor it again.

"No. But there's a Statie right behind him. Lights blazing."

"Are you out of your fucking *minds?*" Dennis was roaring.

I caught Turk's eye in the rear view mirror; it looked like he was trying not to laugh. Dennis, however, was not even remotely amused.

"Do you know how many favors I had to call in just to get you out of there? Excessive speed, reckless endangerment, the gun—"

"I have a permit, Dennis!" They couldn't cite me for that one.

"I cannot *believe* you didn't tell me about the break-in Friday night. We're after a serial killer; you think this is some kind of cops and robbers *game*? Fuck sake Sam."

"I'm sorry, Dennis," I said quietly. "I'm really sorry. I should have told you." I stared at my lap. I was afraid of what he'd say next. Like, "you're off the case."

Dennis leaned around the seat and glared at Milo. "And *you*! You were supposed to keep her in line." They stared at each other. Milo didn't avert his eyes and he didn't apologize.

Finally, he said, "I've done my best to keep her safe, Dennis. Twenty-four seven. She made the decision not to tell you about what happened Friday night and I respected that. I *did* ask her to tell you. But it was Sam's house. Sam's cat. Sam's decision."

Thanks, Milo. But it was the truth.

"Dennis, you can't blame—"

"Shut up, Sam."

I blinked and stared out the window. We were in the back of Turk's Lincoln, leaving the Troop D station house in Middleboro. They were taking us back to North Pembroke, where my car was still parked at the Ninety Nine.

Three hours earlier, on the way *into* Middleboro, Milo and I had been cuffed in the backseat of the state police cruiser. Along with Roald T. Harrington, aka, Tommy, from the Trap.

He'd broken into my house Friday night; *he* was the one who put Pepper in the freezer. While he was there, Tommy saw the murder board and decided he could use the ten thousand dollar reward. He'd been following us around ever since. Based on his rap sheet, and our statements, they'd kept him in custody.

I sighed heavily. Dennis' tirade had finally ended and the only noises in the car were the sounds of traffic on the highway. The sun was low in the sky. We'd missed Anna Fuller's funeral. I stared at the colorful foliage as we left Middleboro. Tonight, another woman might lose her life in Plymouth. I almost wished my stalker *had* been the killer. At least then it would be over. One way or the other.

Forty minutes later we pulled into the Ninety-Nine and Turk pulled up next to my car. I waited for Dennis to speak, but he said nothing.

"So, uh, can we have a look at the tape from the Wine Cellar?" I couldn't help myself.

"Team already looked at it," Dennis said gruffly. "The guy with Reggie Cummins was out of view almost the entire time; they were only there for about forty minutes. Sitting behind a column. All we can see is his lap and his hands. He was wearing khakis. No rings. Kept his back to the camera when they were leaving. Hair was darkish but it's a black and white film. Can't tell if it's brown or grey."

"Oh." I was at a loss.

"Just go home, Sam. Do your thing on the computer and leave the rest to the professionals."

Blinking back tears, I climbed out of the car.

Thirty minutes later we pulled into my driveway. "You want to take Pepper over to my parents' house now?" Milo asked. It was nearly five o'clock.

"That's not really necessary now, is it? Tommy's behind bars; the killer wasn't here." I turned to him. "But you should go see your mom and dad. You've been with me here for days."

"You sure?" Milo looked doubtful. *Disappointed?* Either way, I was on a mission.

I nodded. "I'm sure. I'll probably be up on the computer all night anyway. I'm going to get to the bottom of this. It's that church, or an abortion clinic or the Mayflower Society. One of those places holds the key. I'm not going to quit until I figure it out." I grasped his hand. "Thanks, Milo. For everything. Go home and see your family tonight; sleep in a real bed. Pepper and I will still be here in the morning."

Milo looked me in the eye, and then abruptly leaned in and kissed me softly on the lips. I was still sitting there stunned as he got in his truck and pulled away.

The General Society of Mayflower Descendants was established in Plymouth in 1897 to honor the memory and values of the Plymouth Colony founders. There were fifty state organizations as well as the founding society based in Plymouth. Membership was through the state societies; in order to become a member, you had to document your lineage back to one of fifty-one original Mayflower passengers who survived the first winter in Plymouth.

The Society stopped publishing its membership logs fifty years ago, but with Mrs. Trimble's password I was able to move freely through the site; from there I finally was able to get to the internal databases, which contained all of the state member lists and archival data.

I found Margaret Warren in short order. She was descended from John Howland, Richard Warren and John Billington. I felt butterflies in my stomach. Reggie Cummins was descended from Billington.

A few minutes later I found Charlotte Fuller. She was descended from both Howland and Billington as well as John Alden, John Cooke and Samuel Eaton. So Anna Fuller was also descended from Billington. *Yes!* Now I just needed to figure out if Carolyn Bishop was too.

I leaned back, stretched and stroked Pepper, who was curled up in my lap. It was nearly eight o'clock and I hadn't eaten. I put Pepper on the floor and went to the kitchen. A nice variety of fresh food filled the fridge, thanks to Milo, but that would require preparation and I'd sent the chef home. I stared at the bunch of kale for a moment and struggled not to think about the kiss. I was getting tingles and they were *not* in my face this time. I closed my eyes for a second and then slammed the door shut. I grabbed some granola bars out of the cabinet.

I didn't have time to waste; I had to find *something*. I had to redeem myself with Dennis. Three women were dead and I'd not only wasted Dennis' time this afternoon, I'd wasted his chits, something cops hold dear. I was determined to find the link between John Billington and the victims and Zeke or Charles Smit or whoever this maniac was, even if it took all night.

I put a cup of kibbles in Pepper's dish and went back to my computer.

Carolyn Bishop had a Facebook page, but it didn't look like

she'd been there in months and I couldn't identify any family members. This was going to take some doing.

For the next eight hours I hacked my way through Ancestry.com, Archives.com, and county, state and national census data. I found birth records, marriage certificates and death certificates, most of them hand-written. By four o'clock in the morning I'd worked my way back to the early 1700s; I'd documented ten generations of Carolyn Bishop's ancestors and printed off the supporting documents. And then I found her. Carolyn's great-times-eight grandmother on her mother's side, Mary Cordelia Smith, born in 1719 in Providence, Rhode Island, was listed in the Mayflower Society archives. She was descended from four different surviving Mayflower passengers—including John Billington.

I texted Dennis and Milo. I didn't care if it was four in the morning. "All 3 vics descended from Billington - confirmed," I typed and hit send.

I leaned back and exhaled heavily. There was so much more to do, but I was exhausted and seeing double. I grabbed Pepper and stumbled up to my room. I was asleep by the time my head hit the pillow.

For the generall good of the Colonie

"I assume that you are unaware, Ms. Roberts, that in the early days of the Colony, the ordinaries were established strictly for the benefit of travelers passing through. Of course most Colonists made beer at home for their own consumption. But they were prohibited from drinking in the taverns and anyone who became 'drink drunk' was fined or put in the stockades."

She shrieked through the duct tape that he'd wrapped around her mouth. Sweat was dripping down her forehead and burning in her eyes. She'd fallen over on the cold floor and she squirmed and scooted as far as she could, but there were racks and display cases everywhere. If only she could make enough noise! She threw her head back and smashed it into a tall metal card display that wobbled and then fell on top of her. Lying there covered in envelopes and greeting cards, Margot fought to catch her breath. Above her, dozens of decorative cut paper stars glittered eerily in the dim night light that came through the plate glass windows at the front of the store. If there was anyone outside, they hadn't heard the commotion.

The man in black shook his head. "Was there really any need for that, Margot? No, I don't think so. We both know you won't be leaving here tonight."

Margot moaned as he placed a milk crate on the display case and then climbed easily up. He moved an acoustic ceiling tile aside and tossed a heavy rope over some piping above. He took the end of the cord and looped it around itself.

"Our founders went astray some years later." He continued his story as if he hadn't been interrupted. "Swayed by the excise taxes they collected, they began to allow everyone to frequent the ordinaries. God-fearing men and women were corrupted in these dens of evil, and that corruption now runs rampant across the nation. Today drunken antics are considered a rite of passage and are tolerated with amusement. Encouraged even."

"But I dare say you have no idea of the heavy price of alcohol abuse on our nation today. Allow me to enlighten you, Ms. Roberts. Excessive alcohol consumption kills 79,000 people annually and costs our society $225 billion. Each year. Lives are ruined. It's a disgraceful legacy to the righteous intentions of our forefathers."

"And yet you, you who stands so proudly in support of vile, unholy practices like abortion and homosexual unions, each night you go and happily serve alcohol to your friends and customers. As if you're providing a vital community service."

He climbed down off the counter and stood over her, his hands on his hips.

"Ms. Roberts, you've chosen to spend your golden years in pursuit of sin. From your blasphemous cardboard placards to the very way in which you earn your living, you demean the legacy of the Colony and you commit treason against the laws of our founding fathers. In response, for the generall good of the

Colonie, tonight you must die."

Chapter 25

"They're all descended from John Billington," I said as I walked into the kitchen. "You got my text?"

"Yeah," Milo said. He was scrambling eggs. The scent had awakened me; it was nearly nine o'clock. Five hours of sleep would have to do; I was on a roll. I grabbed a coffee mug out of the cabinet and filled it.

"He wants to cleanse Plymouth of sinners, of Billington's evil descendants. Like Carolyn Bishop, who had an abortion." I hopped up on a bar stool and stirred sugar into my coffee. "Maybe the…."

Milo was pulling toast from the toaster with a frown on his face. I wasn't sure he'd even heard me.

"Milo?"

He looked over at me. "Sorry, Sam. I'm listening." He buttered the toast. He was wearing an old sweat suit and his hair wasn't combed. My bad habits were rubbing off on him.

"Is something wrong?"

He stopped buttering, but didn't reply.

"Milo?"

"It's Mom. She's got a bad cough."

"Oh." I watched him as he made two plates of eggs and toast and added apple slices to each. He put the plates down on the breakfast bar and sat down beside me.

"Is it because of the chemo?"

Milo shook some hot sauce on his eggs and passed it over to me. He took a bite. I watched him nervously. It wasn't like Milo to be so distant. I touched his arm. Finally he looked over at me. He exhaled loudly.

"Yeah. Her immune system's weak and now she's sick. She says I'm overreacting. I wanted to take her to the hospital last night. She wouldn't go."

"What's your Dad say?"

Milo snorted in disgust. "He took Mom's side. Says if it gets serious, they'll go. Told me to get back over here and help you. They think I'm helping you fix your deck." He took another bite, chewed and swallowed. "So, here I am."

I felt a knot in my stomach. Milo didn't want to be here. Suddenly, the idea that Milo might not keep fighting to be with me felt very real. And it felt terrible. Terrible and terribly familiar. ("Cut the crap, Sam," said Dad. "This isn't about you.") As usual, Dad was right.

I stared at my plate and pushed my eggs around with my fork. "How bad is the cough?" I asked softly.

"Bad enough. I kept trying to tell them that it could turn into pneumonia overnight. But Mom says she knows her body. She promised to go see someone if it gets any worse."

"Laura's a smart lady, Milo. Maybe you *are* overreacting. She's come so far, she wouldn't risk it now."

"Do you realize how quickly an infection can go from nothing to practically untreatable in a cancer patient?" he asked in a loud voice. He slammed his napkin down, stood and stormed over to the sliders. He stood with his back to me, arms crossed, looking out at the beach.

"I laid awake all night listening to her cough," he said. "I was afraid to sleep. Afraid I would wake up and not hear anything at all."

I slid off the bar stool and went to stand beside him. I put my hand on his shoulder. "Hey."

He turned and looked down at me with those gorgeous eyes.

"Why don't you just go home and be with her? You're too distracted to be much help anyway," I said with a small smile. "I got this; I'm going to work on the symbols today."

He looked back out at the beach. It was another beautiful Indian summer day. The tide was low and that flock of seagulls was in its usual spot. A little tow-haired toddler ran toward the birds and they took flight. The boy stood there for a moment and then started to cry. A couple holding hands about twenty feet behind him laughed and then the man jogged up to the boy and swooped him up to the sky. I could hear the child's belly laugh through the glass door. The mother caught up to them and put her arm around her husband and the family continued its walk down the beach.

"I want that," said Milo.

I nodded.

"I want that, and I want my *mother* to be there to see it, goddamn it." Milo sighed loudly and turned back to me. A tear slipped out of my eye and rolled down my cheek. Neither my mother *or* my father would be there when—*if*—I ever had a family.

"I'm sorry, Sam." He put his arm around my back and squeezed me into his firm abs. "Come on. Let's eat. And then you're going to pack up your computer and we're going to my place. We can work there."

I smiled. "Pepper too?"

He smiled back. "Pepper too."

"Pull into the Plantation," I said and Milo hit the brakes. We were in his truck heading to Duxbury. Plimoth Plantation had reopened Monday.

"Why?"

"Remember the gift shop? It has all kinds of books. I want to see what they've got on the early Plymouth Colony."

"What? You don't want to read all six hundred pages of Bradford's history?" Milo grinned. His mood had improved once we decided to go back to his house.

"I'm thinking there might be something that will help us figure out the brand and the AD patch. Something that's not written in funky old misspelled English."

Milo turned left and drove down the winding driveway. On both sides, dense evergreens, flaming maples and a few yellow elms gave the impression that we were far from civilization. It was easy to believe we were now in a frontier settlement rather than just a few hundred yards from a busy highway speckled with tourist trap restaurants—until we hit the parking area.

The lot was already half full, and it was only nine thirty. On a Tuesday in October. The rubberneckers were out in force; people couldn't wait to see where it happened. The press was in a frenzy; the Pilgrim Slayer hangings were the talk of the nation.

Oscar Wilde once said "The only thing worse than being talked about is not being talked about." It seemed Liz Smit would have to agree. Could this all be some kind of sick publicity stunt?

"What about Pepper?" Milo asked. Pepper was curled up sleeping in the back seat. We'd interrupted his morning nap when we left my house. Pepper sleeps about eighteen hours a day; I often wish that Pepper and I could trade jobs.

I glanced around the parking lot, remembering his recent escape. "Just leave the windows open a crack; he'll be fine. We won't be long."

We exited the truck and made our way over the wooden stairs and into the welcome center. In the lobby, couples and families with toddlers milled about outside the theater. The old woman standing at the ticket booth looked up at us and frowned. My sweat pants and hoodie were even shabbier than Milo's.

"Uh, we're just going in the gift shop," I said. "We'll only be a few minutes." She nodded and went back to collecting money.

"Let's make this quick," I whispered to Milo. We went into the shop and made a beeline for the book shelves.

"Sharon? Brian?" The click click click of high heels that followed did *not* bode well. Slowly, Milo and I turned around. Liz Smit was smiling broadly, although I was guessing that was probably due to the long queues in the lobby rather than a visit by two new Sight Ministries' followers. It cost like $35 per person to get in to Plimoth Plantation.

I smiled. "Mrs. Smit, what a surprise!" My ears were in flames. "We just stopped in on a whim; we were looking for a book on the history of Plymouth."

"Well, you've come to the right place!" She laughed

loudly; Liz Smit was giddy with all the mobs.

"So, uh, you work here then?" Smit was wearing a name badge. *Way to state the obvious, Sam!*

"Oh, yes, I thought you knew…but then, how would you, being new to the area and all. I've been the executive director here for the past two years." She had spots of color high on her cheeks.

"How interesting that must be," Milo said smoothly. "We can't wait to learn more about the religious roots of the colony. Say, do you have any openings here? As you may recall, I'm still looking for work. Though, I wouldn't come looking for a job dressed like this!" Milo chuckled. "But seriously, I'll take anything at this point."

Smit wrinkled her brow. "Well, now, let me think." She began describing a part-time opening in the café, but I lost track of the conversation when I saw who was heading our way. John Clarkson. *Shit!*

Clarkson was decked out in full John Billington regalia. His head was down but he was walking quickly our way.

"Honey, don't forget, we're on a schedule." I tugged Milo's sleeve and smiled sweetly at Mrs. Smit. "Would it be alright if Brian came back to talk with you? I have an appointment. Really, we were just going to be in and out."

Clarkson had stopped to talk to some kid and his parents outside the theater. "My name is John Billington," I heard him bellow as he launched into his spiel.

Liz Smit glanced over and a bit of the smile left her eyes. *Late again.* She turned back to me and Milo. "Of course, of course, don't let me keep you. Brian, call my assistant Megan and make an appointment sometime later this week. I'm sure we can find something for you here at the Plantation, especially now that it's so busy."

Milo thanked her and we ducked behind a wall of bookshelves, crouching down as if to study the titles on the bottom shelf. I peeked out; Smit went directly to Clarkson's side, who was finishing up his act. I saw him reach for her elbow and guide her away from the tourists, down the hallway to the administrative offices. She leaned into one doorway and said something; a moment later Aaron Stevens emerged and followed Smit and Clarkson. I lost sight of them.

"There's something odd there," I said to Milo, shaking my head. "I don't know what it is, but those three are just plain strange together. We need a fly on the wall in there." Which reminded me: there were cheap listening devices available from the same outfit that sold me my miniature camera. *Hmmm.*

Milo studied my face. "Sam. Have you already forgotten what Dennis said Sunday? Bugs are *his* domain, not ours. Come on, let's find some books and get outta here."

How does he read my mind like that?

Ten minutes later we hurried back up the paved path to the parking lot. We'd chosen three overpriced books on life in the early Colony. Milo paid. *Again.* I needed that reward. I could sort of understand why Tommy'd been following us. But he was still a creep.

As we neared Milo's truck I looked up and stopped. Milo bumped into me and then followed my gaze.

"Who's that?" he asked.

"Injun Bob," I said. He was looking in the window of

Milo's truck and poking the end of his braid through the opening. Pepper was standing up inside and batting at Bob's hair with his paw.

We walked over and stopped in front of Injun Bob.

He looked at me, then over to Milo and then back at me. "You write your article yet?" he asked.

"I'm, uh, still doing some research," I said. I held up the plastic bag containing our books. I was dying to ask him what *he'd* been doing in the research room last week, and who he'd been with, but there didn't seem to be a good way to work that into the conversation.

"That your cat?" he asked.

"Yes."

"You know, we Native Americans have our own stories about black cats." He waited for me to reply.

"Uh, really?"

"In our legend, the black cat is also an evil witch. A shape shifter. Just like in the white man's stories from Europe." He stared at me solemnly. "Makes you wonder a little, doesn't it?"

I tried to laugh it off. Injun Bob didn't smile.

"Well, Pepper's not a witch," I said. "Neither am I, for that matter."

"Not *too* often," said Milo with a wink. Bob still didn't smile.

"Well," I said, "we have to be going."

Injun Bob pulled his skinny grey braid out of the window and nodded at us, then turned and trudged off.

Milo and I got in the truck and he backed out. As he accelerated across the parking lot, Milo said, "That was a little weird."

"Injun Bob's a *lot* weird."

"Maybe we should look at him again."

I nodded and stared out the window. "Maybe you're right. But there's no way he climbed that tree at the Mayflower Society library. But he *was* talking with someone here in the research room last week." But then, I reminded myself, he worked here. "Zeke is still the link here, at least between the first two."

I picked my phone up off the seat; I'd left it in the truck while Milo and I were in the museum store. I had several missed calls and a voice mail message. *Shit.* We'd sort of hoped that when we didn't hear anything from Dennis by nine-thirty that maybe the killer had taken a night off.

As Milo turned left out onto the road, I dialed my voice mail. Before I got to my messages, the phone rang. Dennis. I closed my eyes, sighed, and answered.

"God damn you, Sam, why weren't you answering?" Dennis was mad again. Or maybe still. Probably still.

"Sorry Dennis, I left it in the truck. We were only supposed to be gone a few minutes."

"Scared the shit out of me," he muttered. "This case is gonna be the end of me, I swear."

"Is there…?"

He was quiet a second. I could hear voices in the background. "Yeah. Another one. Inside the Windemere store on Main. Fucking site of Billington's original home. I've seen that plaque a million times, but we didn't have anyone on it. Just the normal patrols on Main."

"We're heading that way right now. Can we stop by?"

"Sorry, Sam. Fucking reporters are swarming, the

forensics guys are everywhere and it's the middle of a business day. Kid found the body when he came in to open, just before ten. It's a zoo here. Turk and I'll be by after with copies of the photos."

"Well, um, Milo and I are going to work from his place today. Can you come by in the evening? Just tell me what the message was."

"Whatever, yeah, later. 'For the general good of the Colony' is the message. There was a rubber snake wrapped around her upper arm." He paused. "Real young one, Sam. I bet she's only twenty-one or twenty-two."

I felt a chill. "Do you know who she is yet?"

"No, not yet. Look, I gotta go. I'll call you later. And keep the goddamn phone with you." He hung up.

I looked at Milo grimly. "You might want to take the highway," I said. "Downtown's gonna be a mess."

Milo pulled into a driveway, backed out, and headed away from town.

Chapter 26

Milo and I walked into his kitchen behind Pepper, who ran over to Lady. Pepper likes his routines. After that he would go into the living room and watch the fish tank for a while. I always thought that seemed like an exercise in frustration, but Pepper didn't seem to mind.

I followed Milo into the living room. Laura was lying on the couch under a quilt with a vaporizer next to her. She opened her eyes in surprise. Her head was uncovered and I could see she was embarrassed. I said, "Hi Laura," and then joined Pepper at the fish tank.

"How're you feeling, Mom?" Milo asked.

"No worse than yesterday." She coughed a thick, wet sounding cough.

"You want anything? Sam and I are going to work for a while out in the sun room."

"I thought you guys were fixing her deck?"

Shit. We hadn't come up with an excuse for being at Milo's house. I wondered what he'd dream up this time. I hoped I'd at least have panties on, whatever the story was.

"We're nearly done with that," Milo said casually. "Sam's

been researching her family tree and I got interested. Thought maybe I'd try to see how far back ours goes. I figured we could do it here and keep an eye on you at the same time. 'Til Dad gets home."

Laura coughed again and put a handkerchief in front of her mouth. She wheezed for a few seconds and then said, "Your dad's side goes back to the Mayflower." Milo stood there as she coughed and wheezed some more.

He turned and went into the kitchen. "I'm going to make you some more hot tea," he said over his shoulder.

Laura sighed and looked over at me. Her face was pale and blue-tinged shadows dulled her large eyes. "Don't ever get sick when your kids are home," she said and coughed. "They're a pain in the ass." She leaned back on the pillow and closed her eyes.

I stared at the colorful fish rounding the tank. Did they mind that their home was just one foot by two feet square? Their faces were inscrutable, mouths opening and closing to some internal metronome. Pepper was enthralled.

Milo brought a steaming mug into the living room. "I'll just put this on the table Mom. You should drink it."

"I will. Thanks, honey. Now let me sleep," she said softly. "That's all I need."

I picked up my backpack and followed Milo out to the sun room. He closed the door behind us.

"You see?" he said.

I nodded. "Yeah, it doesn't sound good."

Milo put his duffel bag on a small white wicker table and withdrew his computer and the books from Plimoth Plantation. "I'm going to try and read. Not sure I can focus on anything else." He chose a book and sank into the loveseat.

I nodded, pulled my laptop out of my backpack and plugged it into the wall. I sat in a matching white wicker chair and stared out at the harbor for a minute. Inside, Laura coughed some more. My stomach clenched.

Finally, I opened the file with my notes and jotted down the information on the latest victim.

I thought about what Dennis said, about how they didn't have anyone on the Billington homestead site. It was a retail store now, filled with light-hearted gifts and whimsical wind chimes and knick-knacks. Right on Main Street. I'd seen the black and gold plaque identifying the brick building a million times myself. In the summer, I always got stuck in traffic right about there.

I decided that before I did any more work on the symbols, I was going to make a list for Dennis of every spot in town related to the Pilgrims, and to John Billington specifically. If nothing else, maybe I could help make sure that enough cops were posted in the right places before tomorrow night. After that I would make a list of all of Billington's descendants who were local members of the Mayflower Society. So far, the victims hadn't actually been members themselves, but I figured the police could at least keep an extra close eye on any young women who were descended from John Billington and lived locally.

"The best offense is a good defense," I mumbled to myself.

"The best defense is a good offense," said Milo.

"What?"

"You got it backwards." He looked at me over his book. "The saying is, 'the best defense is a good offense."

"Yeah, well, our offense has been playing shitty," I replied. "I'm going to put together some info that Dennis can use for *defense."*

Milo nodded. "Good call," he said and went back to his book.

I Googled "Billington Plymouth" and copied down references. There was a Billington Road over by Little Pond and the Billington Bed &Breakfast on Billington Road. There was the Billington Sea, which was one of many large ponds in Plymouth. Expensive homes and summer cottages dotted the shore of the Billington Sea. They would be empty this time of year, providing the killer with plenty of choices.

Then there were all of the major and minor Pilgrim tourist attractions. The town was full of them. In addition to the places where there'd already been killings, there was the Pilgrim Hall Museum, the Forefather's Monument, Plymouth Rock Park, Burial Hill and so on. I worked on the list for another half hour and then composed a text message to Dennis: "Billington Road, Billington B&B and Billington Sea—need extra patrols." A few minutes later, he texted back. "Thx." "Got list 4 u" I replied. This time he didn't respond.

Milo stood and said, "I'm gonna check on Mom." I nodded and logged into the Mayflower Society web site. A few minutes later Milo returned and sat back down. He grabbed his book. "She's sleeping. I don't think she has a fever."

"That's good," I said. "If she's getting worse, she'd have a fever."

He nodded and gave me a small smile. "Thanks for coming over with me, Sam. I woulda been useless at your place."

I looked at him with a serious face. "And that would be different *how?*" I asked.

He grinned at me and I felt that familiar warmth rising up

from my chest toward my face. Maybe I was hitting menopause early. About twenty years early. I seemed to be getting hot flashes about ten times a day. I looked back at my computer screen and tried to figure out where I'd left off on the list of local Billington descendants. I stole another glance at Milo, but he'd gone back to reading his book.

When I finished, I had twenty-six names. Fourteen of them were men, but who knew, the killer might decide it wasn't fair to discriminate based on sex. But, if my theory about the killer being involved with Sight Ministries had any merit at all, that wasn't likely.

Only one of the women was younger than thirty. I put her name at the top of the list and texted Dennis again. "Got list of J.B. descendants in Plmth Cty 4 u from Mflr Soc. Jeanine Harter only woman <30. 52 Wshngtn St." Dennis again texted back "Thx." Such a talker.

I set my laptop down and stood. "I'm going to see what Pepper's getting into," I said.

"He was staring at the fish when I was in there," Milo replied. He looked up at me. "This is pretty interesting stuff."

"I'm more interested in *useful* than interesting," I said and went inside.

Sure enough, Pepper was still crouched on the table by the aquarium. Maybe it was like television for cats. He *was* male; he'd probably be there for hours. I smiled to myself, went and used the bathroom and came back through the living room. Laura was snoring softly. I smiled again.

When I got back to the porch, Milo was leaning forward and making notes on a pad. "I got *useful* for you," he said. He smiled up at me.

"Yeah?"

"In the early days of the Colony, adultery was a capital offense. But rather than execute offenders, they usually banned the guilty from the Colony, or...." Milo stopped and just grinned.

"Come *on* Milo." I was pretty sure I knew where this was going.

"Or made them wear a badge on their sleeve with the letters AD printed in red."

Chapter 27

"Anna Fuller cheated? But she *just* got married."

"I can't believe I didn't think of it sooner," Milo replied. "We studied the shit out of *The Scarlett Letter* in tenth grade."

I hadn't thought of it either. I'd assumed the 'A' and the 'D' were the first initials for *two* words, not the beginning of one. Hester Prynne only had to wear an 'A.'

"Whether she really *was* an adulterer or not," Milo said, "the killer obviously thinks she was. And he thinks Carolyn Bishop was a murderer."

"So what's the triangle brand mean?" I pulled my computer onto my lap and searched for 'triangle symbol.' "What else was a capital offense in the Colony? Which book did you find that in?" I was skimming the Internet article titles that came up.

"This is the one called *The Times of Their Lives*," Milo said. "I *told* you it was interesting."

"Interesting is a bonus," I said. "*Useful* is golden."

"Okay, here it is." He read from the book. "'The 1636 codification of laws of Plymouth Colony incorporated laws already in existence in the colony since its inception, but which had been enforced by the governor on a discretionary basis up—"

"Get on with it."

"Okay, okay. The list of 'capital offenses liable to death were, in order: treason, willful murder, conversing with the devil by way of witchcraft, willful burning of ships or houses, sodomy, rape, buggery and adultery.'"

"Nothing I'm finding here goes with that."

"The triangle was upside down," Milo said.

"Right!"

I searched 'upside down triangle symbol.' In just a few seconds I had it.

"Here we go," I said. "The Nazis used an upside down triangle to mark certain groups in the concentration camps. Especially *gay* people." I looked up at Milo. "It's been adopted as a symbol for lesbians."

Milo flipped through a few pages. "Sodomy, or Homosexuality is the name of the section." He read a bit to himself. "Here. A case in 1637. Two men were found guilty of 'spilling their seed one upon the other.' Blah, blah…. 'John Alexander was therefore censured by the Court to be severely whipped and burnt in the shoulder with a hot iron.'"

"So Reggie Cummins was a lesbian. Maybe. Probably. Carolyn Bishop was a murderer, at least in the killer's mind. And Anna Fuller was either an adulterer, or for some reason the killer thought she was. Either way, she was hanged for it."

"So what's the snake?" Milo asked.

I looked at my scribbled list of capital offenses. "I'd say treason. Is there anything else in the book that talks about treason?"

Milo checked the index. "Nope."

"I guess when Dennis tells us more about her, we can see if it fits," I said. "But I'm pretty sure we've cracked the code."

I leaned back in my chair and rubbed my eyes. "We still don't know *who* he is," I said. "But we're starting to understand him. If we can figure out how he's finding his victims, we can work back from that."

"Well, we've got between now and tomorrow night to do it."

"When did she have time to *study?*" I said.

Dennis and Turk were seated on my couch, Milo was in my reading chair and I was at my desk. We'd met back at my house around four o'clock, after Grady got home from lobstering. Laura was still sleeping on the couch when Milo, Pepper and I left.

I read from the list of student organizations Margot Roberts had belonged to at Johnson & Wales. "AWARE Alliance, Habitat for Humanity, PRIDE Alliance, Silent Witness Program and the Quidditch Club."

"What the hell's the Quidditch Club?" asked Dennis.

"That be where witches and wizards fly 'round on they magic broomsticks, an the Seeker try n catch the Golden Snitch," said Turk.

Dennis looked at Turk like he had two heads. "Where do you *get* this shit?" he asked.

"It's a Harry Potter thing," I said, "but all these other clubs are serious."

Everyone turned back to me. "Silent Witness promotes awareness of women killed by domestic violence. AWARE supports human rights, PRIDE Alliance supports gay rights. She also volunteered at Planned Parenthood and wrote editorials for the school paper. *And* she worked four nights a week at her job and had a 3.8 grade average." When I was in college I'd joined one club. Once. By my sophomore year, I'd quit. Maybe if there'd been a Hacker's Club I would have been more motivated.

"Well, her activism got her killed, looks like," said Dennis. "The question is, by *who?*"

"Whom," said Turk. Dennis stared at him. "It be proper to say 'by whom', not by who."

"Fuck you, Turk," said Dennis.

I tried not to giggle and stared down at the photos on my desk. My amusement quickly faded. Margot Roberts was not only an amazing student; she'd been a beautiful young woman. She was only twenty-two years old. Based on the state of the crime scene, Roberts fought back with everything she had. But in the end, she was found hanging in the middle of the store, bound and gagged just like the others.

I plugged my laptop into the printer and sent my lists to print. I gave them to Dennis. "These are all of the places where I think you want extra patrols. And this is the list of people in the area that we know are descended from John Billington. But there are obviously a *lot* more than that." Dennis nodded and stared at the lists.

"I'm trying to figure out where he finds them," I said. "I went back to searching all of the online dating sites this afternoon. There are several devoted to gays and also a few for swingers. Reggie Cummins wasn't 'out,' but there are sites for people in the closet. And if Anna Fuller *was* sleeping around, maybe that's how he found her too. I can't believe how many hits

I got for 'swingers in Boston.' I'll keep searching, but I think you're going to have to ask the families some...uncomfortable questions."

"How he know they the spawn of Billington?" asked Turk.

I nodded. "It took me *hours* to confirm that Carolyn Bishop was in fact related. He's got access to the Mayflower Society databases somehow. And he knows how to use genealogy web sites like Ancestor.com too."

"So he make a list of people—"

"Women," I said.

"So he make a list of women come from John Billington an he decide which ones he don like," said Turk. "Took some time. Some plannin'."

"He cares about Plymouth's roots, its history," said Milo. "He doesn't approve of the way America has abandoned its religious foundations. He thinks the evil started here, with John Billington. He wants to end it here. Margot Roberts promoted several lifestyle choices that were capital crimes in the Colony. Homosexuality. Abortion, or murder as he sees it. That's why she got the snake. It's a symbol of treason." Milo didn't say much in these meetings, but when he did, he was usually spot on.

"Smit's church is patriarchal. Women are inferior," I said. I wasn't giving up on my Sight Ministries theory just yet. Charles Smit had really gotten to me. "But Liz Smit works *and* they haven't got any kids," I added. "That still bugs me."

"Get me a list of church members," Dennis said, "before you work more on the gay and swinger sites."

Finally, a little respect. I beamed at Dennis. "You got it."

He sighed again and stood. "It's a goddamn shame we don't have the death penalty."

"Accidents happen," said Turk. His usual sarcastic tone was notably absent.

Dennis shook his head. "Let's go. We gotta meet with the task force." He looked over at me. "Nice work, Nance."

I was still grinning when Turk's Lincoln pulled out of the driveway.

Chapter 28

I swirled my wine and took a sip. It was nearly nine. Milo was doing his Tasmanian Devil thing in the kitchen and I was sitting at the breakfast bar watching. God that man could move. He was barefoot and his jeans hung down just a little below his hips; a pair of plaid boxer shorts peeked out. His back muscles rippled under his T-shirt as he pulled pans from the cabinets and set them on the burners. On top of all that, whatever he was concocting smelled divine. *Bonus.*

While I'd hacked the Sight Ministries Intranet in search of a membership list and cried over Margot Roberts' Facebook postings, he'd gone and bought food and some excellent wine. Came in a glass bottle and everything. I figured the least I could do was drink some.

"Where'd you learn to cook?" I asked.

"Just taught myself," he said. "You got any curry?"

I looked at him. "You mean like the chicken dish down at Namaste?"

"Namaste's closed. No, I mean like the yellow powdered spice used to *make* curries."

"It's closed? Damn. That place was good. Spices are up

there," I replied, lifting my wine glass in the general direction of the pantry.

He opened the door. "You got salt, pepper corns—but no grinder that I've been able to find—and...." He pulled a little round container out. "Sesame seeds." He looked at me and shook his head. "Don't you ever cook?"

"I'm really quite fond of cold cereal," I said.

Still shaking his head, he put some oil in a pan and dumped the sesame seeds in. "Change of plan. I'll do a stir fry. You got soy sauce at least?"

I wrinkled up my brow. "I think there're some little packets in the butter compartment in the fridge." I'd ordered Chinese a few weeks back, after Mrs. Jansen paid me a hundred dollars for raking her leaves.

He found the packets of soy sauce, dumped them in a bowl and added some sugar. Then he removed the chicken breasts he'd sautéed from the pan and added some water. "Just have to make the broth," he mumbled. He let the liquid simmer and then added the soy sauce and sugar mixture. "Cornstarch?" he asked.

I shrugged. "Can you make that from cornflakes?"

"Hopeless," he said, as he opened every cupboard. He pulled some boxes out and put them on the counter, then got some garlic out of his grocery bag and began to chop. I decided not to tell him that most of those boxes, whatever they were, dated back to before Dad died. Maybe before *Mom* died. Milo stopped chopping, whirled around to shake the sesame seed pan, then went back to chopping.

"So, Milo."

"Hmmm."

"Why'd you quit school?" The wine was loosening me up.

And besides, who quits Harvard?

He stopped chopping for a second, knife poised above the minced garlic.

"Just didn't like it anymore."

I waited. Finally, I said, "But Milo, why? I mean, you were at *Harvard.* You could be making big money now. Probably on Wall Street or some shit like that. Instead you're lobstering and playing detective with me." I took another gulp of wine.

He looked at me. "Why'd you quit the NSA?"

I didn't answer.

"I'll show you mine if you show me yours," he said with a half smile.

"It—I just—I didn't agree with our mission, I guess." I raised my eyes and smiled. "That's all I can tell you or I'd have to shoot you. Your turn."

He sighed. "Similar, I guess. I didn't like who I was becoming. Who I *was* for a while."

I waited, but he didn't elaborate. After another minute, I said, "Do you like who you are *now?*"

He stirred the garlic into his sauce and stirred some five-year-old cornstarch into a cup of water and then added it too. "Yeah, I think so. Yes."

There was obviously more to the story, but I decided to let it go. He would tell me when he was ready. And there really wasn't more that I could say about my resignation from the NSA, otherwise known as 'No Such Agency.' If only I'd had 'No Such Job.'

I drank some more wine. "Me too," I said after a while.

"You too what?" He was adding the sliced chicken breasts back to the sauce and chopping peppers and measuring rice into boiling water. It was like he had six arms.

"I like who you are now."

He stopped for a second, looked me in the eye and smiled. "*Good.*"

"This is really good," I said. I took another big bite of stir fry and chewed. "Let's go to the Mayflower Society Library tomorrow morning. Dennis said they have a log book. Let's see who went there over the past few months. Compare that with the Sight Ministries membership. Talk to the Historian General."

"You're really convinced that church has something to do with it." Milo poured a little more wine for himself. I'd already consumed about half the bottle.

"No, I'm not *convinced.* But you heard the guy. Everything he preaches goes along with what the killer seems to believe. Either way, there might be a name that stands out."

"Didn't Dennis and Turk already review it?"

"Yeah, after Carolyn Bishop, but they haven't read months' worth of Facebook comments and emails like I have. Just seeing a name might trigger something."

Milo nodded.

"Anyway, I just want to see what's there. I never really paid attention before. To the Pilgrims and all that." No one does touristy stuff in their own home town, and I was as guilty as the next person. "Sounds like you could be a member if you wanted, Mr. *Cooke.*"

"You too," Milo said.

I raised my eyebrows.

"Name like Warren? In Plymouth since forever? Safe to

say you're probably a descendant, too."

"Huh." I thought about that. "I guess you're right. Mrs. Trimble said that too, and she knows *everything.*"

He laughed. "She's definitely sharp."

"As a tack," I said.

We ate some more in silence. It was a comfortable silence; neither one of us seemed to feel the need to keep talking. Unfortunately, my brain filled the void with all of the pictures and life I'd found in Margot Roberts' Facebook pages.

"Margot Roberts' sister is going to have a baby any day now," I said after a while. Tears welled in my eyes. Okay, so maybe half a bottle of wine isn't the best idea when you're exhausted and emotional. "Now every year she'll be planning that kid's birthday party and she'll be reminded of what happened to her little sister."

Milo took my hand. "Hey."

I shook my head; tears were running down my cheeks now. "Who am I *kidding*? Just because I can hack into databases doesn't mean I can solve *crimes.* Women are being *killed.* The FBI and that whole fricking task force haven't figured it out. Like *I'm* going to? Stupid."

"Look at me," Milo said. He put his hand under my chin and lifted it. Then he wiped my tears away and caressed my hair. "We've already given Dennis a lot of good stuff. Stuff that *you* figured out. *Before* the FBI, with all its analysts and resources. They didn't know Anna Fuller was a swinger. *We* figured that out. And you found her on that site in about, what, thirty minutes this afternoon?"

I nodded.

"Now they have another way to look for the guy. Now

they know one more thing. And we'll keep giving them one more thing and one more thing until it comes together. Doesn't matter if *you* figure it out yourself, or if you provide the clue that helps *them* figure it out."

I leaned back, pulling away from Milo. *God* his touch felt nice. "Sorry," I said. I blew my nose in my napkin.

"For what? Being human?" Milo shook his head at me. "I'm not."

He stood, picked up his dishes and carried them into the kitchen, and I did the same. By mutual, unspoken agreement, we rinsed them and left them stacked on the counter. I got Milo his pillow and blankets and put them on the couch. Then I grabbed Pepper out of his tree and headed up the stairs. Halfway up I paused and watched Milo get a glass of water. *Sweet dreams Milo*, I thought, and continued up the stairs.

Chapter 29

Indian summer turned to fall with a vengeance while we slept. I awoke early to the drone of heavy rain on the roof and the branches of my small maple tree swiping the siding. I lay there for a moment listening, then rose and peered out the window. The tide was about half and the water was choppy; white caps danced across the dark grey surface. There would be no young families or martini-swilling seniors on the beach today. In the distance, over Duxbury, a huge lightning flash appeared, followed seconds later by a sharp clap of thunder. The wind was blowing rain in on my T-shirt and I forced the window down.

I took a quick shower and pulled on jeans and a turtleneck. The outside temperature had fallen by at least twenty degrees overnight. I put on thick socks and hiking boots, grabbed my hoodie and went downstairs.

Milo had a small fire going in the fireplace. The man was a fricking saint. I filled my coffee mug and went and sat in my chair by the fire. He was reading another one of the books we'd purchased yesterday.

Finally he looked up at me.

"Nice fire," I said.

"You're welcome."

"Any more useful stuff?" I nodded toward the book.

"Useful, no. Lots of interesting, but as you said, that's not what we're after."

I nodded and sipped my coffee. A really loud clap of thunder made us both jump.

"Sheesh," I said. "Nasty out there."

"I like storms."

"Yeah, me too actually. Good day for a book by the fire." Or to curl up on the couch with Milo. "*But*," I added. "Not for Batgirl and Robin."

"Breakfast?" he asked after a moment.

"I'll just have some cereal."

"I *like* to cook, Sam. You know that."

"And I *like* cereal. Go ahead if you want, but I haven't had my Wheaties in days. My cholesterol's probably about a thousand by now."

He laughed. "I don't suppose you want a smoothie."

I made a face. "I want Wheaties."

"Fair enough."

We went into the kitchen, made our breakfasts and sat comfortably side by side eating. We were like an old married couple, except for the part about no sex. I was starting to think I might like to add that feature. ("Focus Sam," said Dad.). *Right.*

When the kitchen was clean and Pepper'd been given his kibbles and fresh water, we gathered up our computers and books and I found one of Dad's raincoats for Milo to wear. Then we ran out, leaning into the driving rain. We climbed into Milo's truck and headed for town.

We swung into the parking lot of the Mayflower Society House and library about fifteen minutes later. The main house was a grand white building with a columned front porch, lots of tiny-paned windows and black shutters. In the summer, the gardens around the house were spectacular. Rocking chairs were scattered across the veranda, but on a cold, stormy October day, the invisible hand of the wind was all that moved them. Eerie. We drove past the main building to the parking area in back. A lone car sat next to the library.

On the left, the yellow crime scene tape that enclosed the tree where Carolyn Bishop was hanged now lay tangled in puddles on the pavement. A single patrolman in rain gear huddled nearby. Milo and I stared silently at the huge tree for a few seconds. The images we'd seen of Bishop's body hanging there were imprinted in our minds. The wind howled, lifting dead leaves into the air.

Finally, Milo turned to me. "Ready?"

I nodded. We got out and jogged around puddles to the entrance.

The Mayflower Society library was in a small, one-story building with greying cedar shingles and white trim. Dark green shutters framed the windows and a long handicap ramp angled up to the doors. I guessed a lot of older people wanted to find out if they were descended from the Pilgrims. Younger people didn't seem to care much about such things. Until now, I'd never given it a second thought.

We took our raincoats off between the double doors, shook the rain onto the floor and hung them on hooks. Inside, a small sign on the desk requested a five dollar user's fee. The log book lay right in front of us. Behind the desk, a small salt and pepper-haired woman was reading a text and taking notes. She had reading glasses perched on the tip of her nose; she looked up at us and smiled.

"Aren't *you* the determined genealogists," she said. "I didn't expect to see a soul today. Please sign in right there," she added.

After we'd signed in and Milo gave her five dollars, she said, "Now, is there something I can help you find?"

"Actually, Ms....," Milo began. I was learning to let him do the talking with women. They were generally much more accommodating for him; when I tried to be our spokesperson, they just got irritated.

"Meredith Bradley," she said. "I'm the Assistant Historian General for the Mayflower Society."

"That sounds impressive."

"Oh, not really." She blushed. "But I enjoy it."

"Well, Ms. Bradley, could we start out by looking through this?" Milo held up the log book.

She looked puzzled. "You want to look at the log book?" A second or two later she frowned. "You're after the reward. For the Pilgrim Slayer."

"Oh no, nothing like that," Milo said smoothly. "We're interested in talking with genealogists. See, I'm writing a book of interesting family stories that amateur genealogists have uncovered. I want to get in touch with some of your visitors and see if they'll agree to an interview. I just need a few names of people who don't live too far away."

She looked uncertain. *Go along with the nice looking man or follow protocol?* My money was on the nice looking man.

"Do *you* have any interesting family stories you've uncovered?" Milo asked. "You must have traced your roots, considering..."

She giggled. "I have indeed done my family tree, but unfortunately my family's only been here for a few generations. Nothing very interesting at all."

"Oh, I'm sure *that's* not true," said Milo. "But if I could just look through the log...?"

Finally she said, "I guess so. Let me know if I can help with anything else." She smiled broadly at Milo.

Milo carried the log book over to a long wooden table. I sat down beside him and pulled my laptop out of my backpack.

"You're pretty good at this lying business," I whispered with a smile.

Milo frowned. I looked at him, eyebrows raised, but he just shook his head.

Flushing, I grabbed the log book and got to work.

For the next hour we reviewed the names of visitors to the library and compared them with all of the other names we'd gathered, including the members of Charles Smit's church.

Finally, I leaned back. With only one exception, there weren't any names that we recognized or that were listed as members of the Sight Ministries congregation.

"Well, Liz Smit comes here a lot," I said.

"Yeah, but considering her job..."

"I know Milo. I *know*." I thought for a few minutes. "But really, she's an administrator. Why does she need to come here so often?"

"They probably do special projects or exhibits. There's a research room at Plimoth Plantation too. Maybe they cooperate on stuff. Share resources," said Milo.

"Right."

I was disappointed. I'd been so sure we'd find a link between the church and visitors to the library.

"Some of the people only gave a first initial," I said finally. "I'm going to make a quick list of them, and when they came."

Milo shrugged. "Can't hurt."

Outside the wind was still strong and the rain showed no sign of easing. Milo wandered around the book-filled room, looking at titles and occasionally pulling one off the shelf for a closer look. The phone rang and Ms. Bradley answered.

"General Society of Mayflower Descendants Library. This is Meredith, may I help you?"

"Hi, honey."

"No, probably not today—"

"I know but—"

"Sorry, but I can't. I'm the only—"

"Zeke! I said no, I'll call you later."

The hair rose on the back of my neck. I looked at Milo. He nodded at me and strolled toward the desk.

"Your son?" he said.

She looked up at Milo. "Yes."

"I hope he's not sick? I mean, shouldn't he be in school?"

"Oh no, he's out of school."

"You don't look *old* enough to have a kid out of school," he said and winked.

She giggled. I pretended to be busily typing; I'd already finished my list.

"Well, I do. He wanted to come down; he hangs out with me here some days. But I have the car and I'm the only one here now."

Milo laughed. "Tell him to do the laundry and clean the house if he's bored."

"Believe it or not, he probably already did," she said and chuckled. "He's very particular."

"Oh. Well, you must have done *something* right," Milo added with a smile. He gave her the look for a few seconds. She giggled. Again. Frumpy librarians should *not* giggle.

Finally, Milo walked back over to me. "You almost done, Sam?"

"Yep." I packed up my laptop and we put our coats on. I placed the visitors log book back on Meredith Bradley's desk. "Thanks again," I said, and we grabbed our coats and rushed out into the rain. I had my phone out dialing Dennis before we got to the truck.

Chapter 30

"Got it!" I said.

Milo was pacing back and forth in front of the fire. He stopped and his gaze found mine.

"I found it in their newsletter. She took the position in April. Moved here from Vermont. Now, to the Vermont DMV..."

Dennis still hadn't called me back, but I was flying high on adrenaline.

"It's *him*, Milo."

"Maybe..."

"Come on. *Nobody* has the name Zeke. Yet we found it in Anna Fuller's calendar, in Reggie Cummins' planner, and at the Mayflower Society library? His mother *works* there? *Way* too much coincidence."

My fingers were flying as I worked my way through the layers of the Vermont Department of Motor Vehicle database.

"Plus, Ezekiel's the name of a book in the Bible. Maybe Meredith and Zeke go to Smit's church. Maybe the membership just hasn't been updated recently. Or maybe they had their own whack-job church up in Vermont. It *still* works."

I paused as my search came up empty.

"Okay, no Ezekiel Bradleys...And no plain Zekes either. What else could Zeke be short for? Maybe it's a middle name..."

I searched for middle initials 'Z'. Quite a few came up, but full middle names weren't given. I hit 'print' and then searched for Meredith. "I'll just compare addresses," I mumbled to myself. "He still lives with his mother; he's probably under thirty."

A few minutes later I found Meredith Bradley's Vermont driver's license. The address didn't match that of any of the 'Z' middle names I'd printed, so I switched over to the Massachusetts DMV.

"If she got a new license like she's supposed to...She's a librarian, so she's anal..." I kept typing and scanning the screen.

"She's not a librarian, she's a historian."

"That might be her title, but did you see a frumpy, middle-aged woman manning the desk in a room full of books? Cuz that's what *I* saw."

"Ah yes, your theory of types," Milo said.

I looked up at him. "*What?* Don't you think it's him?"

"Maybe, Sam. I'm just saying, we don't really have much yet. Just a bunch of coincidences."

"All the detectives, in all the books I read, don't believe in coincidences. Doesn't happen. That's *always* how they find the bad guy."

"That's fiction."

"That's common *sense.* Here she is; I got her address. Sixty-two Summer Street. Should we go there?" I didn't want to wait for Dennis. I was pumped.

"No," Milo said firmly. "Find her kid. Find a birth

certificate with her name on it. Then we can find out more about him."

"Okay, I can do that," I said. I typed some more. "But he may not have been born in Vermont."

We were both quiet while I searched the Vermont state archives.

Twenty minutes later I leaned back and sighed. "Meredith L. Bradley didn't give birth in Vermont, at least not between 1980 and now. They must have moved there. Or maybe he was adopted." I looked up at Milo. "Let's just go to the house and watch from the street. At *least* until Dennis calls."

"Search the adoption—"

A muffled Red Hot Chili Peppers ringtone emerged from Milo's pocket. He dug in and pulled out his phone. "Dad?" He listened for a few seconds. "I'll be right there," he said and hung up.

Oh no. "Your mom?"

He nodded. He was gathering his things and packing his bag. "I gotta go; Dad's taking her to Jordan." Jordan Hospital was in Plymouth; there wasn't a hospital in Duxbury.

I just sat there as he shoved things into his duffel bag. I didn't know what to do. Should I go with him? But I'd just about found the killer. Maybe. But this was *Laura*.

I stood up. "I'll go with you."

Milo paused and looked over at me. "Thanks, Sam, but no. Stay here and finish what you're doing. He's going to strike again tonight. I'll call you from the hospital."

"But, Milo." Tears filled my eyes. Milo came over to me and grasped my shoulders.

"She'll be okay, Sam. And even if she's not…You might

have him; this might be the guy that's killed four women in a week. You can't make Mom better, but you *can* do this." He looked me hard in the eyes. "*Don't* go to that house alone. Wait for Dennis; let them do their jobs."

I nodded and put my head on his chest. He wrapped his arms around me and we stood like that for a minute. Finally, I pulled away.

"Go," I said.

He grabbed his bag and made for the front door. "Don't go to that house, Sam," he yelled and then the door slammed shut.

An hour later I was parked just down the road from sixty-two Summer Street. It was a traditional boxy, New England style home that had been divided into apartments or condos; the siding was cream colored and the windows were adorned with white shutters and flower boxes. A freshly paved parking area on the left would accommodate four or five cars. One of Plymouth's many ponds backed up to the yard.

The storm had sunk in its teeth; the sky was dark and gloomy, but in better weather the units would have nice views. From this location, one could easily walk to downtown—to the waterfront where the Mayflower II was anchored, to the Windemere store and also to the Mayflower Society library. I guessed that the weather had kept him from walking down to the library today, but in general Zeke Bradley could have made it on foot to three of the four crime scenes. I wondered how old he was. A guy out of school could be anywhere from eighteen to his late-twenties and still living at home, especially in this economy. His mother implied that he didn't have his own car. Maybe the night Anna Fuller died, he used his mother's car. It could work, although I still had no driver's license for the guy.

It was almost one in the afternoon, but the lack of sunlight and the hard weather made it feel more like evening. Best I could tell, the house was divided into two units—upper and lower. All of the first floor windows were dark, but light shone out of the back windows for the upper unit. I turned up the heater and hunkered down in my seat. I would just sit here and watch until Dennis called me back.

Fifteen uneventful minutes passed before the proverbial light bulb switched on. I pulled my laptop out of my backpack. If I could find their WiFi network, I would be able to hack into any computers that were turned on. The trick was finding the right network.

I searched for available wireless networks and nearly a dozen came up. I turned the key, shifted into first and moved the Mini to a parking spot closer to the building's driveway.

Now I had three networks with strong signals. One was unprotected, so I checked it first. Five minutes of scanning the email account confirmed that it wasn't the Bradleys' network, though I figured I should probably tell Dennis about the guy's recent purchases. Grow lights, a reflector, and an ozone filter. Classic weed-growing starter kit. The guy was so clueless, he'd arranged to have UPS deliver the goodies right to his house. With a disgusted sigh, I moved on to the second network and worked my way around the password.

Now I was getting somewhere. There were two IP addresses associated with the network. I worked my way through the first, which turned out to be Meredith's. I checked her browsing history and read a week's worth of emails. Ms. Bradley had researched chemical peels and boob jobs in the past week. Huh. Guess she was tired of the frumpy look. I checked her Facebook account. She had a lot of friends based in Vermont, and also about a dozen in Montana. *Ah ha!* Maybe I would find Zeke's birth records there. But first I needed to see what Zeke himself was getting up to online. My palms were sweating.

My phone rang. Dennis.

"Dennis, I found Zeke," I said in a low voice. It's not like the guy could hear me from his apartment a hundred feet away. I was closed up in my car, the wind was loud and the rain was heavy. Still, I somehow felt the need to be furtive.

"Talk to me," he said.

"I'm outside his house now, we—"

"You're *what*? Sam, start your car right now and get out of there."

"It's fine; I'm just parked on the road. I haven't seen anyone. But I—"

"I'm ordering you to get the fuck out of there. *Now.*"

"But I—"

"Now!" *Sheesh.*

"Okay, okay. I'm starting the car now." I made a U-turn out onto the street, continued to the corner and turned right onto Spring Lane.

"You still there?" I asked.

"Yeah."

I pulled into a parking spot facing the pond; across the water I could still see part of Zeke's building, but my view was obscured by the neighboring house.

"Okay, I'm parked on Spring Lane. Across the pond from his back yard. The address is sixty-two Summer Street. Where are you?" I was frantically typing to see if I still had a connection to the Bradley's WiFi network.

"We're at the station."

"Can you come here? I'm getting into his computer."

"Be there in ten." He ended the call.

I glanced around. Mine was the only car in the parking area for the park that bordered the pond. The wind was coaxing foamy, white tipped waves from the dark water and the tree beside my car was swinging its bare branches back and forth in a macabre dance. Dennis' freak out left me nervous. I turned off the engine and my lights and locked the doors. *Dennis and Turk will be here in ten minutes.*

I was still connected to the Bradley's network, but the signal was very weak and each step took forever. Five minutes later I was looking at Zeke Bradley's Internet browsing history. Slowly, I compiled a list of recent web sites visited. Mayflowerhistory.com, plimoth.org, themayflowersociety.com, americanancestors.org, ancestry.com. My hands were shaking. This was it, I'd found him! I checked his email account but didn't find any recent personal communications, just some newsletters and promotional stuff from the sites he frequented. But his email account gave me a full name. Zedekiah R. Bradley.

There was a knock at my window and I just about jumped out of my skin. Turk was bent over, peering in the passenger window. My heart was hammering as I lowered the window. "You be on a stakeout, usually you wanna pay attention to what shit be going down," he said with a smile.

I gulped and nodded. Behind Turk I could see Dennis in the passenger seat of Turk's Lincoln. I didn't even hear them pull in. "I'll come to your car," I said and shoved my laptop in my backpack. I hurried through the rain, slid into the back seat and pulled my hood off.

"It's him, Dennis, it's him! That's his house, right over there." I pointed through the seats at the Bradley's house.

"He home?" Turk asked.

"I think so, he called his mom—"

"Whoa, Nelly," Dennis said. "Start at the beginning. I got an unmarked watching the other side of the house. He's there, we'll know if he leaves. Just start at the beginning."

I took a deep breath and explained to them everything we'd learned at the library and what I'd uncovered since.

"So it be dumb luck you find him," Turk said.

"Dumb luck didn't find his address, Turk," I said irritably. "He's in there, I'm almost positive. Can't you take him in for questioning or something?"

Dennis stared across the water at the house for a couple of minutes.

"We got his *nick*name in some notes by two of the vics, out of *four*, and his mom works at the Mayflower Society Library. It's not enough. We need more."

"I just told you, all of his Internet browsing is related to Plymouth history. *And* Ancestry.com. He's into genealogy too."

Dennis sighed. "That's not illegal, Sam. You didn't even see the guy; he could have one leg, for all you know. We're not going in half-cocked. We'll keep him under surveillance. If it's him, he won't be keeping his appointment for tonight."

I leaned back and sighed. My balloon was deflating.

Dennis turned and faced me. His expression was softer now. "You done good, Sam. But we got to make sure this thing is air tight first. Fucking lawyers have a field day if there's the slightest problem with the bust. The burden's on us to make sure it's all by the book, or the fucker might walk. You know that."

I nodded. It was so frustrating.

"Don't worry, Sam. If this is the guy, we'll get him. And you'll get that reward." He smiled and I got a glimpse of the handsome man Dennis had once been, before the stresses of police work and three divorces did a Dorian Gray on his face.

"You're right." I forced myself to smile. "I've got his full name now; I'll go home and see what else I can dig up." I put my computer in my backpack, pulled my hood back up over my head and opened the car door.

"Sam," said Turk. "Keep bombin' that shit."

I smiled. I wasn't sure, but I thought he said, "Nice job."

Chapter 31

Through the window I could see Laura. She looked much the same as she did the day before on her couch, except now she had nasal prongs delivering oxygen to her nostrils and an IV hooked up to her arm. She appeared to be sleeping. Grady was sitting in a chair next to the bed, flipping idly through a magazine. I didn't see Milo.

"Hey, Sam." Milo's voice came to me from behind. I turned.

"Hey."

He approached carrying two Styrofoam cups of coffee. Behind him, I could see a couple of the nurses eyeing him from their station. Milo was oblivious.

He gave me a weary smile.

"How's she doing?"

"Could be better, but could be worse. Doctors said it was a good thing she came in today. They're pumping her full of antibiotics. Should see improvement by tomorrow. They hope."

"That's encouraging," I said.

"Yeah. You want a coffee? I'll just leave this with Dad and we can go to the cafeteria." Milo opened the door and handed the coffee to his father. I hovered by the door and smiled at Grady. "Hey old man," I said.

"Hey there, Samantha." He gave me a small smile. Then he scowled at Milo, who shook his head and walked back out of the room. *What the heck?*

Puzzled, I walked over and sat in the chair next to Grady. I put my arm around his shoulders. "She'll be good as new in a few days," I said in his ear. I squeezed him a bit and took my arm back.

He shook his head. "Damn sure hope so," he said.

"She's the toughest lady I know," I replied.

He stared at Laura. Her face was still pale and her naturally high cheekbones jutted sharply from her thin face. She had a red stocking cap on her head.

"Doc says she'll be back home giving me hell in no time," he said.

"Someone's got to do it," I said with a wink.

"And she's got it down to an art, that one," he replied.

"I've spent nearly…forty years perfecting my…giving-Grady-hell skills," Laura said between breaths and opened her eyes. "Hi, Sam."

I reached over and squeezed her hand. "Hey, you. How you feeling?"

"Just tired," she replied. "Really tired."

"Well, go back to sleep, Laura. We'll stop yammering now so you can rest." I stood. "Take care of her, Grady. He nodded without taking his eyes off Laura.

I closed the door quietly and Milo and I walked down the hall to the elevator. The nurses giggled as we waited by the stainless steel doors. I couldn't help but wonder if they were laughing at the frizz-haired, freckle-faced woman with the tall, handsome god. Probably.

The elevator dinged and the doors opened. A couple of doctors in scrubs exited without giving us a glance. We stepped into the elevator and Milo pushed the 'one.'

"Did you find more on Zeke?" he asked as we descended.

"What was that with your dad?"

He shook his head. "Don't worry about it."

I stared at Milo. "Seriously, what's going on?"

"He's mad at me." He didn't offer more.

"Why?"

He sighed. "It's complicated, Sam. Don't worry about it; he'll get over it. So, did you find more on Zeke?"

I searched his eyes but Milo was inscrutable. I'd have to wait to learn about the trouble between him and Grady. "Um, yes. Yes, I did."

He eyed me suspiciously. "You went there, didn't you?"

"I might have parked sort of close to the house and hacked the Wifi network for a bit," I said with a grin. "I got his name, Milo. Zedekiah Bradley." I was excited enough to let go of the Milo/Grady drama. "That's why we couldn't find him; who ever heard of Zedekiah? *And,* I got his browsing history. Guy's been all over Plymouth history web sites. And Ancestry.com." I looked up into Milo's eyes. "Dennis has him under surveillance. This might be it." I figured I was about to get a tongue-lashing, but I had to brag a little. I was proud of myself.

Milo didn't smile, but I could see amusement in his eyes. "You're incorrigible. But that's great, Sam. So you really think it's him?" We exited the elevator and headed toward the cafeteria.

"It sure looks that way. Everything we've got *could* be

coincidence. Hell of a coincidence though. If it *is* him, he's all done. They'll be watching his every move from here on out. Now that I have his full name, I'm going to see what else I can find out when I get home."

Milo nodded. We entered the cafeteria and got in line; I suddenly realized I was starving. I hadn't eaten anything since my bowl of Wheaties that morning. I got a cheeseburger with fries and a large coffee. Milo got a banana. I raised my eyebrow at him. "I had a sandwich earlier," he said.

After Milo paid the cashier, we took a seat by the windows. Outside, it was still pouring, and the sky was ten different shades of grey. If the sun was still up there, it was taking a personal day. The small trees and bushes in the landscaped courtyard swayed and twisted in the wind like dancers at a disco.

I smothered my burger with mustard and hot sauce and put some mayonnaise on my plate for the fries.

Milo smiled. "You appear to have a case of condiment confusion," he said.

With a grin I took a big bite. "Yum." I chewed for a minute. "So Laura's really going to be all right?" I asked.

He sighed. "They think so. They'll have to delay the last round of chemo now, but the doctor said he thinks it'll be fine. They're 'cautiously optimistic,'" he said, making finger quotes.

I nodded, still chewing. That was more than I'd ever had. Mom was killed instantly and Dad died after a heart attack. He was still alive when I found him, but just barely. He didn't even make it to the hospital.

Milo took my hand. "Hey," he said, looking at me seriously. I swallowed and raised my eyebrows. "You gonna go out with me when the case is over?"

Instant heat. The chest. The neck. The face. Further down. My ears were burning. I looked at his large tan hand over my smaller freckly one. Finally, I nodded, still staring at our hands. When I looked back up, he was smiling. I smiled nervously back. I still couldn't believe he really wanted to date me. ("He'd be lucky to have you, Sam," said Dad.)

He took his hand back and peeled his banana. Relieved, I took some fries and swiped them through the mayonnaise and put them in my mouth.

Shaking his head, Milo said, "*Gross.*"

I just smiled.

A half an hour later I pulled the Mini into my driveway and ran to the door with my backpack. I hadn't heard any more from Dennis, but I was going to find out everything there was to know about Zedekiah Bradley and his mother.

I walked into the living room, dropped my backpack on the couch, tossed my raincoat on its hook and threw another log on the embers. If I were lucky, the fire would revive without too much effort. Pepper was curled in a ball in my chair.

"Tough life, Pep," I muttered and stroked him. He stretched and yawned, making that funny snorty sound he makes when he yawns. I giggled and took my laptop out of my backpack. I connected it to my monitor and keyboard, went into the kitchen and put some water in a pan to boil. I pulled the Red Zinger out of the cabinet and waited.

I ran through everything I'd found on Zeke so far, which now didn't seem like that much. When push came to shove,

Dennis was right. We didn't have enough to storm in on the guy. His mom worked at the Mayflower Society library; theoretically that might give him access to their databases. But unless he was very computer savvy, it wasn't clear that he'd be able to find everything necessary to work out the lineage on non-members the way that I'd done Carolyn Bishop. Meredith admitted he spent time at the library when she was there working, and his browsing history made it clear he was deeply interested in the history of Plymouth. But then, so was she; she worked there. He might just be a history buff.

Most damning was the fact that both Anna Fuller and Reggie Cummins had met with him—or someone else named Zeke—in the weeks leading up to their murders. How many people named Zeke could there be? I needed to find a picture of the guy; if I could, I would take a ride up to the Wine Cellar and see if the bartender there recognized him as the Average Joe that came in with Reggie Cummins. If I could do *that*, I'd feel a whole lot better about Zedekiah Bradley as our primary suspect. I poured the boiling water into a mug, added a teabag and went back to my desk.

I started with the DMV for Massachusetts. Nada. I went back to Vermont. Zilch. I checked Facebook. Still nothing. Who doesn't have a Facebook account these days? I knew eight-year-olds who were already slaves to social media. Finally, I just Googled his name. I got numerous responses, but none with Zedekiah and Bradley combined. This guy really flew under the radar. Which, I reasoned, would make sense for a serial killer.

Leaning back, I sighed and thought. Nothing brilliant came to me. I got up and put another log on the fire, which was now dancing merrily. I stood looking out the sliding glass door.

It was nearly seven and while the thunder and lightning seemed to have passed, the rain was still hard and steady. I flipped the switch at the side of the door, but the outside light remained dark. Time to buy light bulbs.

As I stared out into the black, I noticed that my umbrella was lying sideways on the deck, about to blow away. It had come out of the table stand. I pulled the broom handle out of the slider, opened it and ran out to retrieve my umbrella. I rushed back to the door, maneuvered the umbrella through the opening and slammed the door closed. It had gotten colder. I put the umbrella off to the side of the fire so it could dry.

I went into the kitchen and stared into the refrigerator. I closed it and opened the cupboards. Sighing, I grabbed some sunflower seeds and went back to my desk. I hacked into the IRS' electronic filing system. No returns in his name. I searched for his mother's returns. *Finally,* something. Her Form 1040 told me that Zedekiah was twenty-four and that Meredith still claimed him as a dependent.

From there I checked the student registration files for every community college and university in eastern Massachusetts and then in Vermont. That took nearly two hours and still nothing. *What the hell?*

I decided to come at it from a different angle. Serial killers sometimes start smaller, with wild animals or pets, when they're young. I hacked the Brattleboro PD and searched from 1995 until now for reports of seriously injured or malicious acts against pets. Sadly, all I found were a few examples of animal neglect or cruelty by their owners. I checked for unsolved murders. Nothing.

Finally, it dawned on me. I looked up pediatricians in the

Brattleboro, Vermont area. A dozen men and women treated children in the region, and the security for medical records was decent, but about an hour later I found what I was looking for. I read the transcript quickly, and as I did, my stress level rose. *Shit!*

I grabbed my phone. It was nearly midnight, but I needed to talk to Dennis. Before I could dial, however, my slider opened and a man wearing a black ski mask and rain gear stepped in. His gloved hand held a gun; it was pointed straight at me.

Chapter 32

"Please put the phone down on the desk, Ms. Warren," he said in a smooth voice as he closed the door. Slowly, I did as he asked and raised my hands. He looked over at Pepper, who was still curled up by the fire. Good companion? *Yes.* Guard cat? *Not hardly.*

"A familiar," he said, staring at the cat. "*Of course.*"

"What?" I said shakily. *Stall,* I thought to myself. Stall as long as possible. I glanced at my backpack, which was still on the couch. The man was standing between me and my weapon.

"Not to worry, Samantha." He glanced around the room and, finding the light switch on the side of the sliding door, he turned off the overhead light. The yellow glow of the fire danced on the walls. The only other light in the room now was the blue glow of my computer monitor. I wondered if Mrs. Trimble might be up for a pee break.

He pulled a roll of duct tape out of his pocket and, still aiming his gun at me, said, "Please come stand in front of me. Put your hands behind your back. I'd really rather not have to shoot you here, so your full cooperation would be appreciated."

I rose slowly, my mind racing. In the dim light, maybe I could fall, roll and then run out the front door. Getting shot in the back, however, would be a very real possibility. I stepped toward him. I'd taken self-defense classes, and I wasn't bad with a roundhouse kick. But if I missed the gun, if he didn't drop it, I was probably dead. ("Stall, Samantha!" said Dad.)

"What did you mean by that?" I asked. I was still behind my desk.

Impatiently he strode over to me and jerked my shoulder around so that I was facing away from him. The cold metal of the gun was now pressed into the side of my head. It wasn't a good feeling. I raised my eyes up toward Mrs. Trimble's bathroom window, but all was dark.

Still holding his gun to my head, he put the loose edge of the tape on my desk and jerked the roll so that a two-foot strip came free. With one hand he wrapped the tape around my left wrist once, then pulled the roll to the right and did the same with my other wrist. He pulled more of the tape from the roll and wrapped it around both wrists. I tried to keep my wrists apart, but he tightened the binding with each turn of the tape. When my arms were securely fastened behind me, he pulled me roughly away from my desk.

I wondered if screaming would help. With the wind and the rain it was doubtful, but it might earn me a bullet in my brain. The man wound duct tape around my head, and pulled it between my teeth. So much for that idea.

When I was gagged so tightly I had to concentrate in order not to panic, he pulled a plastic garbage bag out of his pocket. He put the gun down on the mantle, shook the bag open, grabbed Pepper by the scruff of his neck and shoved him into the bag. Now I was *mad.*

I kicked the back of his knees and the man fell into the

chair. I rushed the couch, where my backpack and nine were. He jumped up and grabbed my shoulder and pulled me backward. I fell over onto the coffee table, flat on my back, and then rolled to the side onto the floor.

Suddenly, his gun was back at the side of my head. "Don't move, Ms. Warren, or we'll end this right here." I froze. There's something about the cold, hard metal of a gun pushed firmly into the side of your head that makes you stop and think. He jerked me up to my feet and pushed me onto the couch. Pepper had jumped out of the bag and was crouched under the coffee table growling. Pointing his gun at me still, he grabbed Pepper again. He moved slowly back to where the bag lay, crouched down and, never letting me out of his sight, put Pepper back in the bag. For a minute he just stood there, holding the bag and aiming his gun at me.

Finally, he spoke. "The weather has been remarkably cooperative this evening," he said. "I was concerned about your nearby neighbors, but it's a very dark night. We'll be leaving by the beach. You will walk in front of me up to the boat ramp where my car is parked. If you try to run, I will shoot you." In the bag, Pepper was yowling and squirming. "I will also kill your cat," he added. He moved his gun toward the slider and said, "Go."

I got up and walked out into the rain.

The ramp was about two hundred yards down the beach from my stairs. I walked as slowly as he would allow, darting my eyes back and forth in the hope that someone would be out with their dog or looking through a window at the storm. No luck. I was soaking wet by the time we got to the gravel driveway; all I was wearing was my turtleneck and jeans. At least I still had my hiking boots on; if I did somehow manage to escape I'd be able to run.

A darkish sedan was parked facing out by the boat ramp, close to the bluff on the side. The car I'd seen by the Mayflower II. The man put a key in the trunk and popped the lid. He tied a knot in the garbage bag with Pepper and put him against the side of the trunk. Then he leaned down and wrapped duct tape around my feet, holding his gun against my kneecap. No way now to run. I stared up at the house perched on the bluff. The windows were completely dark. Weekenders. Then he shoved me down into the trunk, arranged my legs and softly closed the lid.

He got into the car; my head sank and then rose with the motion. The door closed. The engine turned over and we began to move. I squirmed around, trying to position my face toward the bag that held Pepper. If I could somehow bite a hole in the bag at least he'd be able to breathe. I got my face turned up against the plastic and worked my jaw up and down. The gag was tight, pressing down on the back of my tongue. I felt like I was choking. But I could still clench my teeth; I worked my jaw up and down furiously, fighting my gag reflex, trying to stretch the tape. If I vomited now I would almost certainly asphyxiate. I got a bit of the plastic in my mouth and pulled, tearing a small hole. Panting, I did it again twice, making the hole bigger each time. Pepper was growling and squirming but I thought he'd have enough air now.

My neck was cramped from the effort; I turned my head back and bent my chin down toward my chest to ease the ache.

He'd put me in the trunk facing away from the opening. I craned my neck, searching in vain for a release; in newer cars there's a glow-in-the-dark handle that will open the trunk. Nothing. He was surely insane, but the guy wasn't stupid.

If I could get myself rolled over, maybe I could get the brake or taillight wires in my mouth and yank them out. I felt around with my hands first; blindly, I moved my arms away from my back in search of a wire, *any* wire, to pull. I could feel the smooth metal and felt the occasional hole or protrusion, but there was nothing I could grab. I tried to roll over but it was too shallow and I couldn't straighten my legs enough. Finally, I lay still, fighting to catch my breath.

I was blind inside the dark trunk; my hair was plastered to my head and getting in my eyes. I was shivering from the cold and wet. *Think, Sam. Think!* I kicked back with my feet, hoping vainly that I might get lucky and kick out the brake light. I struggled for a few more minutes, then lay still again. It was difficult to breathe through my nose and not gag.

We'd been driving for about ten minutes. Only twice did I hear the sound of a passing car. Late on a miserable, wet, midweek night, there wouldn't be a lot of traffic.

Pepper was quiet. We were both accepting the futility of struggle. The rain beat on the roof of the trunk, teasing me, as if someone were out there knocking. A few more surges of adrenaline, a few more moments where I thrashed and kicked and banged my head against the roof. For my efforts, I had sharp pains on the side of my head and knees. I was bound and bruised and helpless.

Chapter 33

The car slowed and turned sharply. The crunch and vibration of gravel rose from the tires below. We were travelling slowly, down a driveway or a secondary road. After several minutes, we rolled to a stop. I heard his car door open. Steps on the gravel. A key in the lock. Then the trunk lid popped open. I blinked.

The man's dark figure was silhouetted; a bright light shone from somewhere and it wasn't the dark sky. I felt a surge of hope; maybe we were somewhere near civilization. Near people. I wondered if Dennis or Milo had tried to reach me or gone by my house.

He pulled me up by my shoulders, lifted me out of the trunk, and stood me against it. I was unsteady on my feet, but I managed to stay upright. As my eyes adjusted, I could see that we were parked close to a very large home, a McMansion. In front of me was one of Plymouth's large ponds. My money was on the Billington Sea. *That's good.* There should be extra patrols. I looked to my side, but all I could see beyond the home was heavy forest. The driveway was long. My hopeful thoughts flitted away.

He picked me up and flung me over his shoulder, then

grabbed the bag with Pepper, who yowled loudly and thrashed about inside the bag. He carried us easily; the man was strong. He was also tall; not as tall as Milo, but I figured six foot. He stepped onto a dock and walked quickly to the end, where he dropped Pepper and then roughly dumped me into a canoe. He turned around and went back up to his car. I struggled to sit up. I could see the back of the large house, no doubt a summer retreat for wealthy Bostonians. The man was pulling a large duffel bag out of the sedan. *His ropes.*

Shit! Shit! Shit! I considered throwing myself out of the canoe, into the water. I could probably hold enough air in my lungs to float. But then he'd either pull me back out or shoot me. There was no way I could get far enough away from him with my hands and feet bound. The rain was stinging my eyes as I looked around frantically for a way to escape.

A moment later he was back on the pier. As he approached, he chuckled. He dropped his duffel bag into the canoe, untied the small craft from the dock, and climbed in. He pulled an oar out of the bottom and began to row. Still chortling.

"I do so appreciate irony," he said. "The road that brought us to this lovely estate? It's called Black *Cat* Road." He laughed loudly, a warm, melodious laugh. "It's just so fitting, isn't it?" His voice was deep; it had a radio announcer's warm tone. It wasn't Charles Smit or John Clarkson. And I now knew that it wasn't Zeke Bradley. He continued to chuckle as he worked the oar. We were gliding rapidly across the surface. I was shaking from the cold.

"Do you know the story of the Billington Sea, Ms. Warren?" he asked a few minutes later. I just stared at him. The ski mask hid his features; the eyes that peered out were dark.

We'd left behind the glow of the outside lights that surrounded the home on shore; I couldn't make out the color of his eyes.

"Young Francis Billington was exploring in the early days of Plymouth Colony; just a month after the Mayflower arrived. He climbed a tree, the story goes, and saw a great body of water surrounded by thick forest. They actually thought it might be a passage to the Pacific. That's why they called it a 'sea.' Of course, some days later, Francis and a shipmate came and found it was just a pond." He paused and glanced around. The cold rain seemed to have no effect on him. *He* was wearing rain gear.

"Imagine. Four hundred years ago, this pond looked much as it does now, absent the summer homes and cabins." He continued rowing, staring at me as if he expected me to reply. *Oh yes, it's a lovely spot, Mr. Murderer.*

I was already shivering violently, but again, I considered throwing myself out of the canoe. We were far from the shore now and the night was dark. It would be more difficult for him to shoot me. But not impossible. Not nearly as impossible as it would be for me to reach land before drowning. Tears joined the raindrops on my face. A minute later I grew angry. I screamed, making as much noise as I could through the gag. I thrashed around, lurching from side to side in the canoe. I didn't care now if we capsized. I screamed until I was choking; I gasped and sobbed a few times, caught my breath and then started up again.

The man didn't react and he didn't pause; he rowed steadily. We were several hundred yards from the home on the shore now. A few lights flickered around the pond, but they were all quite far away. After a couple more minutes, the canoe scraped sand and we came to a stop.

He climbed out of the canoe and dragged it up on the

shore. He lifted out his duffel bag and put his arms through the handles and shrugged it up onto his shoulders. Next he leaned down, grabbed me from behind and dragged me out onto the ground. He left me lying on my back amid the brush. I turned my head back and forth, but I could see little and rain was pelting my face. He left my field of vision for a few seconds, and then he was back holding the bag with Pepper in it. Pepper wasn't moving anymore. Was he unconscious? *Or worse?* I wasn't sure if I'd made the hole in the bag large enough. I screamed again through the duct tape, the rain and my tears blinding me. He picked me up, threw me over his shoulder and climbed into the woods.

We were on Seymour's Island, I was nearly certain. It was small; maybe four hundred feet across at its widest point. I'd walked it once, as a teenager, when friends and I were boating on the pond. With his duffel bag in my face I couldn't breathe; I struggled to turn my head the other way. I could barely make out the trunks of the trees as he walked through the forest, but the dark didn't seem to bother him. He continued briskly for about two minutes and then stopped, dropped me and Pepper to the ground and shrugged off his duffel bag.

Chapter 34

"Did you know, Ms. Warren, that after Margaret Jones was hanged, a brutal storm ensued? The sky filled with great bouts of thunder and lightning; trees fell and the people believed that God was pleased."

Who the fuck is Margaret Jones?

The man stood staring at the sky for a moment. "It really is perfect," he added. With that, he took the roll of duct tape out of his pocket, turned me on my side and jerked my feet up behind me. I struggled briefly, but it was useless; I was numb with the cold and had no strength left. He wrapped more tape around the bindings, connecting my feet to my wrists the same way he'd done to the other victims. I was stretched backwards; the right side of my face was lying in soaking wet pine needles. When he released me and stood, I struggled not to roll all the way over onto my face. I strained in the dark with my left eye to see what he was doing, but only when he moved right by my face could I see anything at all.

Hope was seeping out of me like the last few grains of sand in an hourglass. Four women had been in this position before me; four women had *died* in this position. I whimpered, quietly now. I could only hope that the wet cold would fully numb me to the pain. Maybe I would even lose consciousness; it was below thirty degrees and I was soaked to my skin. By my head, I felt Pepper move in the garbage bag and felt a moment of relief—until I realized that it might have been kinder if he'd suffocated.

A couple of minutes later the man's legs came into view again. He'd changed out of his rubber waders and was now wearing tall black leather boots with light colored laces. Strapped to the boot near my face was a metal spike that glowed in the dim light. He leaned over, picked up something that I couldn't see and walked away. He spoke again.

"Yes, they said Ms. Jones had two nipples hidden near her womanly parts. They believed she used them to suckle her familiars. She was put to death long before the Salem witch trials. Of course, here in Plymouth our forefathers were rather more lenient with witches. But no matter." Now I understood why he'd brought Pepper.

I heard scraping on tree bark. He was climbing the tree, carrying his rope up to the branch from which I would hang. For a couple of minutes, all was quiet. Now he would be making my noose.

I was entering a fugue. It was like watching a movie. A really bad B-rated movie where you knew right from the start that the heroine is doomed, only this time *I* was the stupid bimbo who hadn't locked her doors.

In the tree somewhere above me I heard more shuffling. I was growing sleepy, but I was no longer cold. I no longer felt the pain of my bruises or the discomfort of my contorted limbs. I wondered where Milo was and hoped that Laura was responding to her medication. I nuzzled deeper into the pine needles; they felt soft and comfortable and warm now. The man said something else above me, but I could no longer understand his words. *So this is how it feels to die. Not so bad, really.*

Minutes passed; I didn't know how many. Then, abruptly, the man lifted me up into his arms and we were running. Or rather, he was running, clutching me awkwardly. I felt myself slipping and he stopped, adjusted my weight and then took off again. That didn't make sense; I struggled to think clearly. The jarring motion was bringing me back to consciousness, but I was confused. *Why is he running?*

"No, no, no," he was mumbling. I felt him stumble and then we were moving again. Just a few seconds later, I was launched into the air. I braced for impact, but when I hit the surface I continued to descend. He'd thrown me into the water.

I was sinking quickly; I'd had no time to prepare or take a deep breath. The water was freezing. I clamped my lips around the duct tape but already my lungs were screaming for air. I squirmed and looked frantically around, but everything was black. My chin and stomach hit the bottom, hard, and my mouth opened. Ice cold water filled my throat. I was going to die, hog-tied and face-planted at the bottom of the Billington Sea.

"Get her clothes off!"

I heard the voice from far away. I sensed motion all around me. Something cold touched my skin near my waist; I heard more than felt my jeans being cut away. Did I have nice panties on? What felt like more than one pair of hands was rubbing my chest, my stomach and my sides. Slowly, I opened my eyes.

I was in an ambulance; three men in navy blue jackets moved rapidly in and out of my line of sight. Rough hands still massaged my torso, but now a blanket was covering me.

"She's awake!" one of them shouted, and a red-faced man with sandy hair came into view. "Can you hear me, honey?" he asked. I tried to speak, but my throat was raw. I nodded. Someone pulled a warm hat over my head.

"Can you drink something?" he asked.

I didn't know if I could, but I nodded again and he smiled.

"Get me some coffee out of that thermos," he yelled. I heard a flurry of activity and then he was holding a plastic thermos lid cup in front of me. From behind me, someone eased me up until I was at enough of an angle to drink. The ambulance was moving, but he managed to give me a sip without spilling it all over. The hot coffee burned as it went down.

"A little more," he said. I drank some more. The coffee was strong and had too much sugar in it, but the warmth felt good. I took another sip, and Sandy Hair said, "Good girl." I smiled faintly and I was eased back down. The activity continued; I was massaged from all sides and something warm was laid on my stomach. Slowly, I drifted away.

Chapter 35

I was floating, drifting, surrounded by blackness. I moved my hands and feet—they were no longer bound. I flailed wildly, felt a sensation of falling, and then, with a jerk, I was awake. "Pepper?" I struggled to sit up.

Next to me, Milo jumped up and clutched my arms. "Hey, hey, it's okay." He leaned over me, slid his hands up to my shoulders and eased me back onto my pillow. He gazed into my eyes with a small smile and smoothed back my hair.

"He's safe, Sam. You're at Jordan. Pepper's safe at Turk's condo."

I searched his eyes, those wonderful, chocolate fondue eyes. "He was in a garbage bag."

"And Dennis found him, and they took him to the vet this morning, and he's *fine. Promise.*" Milo sat back down and stroked the palm of my hand.

I closed my eyes and enjoyed the sensation for a few minutes. Then I reopened them and turned to Milo. "Did they get—"

Milo's smile disappeared. "No. They were busy saving you—thank God—but he got away. They think he swam to

Morton Park. In fact, I should call Dennis now." He stood. "You want some water?"

I nodded. He took a plastic cup with a straw from the nightstand and held it to my lips. It hurt to swallow, and as I leaned up I felt pain in my shoulders and my knees. My head was pounding. Slowly, I lowered myself back.

"They got the guy's car and his bag from the crime scene and the forensics guys are going over them," Milo said. "Dennis asked me to call as soon as you woke up. Do you feel up to talking?"

I shook my head 'no' and said, "Sure. But how—"

"Let me call him and tell him you're awake and then I'll tell you what I know." He pulled his phone out of his pocket, and then looked back at me. "You scared the *shit* out of me," he said. "Don't *ever* do that again." He turned around and faced the window as he dialed.

I'll try to keep that in mind the next time a masked gunman comes into my house.

Milo spoke into the phone briefly and then came and sat back down next to me. The door opened and a smiling nurse with long straight blonde hair and small round glasses walked in. *Marcia Brady meets John Lennon.* Her scrubs were tie-dyed. Behind her I could see a uniformed cop standing outside my door.

"Are we ready for some good drugs?" she asked. "The doctor said you'd be pretty sore once you thawed out." She handed me some pills.

"Thanks," I said. "He wasn't kidding."

"Well, nothing's broken, but they want to keep you one more night." She brought the water cup to my lips and I swallowed the pills. "Just wanna make sure your heartbeat's regular. You had a pretty close call last night," she added.

You have no idea.

She fussed around the monitors for a bit and finally left my room, closing the door behind her.

I looked at Milo. "So what happened? How did they find me?"

He sighed. "Turk gets the credit. The *one* night I leave you alone." He took my hand again and looked down at his lap for a minute. Finally his eyes met mine. "Around twelve, I texted you and you didn't reply, so then I called, like four times. When you didn't answer, I got worried. I started over to your house and on the way I called Dennis. He didn't know anything. I told him I was going to your house to check on you. I thought maybe you fell asleep and left your phone downstairs.

"So then I get there and you're not there but your car and your phone and your backpack *are*. I called Dennis back, but he says they think they got the killer on a security video, out by Billington Sea. He and his teams are on the way there, he can't talk. I didn't know what to do; I didn't know *you* were the one with the killer. I called Middleboro to see if Tommy was still locked up, but he is. So then I called Dennis *again*, but this time he didn't answer. I went next door and woke Mrs. Trimble up, but of course she didn't know anything either.

"I was going crazy. I went out on the beach with a flashlight, but you know, it was pouring, and there was no one there. Finally, I just sat down on your couch and waited. Maybe thirty minutes later, Dennis calls me back and says it was *you* with the killer. They're taking you to the hospital. I ran to my truck and got here in like five minutes; I beat the ambulance.

"Turns out that after you suggested extra patrols on Billington Sea, Turk contacted all the security firms in town. Bunch of those big houses have monitoring; they had extra guys watching the video feeds in real time. They saw the car arrive and disappear around the side of the house." I remembered blinking up at the light when the man opened the trunk.

"The first patrol unit got there about seven minutes after it was called in. They couldn't see anyone in the rain, but no one was in the house, so Dennis guessed that he was heading for the island. They got a dinghy with a motor from the kayak place. I guess the killer heard the motor when they got near the island and that's when he decided to throw you in. When they got off the boat; they heard him running through the brush and they went after him. Then they heard the splash. Officer Wills and Officer Hartfield both dove in. They saved you; they got you out and did CPR. By the time the SWAT guys and the other teams arrived, he'd gotten away."

"They had to do CPR?" I shuddered.

"Yeah. They got your heart going again, wrapped you up in a couple of jackets and took you in the dinghy back to shore. I guess you woke up in the ambulance."

I looked up at the heart monitor with new respect. I'd thought they were just being cautious.

"I was here when they brought you in," he continued. "They rushed you away and I didn't know what was going on for almost another hour. I was losing it."

"Sorry," I said with a weak smile. "My nine was on the couch when he came in. I tried to fight, but he put a gun to my head. I'd just figured out about Zeke. I guess I'm descended from Billington. You should have heard him, Milo." I closed my eyes.

All of my muscles hurt, and I was remembering the crazy things he'd said. The sound of his voice. "He was going to kill Pepper too."

I felt Milo's hand on mine. "Just rest until Dennis gets here. They were at the island when I called; it might be a while. I'll be right here."

"Is Laura okay?" I mumbled.

"She will be. She's a lot better. Now it's your turn. *Rest.*"

So I did.

When I opened my eyes again, seven people stood around my bed. I'd heard the mumbling, like they were trying to be quiet, but really they wanted me to wake up. I stared around the room. Outside the sky was nearly dark. I'd slept the day away.

Dennis and Turk were on my left; Milo was standing behind them. On my right were a tall blond man with pink skin and a big-boned woman with short dark hair; they were both wearing suits. *FBI.* At the foot of my bed were two more suit types, one with a greying beard and glasses; the other looked like he was just out of high school, too-big suit, zits and all. They were all looking at me.

"I hope you guys brought the beer and pizza," I said.

They all smiled. Nervous.

"You want anchovies? They gots a special down at Rose and Vicki's," said Turk.

I smiled. "Think I'll pass on that, Turk. Got my fill of bottom feeders last night." I squirmed and tried to sit up.

"Here," said Milo. He reached around Dennis and pushed a button on the bedrail. The mattress beneath my pillow rose.

"Thanks, Milo." I looked around at everyone. I tried to smooth my hair back; I could only imagine what I looked like right now. I sighed. "Okay, let's do this." I might look like shit but at least I felt a whole lot better after my nap; the painkillers Marcia Lennon doled out really *were* good drugs.

Dennis moved closer to the bed. I glanced at him and felt my face flush. I was *never* going to be a Tough Bitch in his eyes now.

"Hi, Dennis," I said.

"Scared the piss outta me, Sam." His eyes were inscrutable.

"I scared me a little myself," I said with a smirk.

Dennis didn't smile. He turned to Milo. "Have to ask you to leave while we take her statement," he said. "You understand," he added with raised eyebrows.

Milo nodded. "I'll be in my mom's room, Sam," he said. "Text me when you're done; I put your phone on the nightstand."

"Thanks." My eyes followed him until the door closed and then I looked back at Dennis. "Where do you want me to start?"

Chapter 36

The wind was cutting and the sky still mottled with rain clouds, but for the time being at least, they held back the waterworks. I didn't care if I never saw rain again. Maybe I would move to the desert. I might have good hair in the desert. I shifted my cap lower. The automated doors made a smooth ssshhh sound as they slid open. Then the voices assaulted me.

"What can you tell us about the killer?"

"How did you survive the Pilgrim Slayer?"

"How did you feel when you realized what was happening?"

"Do you have a statement for us, Ms. Warren?"

Flashes exploded. I shuddered involuntarily and Milo squeezed my hand. Dennis had warned me, but I didn't expect *this*. Some fifty newshounds were shouting and shoving near the hospital entrance as Milo pushed me through the doors. The nurse had insisted I use a wheelchair, which just deepened my embarrassment. Cameramen were zooming in on us; this would make the evening news. The *national* news. And I had no mascara.

I rose from the chair, waved to the crowd and took Milo's arm as we followed the path the police had constructed out of a dozen white sawhorses and a few hundred yards of yellow tape. I studied my feet as we crossed the parking lot. "Don't talk to the press!" Dennis had said.

We made it to Milo's truck and climbed inside. The great black eyes of the cameramen stayed with us as we exited the parking lot.

"*Jeeeesus*," I said.

Milo grinned. "You survived the Pilgrim Slayer. It's all over the news. You're famous now. Talk shows will be calling."

"*I* didn't survive him; I got rescued *from* him. I'd be fish food if Turk hadn't alerted those security guys." I stared out the window. "*He*'s the hero.

"Don't forget the guys who pulled you out, and the EMTs, and the doctors."

"Exactly my point. I'm nothing more than a victim. A lucky victim."

"Lucky, but also tough, Sam," Milo said. "Not everyone would have lasted as long as you did. You could have died before he even threw you in. If anything, the water temperature was warmer than the air. That might actually have saved you."

"Great. I owe my life to a murderer. He did say he appreciates irony. Doesn't matter. I just don't want all this attention," I said grumpily.

Milo reached over and took my hand. "It's a lot better than the alternative," he said softly. "And anyway, *you're* the one who told Dennis to cover Billington Sea. So really you *did* save yourself."

I squeezed his hand. "I guess," I said. I was still

overwhelmed by all that had happened, and I was glad to be going home, even if there would be no privacy until the killer was found. An unmarked car followed us even now; I would be under surveillance twenty-four seven. Dennis believed, and the FBI stiffs concurred, that the guy would make another run at me. I was now, officially, *bait.* Before heading home, though, we were going to pick up Pepper.

We parked outside Turk's condo about ten minutes later. He and his girlfriend lived in a newer complex overlooking a golf course on the edge of town. We climbed the stairs to his unit and Turk opened before we could knock. He nodded at my babysitter in the parking lot below. Handoff complete.

Dennis was sitting at Turk's kitchenette, shuffling through paperwork. I looked around for Pepper.

"He be under the ottoman," Turk said.

I hurried into Turk's living room. It was stylishly decorated with an eclectic mix of contemporary leather and classy antiques. There was no end to the many faces of Turk. I knelt down on a fluffy, white Flokati rug and peered under the ottoman. Pepper was lying on his side, legs sprawled.

"Pepper," I said softly. His yellow eyes opened and I'd have bet the Pilgrim Slayer reward money that he smiled. He crawled out from under the footstool and stretched his Halloween cat stretch. I scooped him up and hugged him to my chest; his purring vibrated through me. Awesome. "You're down two lives now, Pep," I said. "Let's keep the rest in the bank for a while, eh?"

I stood and carried him back to the kitchen. I sat down at the table next to Dennis and Pepper curled up on my lap. "So what's the latest?" I asked.

"We were finally able to talk with Zeke Bradley this

morning," Dennis replied.

"Talk *at* him; he ain't talk to us," said Turk. "He just recite shit. *Boring* history shit."

Dennis shook his head. "Guy's just this side of Rain Man. But there's a chance he can identify the killer. We think Zeke either spoke to him at the library himself, or else the killer overheard his mother use Zeke's name and took it as an alias. He's a savant, can quote whole passages from historical documents word for word. And tell you what page it's on in what book, and where that book is shelved in the library. He's also a computer whiz."

"Ain't got nothin' to say on nothin' else though," Turk added.

"What about Meredith?"

"She says there are a few regulars who come in weekly. But we've already gone through the log book." I nodded. So had I. "She said Zeke was outside with his books a lot over the summer, so she doesn't know everyone he might have talked with, or who might have seen him there. She couldn't—"

"Wouldn't," Turk interrupted.

"Couldn't or wouldn't say if there was any one guy that fit your 'tall, strong and radio voice' description. Said she just doesn't pay that much attention. Said more than two thousand people have come through since she started working there."

I thought about that. Meredith Bradley was forty-five years old, single and lived with her autistic son. She'd been researching boob jobs and face peels. She either had a new man in her life or she was looking for one.

"I think she's holding back," I said, and proceeded to explain my rationale.

Turk laughed. "We tell the Feebs we got a 'boob job theory.'"

We all laughed, but Milo said, "I think Sam's right. Meredith Bradley's a single, middle-aged woman. She'd notice a tall, well-built guy, especially one who came in more than once."

"I'll dig deeper in her email account, go back further," I said. "I only saw a bit the other day." I leaned back, stroking Pepper. "You get anything on the boots?" The killer's climbing boots and spurs had looked new to me; the FBI was tracing purchases.

"Not yet, they're still on it. We put someone in the library too," Dennis said. "One of the Feebs, the woman, is going to work there for a while."

"If he's smart, the killer's going to take a break," Milo said.

"Depends," said Dennis. "These guys like their routines; either that or they escalate. Have a hard time stopping once they're on a roll." He exhaled loudly. "But you're right. He could sit tight for a few weeks while we blow up our budget watching Sam. But that's what we're going to do. I *want* this guy."

With that he stood. "We should be going. Lots of paperwork with the damn Feds. They got a form for taking a shit and another one for wiping."

Chapter 37

Milo pulled slowly into my driveway and parked behind my Mini. He *had* to go slow or he'd run over a journalist. I suggested he floor it. He snorted, but I was serious. A gaggle of twenty or more reporters and cameramen stood shivering on the road in front of my house. A young uniform battled to keep them from crossing onto my postage stamp of a yard, but he was seriously outnumbered.

Pepper put his front paws up on the window and peered out. A flurry of flashes went off. Tomorrow my cat's face would be on front pages all over the nation. At least it took some of the spotlight off me. I pulled my cap down further and opened the door.

Pepper jumped down and strutted up the driveway with his tail high. He was loving it. Maybe I should give up the P.I. thing altogether and get him into show business. He could do a reality show. If Honey Boo Boo could do it, Pepper was a shoe-in.

The reporters were loud and obnoxious, but we ignored them and made it into the house unscathed. I went into the kitchen and watched through the window as the police officer fought to keep them from trampling my grass. How long would they stay out there? A good Arctic cold wave would be welcome right about now. Maybe a hurricane. Sighing, I backed away from the window. Right into Milo.

He put his arms around me and I turned around. He looked down at me. "*Finally,* I have you to myself," he said.

I looked up at that pretty face, into his eyes. If he wanted to kiss me now, I was up for that. I nearly died two nights ago and I hadn't had sex in something like two years. I really didn't want to go out at the tail end of a dry spell. *And* I was probably still the target of a deranged serial killer. No time like the present. I put my arms around him and stroked his back. I looked up again. "You want to make a fire and get cozy on the couch?"

He smiled. "I *like* cozy." He released me and walked into the living room.

I followed him slowly. "I haven't gotten cozy in a long time," I said. All of a sudden I was nervous. Did I really want to get cozy with Milo? *Yes, I did.* But could I remember *how* to get cozy? What if I was really bad at getting cozy? I had the feeling Milo's experience with coziness greatly exceeded my own.

He laughed. He was bent down putting newspaper under the log holder. "Sam, getting cozy is just getting cozy. If things get cozi*er,* that's cool. If they don't, *for now,*"—he grinned at me—"that's cool too."

Okay, I could work with that.

A few minutes later, Milo had the fire burning nicely and he joined me on the couch. I snuggled up against him. After a few seconds he leaned down and kissed me, slowly. *Holy cow!* Suddenly, I remembered *exactly* how to get cozy. And I wanted to get cozy *right now.*

Milo was pulling my sweater over my head when I heard a loud crash right outside my window. It sounded like something big and heavy had fallen onto the brick walkway that ran alongside the house. Milo jumped up and ran to the window. I sat up. My face was smashed inside my turtleneck. I pulled it off and held it in front of my chest. My heart was pounding. "What *was* that?"

Milo laughed. Then he laughed even louder. He turned around. He was naked from the waist up and, if we weren't in danger, I wanted to go back to being cozy.

"*What?*" I said.

"Come see, Sam," he managed to sputter. Sighing, I rose and joined him at the window; I still had my shirt pressed against my naked chest. I peered down.

On the sidewalk below my window, a reporter was crawling around on the ground recovering pieces of what was probably once an expensive camera. Mrs. Trimble was standing next to him with her arms crossed and a small smile on her face. The uniform was next to her, his jaw hanging open. The reporter looked up and yelled at the cop and now I could see why Milo was losing it. The reporter's face and neck and the front of his jacket were covered in what had been, no doubt, a very delicious chocolate cake.

Milo and I pulled our shirts and jackets on, went out the back door and around to the side of the house.

"I want you to *do* something," the reporter was shouting.

The cop had finally closed his mouth. Now he was struggling not to laugh.

"She assaulted me!"

"You were trespassing," said Mrs. Trimble primly.

"You smashed a cake in my face!"

"I was bringing a cake to a dear friend who's had a traumatic experience." Mrs. Trimble turned to the cop. "So you can imagine my *fright* when I saw someone sneaking around outside Samantha's house. And after everything she's been through…" Mrs. Trimble shook her head. She had her hand to her chest now and was making wide-eyes behind those thick glasses. "I just reacted the only way I could think of."

I thought she was laying it on a little thick, but then, the cop didn't know Mrs. Trimble.

"I suggest you take off now, buddy. There's a clear line at the front of the house and you crossed it. You were trespassing, like the lady said." The cop winked at me.

The reporter was still on his knees and he dropped his head. A chunk of frosting fell from his hair onto his pants. He tried to pick it off, but wound up smearing it into his chinos. "Fucking *great*," he said. He got up and stormed past the police officer.

When he disappeared around the front of the house, I giggled. Milo joined in and soon all four of us were busting a gut.

Finally the officer stopped laughing. "I better get back out front before one of these idiots tries to go in the front door." He turned around and strode off with a wave.

I surveyed the mess on the sidewalk. I guess we were stuck with the cleanup, but I was awfully glad that Mrs. Trimble and her cake had come by *before* the guy snapped a shot of me and Milo getting cozy.

Chapter 38

Milo set a glass of wine down on my desk, then came around, stood behind me and caressed my neck. He bent down and kissed my forehead. I looked up and we kissed upside down. I immediately felt that spark, the one just below my belly button, which was becoming delightfully familiar. I wondered if he were up for yet another round of cozy. We'd spent the whole afternoon upstairs in my bed, but I was, after all, coming off a two-year hiatus.

"Dinner's almost ready," he said.

Damn.

"Okay," I said and stood. "I've already got dessert on my mind." I put my arms around his waist and smiled up at him.

He looked down at me and shook his head. "*Wow,*" he said.

"I know," I replied. "I *told* you I hadn't gotten cozy in a long time. I'm just getting warm."

He laughed. "Yeah, well, as much as I'd love a little dessert before dinner," he said, "Dennis and Turk will be here any minute. We better hold off."

"Lightweight," I said.

"Oh, I can hang," he said and pressed himself closer to me. "See?"

He wasn't kidding. *Damn.* I grabbed my wine and took a sip, one hand still clutching his butt. Pepper jumped up on the desk, sat down and stared suspiciously up at Milo.

"He's jealous," I said.

"Yeah, well, he better get used to it."

Excellent. I was already getting used to it. We were right in front of the window; I looked over, but for once Mrs. Trimble wasn't hovering in her kitchen. I let go of Milo and walked around my desk.

"So, I'm back to 1670 or so and I still don't have a Billington ancestor," I said. I'd been working on my genealogy. "I got Warren and Browne and Chilton. No Billington."

Milo frowned. "What does *that* mean?"

"I don't know. I'm not done yet, but getting close. There's only two more generations." This genealogy business wasn't easy, but it wasn't rocket science either, especially not when you had free reign of every online database imaginable. Had the killer made a mistake? Changed his MO? "So far, I'm not descended from Billington."

My front door opened and I heard Dennis and Turk shuffling in. "Honey, I'm home," Dennis called. I could feel my cheeks flush as Dennis walked into the living room. Milo was a good eight feet away but I felt like I was wearing a neon sign. One of the blinking ones. *Sam had sex today. Sam had sex today. Sam had...*

Milo stayed behind my desk. Dennis looked at us blankly. Turk came into the room behind Dennis and stopped. "Sheeet," he said and winked at me. *Wow.* Turk really did have freakishly good instincts. He pulled off his coat.

"Smells good," said Dennis, apparently none the wiser.

Out of nowhere, a knock sounded at the door. We all looked at each other. Dennis put his hand on his gun and followed me to the front door.

I peered through the peephole. I turned to Dennis. "It's *Barbie,*" I said with a smirk.

He stared at me. "Oh, for God's sake." He opened the door.

Barbie stood under the front porch light smiling. She held up a bottle of wine. "Hi...?"

"What are you *doing* here?" Dennis asked.

Her face held the smile, but her eyes lost it. "Well, I saw you leaving the station and..."

"And you *followed* me?"

"I just thought...things didn't end so well at that...*place* the other night," she said. "I had some wine, so I thought...well, I *thought* you were going home but then you passed..."

"Come on in, Barbie," I said, giving Dennis a look. It wouldn't be good if Judge Barbie figured out that Milo and I were working with Dennis. She *knew* people. Like Chief Hastings. Time to pour Barbie a drink. "Here, let me," I said, reaching for her bottle. "We were just getting ready to have some drinks before dinner."

She smiled at me appreciatively. Handing me her bottle, she stepped inside and followed me into the kitchen. Grunting, Dennis followed. Barbie was wearing a long cashmere coat and designer boots. Jimmy Choo or Manolo Blahnik. I sometimes read *Vogue* in the checkout line; I'm a little bit better with shoes than I am with cars.

"Can I take your coat?"

She shrugged it off and handed it to me. When I went into the foyer to hang it, I saw Milo in the living room cleaning the murder board. *Good man.*

A minute later Milo came into the kitchen and went to the oven, opened the door and had a peek. He was making a pork roast in pastry with Dijon mustard and tarragon.

"Oh, it smells wonderful," Barbie said. "Are you sure—"

"It's *fine*," I said with a smile. "Here, let me open that. We were having red." I grabbed the corkscrew off the counter and went to work on Barbie's bottle. It was a 2008 Pinot Grigio.

"Got any Scotch?" Dennis asked. I pointed to the cabinet above the fridge. He took down my bottle of Dewars and poured himself four fingers. *Shit.* That was expensive Scotch. But Dennis looked like he needed it.

Turk approached Barbie. "I'd *kill* for a taste of that Pinot Grigio," he said. "So to speak," he added with a chuckle. The ghetto accent was nowhere to be heard.

"Oh, of course!" she said, pleased to be of use. Milo put ice cubes in two wine glasses and served Barbie and Turk. We all went into the living room and sat. An uncomfortable silence ensued. Dennis chugged his Scotch. Barbie put her hand on his thigh. Dennis picked it up and moved it off.

"Sooo," Barbie said, turning to me, "I guess *you* had a bit of a scare the other night."

A bit of a scare? How about I was kidnapped at gunpoint, tied up, shoved into a trunk, and nearly froze to death just before I nearly drowned?

"Uh...yeah," I said. I took a swig of wine.

"Sam can't talk about what happened," Dennis said crossly.

"Oh, I'm sorry, I know that," said Barbie. She uncrossed

her legs and then crossed them the other way. Pepper chose that moment to walk over to the couch and jump up. He looked at Barbie and dug his paws into her thigh. Left, right, left right. Was she wearing *Spanx*? She looked thin, but Pepper doesn't waste his time kneading muscle. He has a sixth sense for cellulite.

"Oh," she said, and pushed Pepper onto the floor. She looked at me apologetically. "I'm allergic," she said. Pepper jumped back up and resumed in earnest. Barbie's eyes turned anxious. They were watering. She stood and Pepper fell onto the couch.

Dennis rubbed Pepper's chin. I wasn't sure Dennis even remembered Pepper's *name*, but suddenly they were best friends. Barbie stood there uncertainly.

Milo stood. "Here, Barbie, take my seat. Pepper doesn't bother me," he said.

"Thank you, Michael," she replied. I stifled a giggle. They maneuvered around the coffee table and each took their new seats.

Just then, there was another knock at my door. *Seriously?*

I rose again and Dennis followed me to the door. I looked out the peephole. *Shit.* I looked at Dennis. "It's the chief," I whispered.

He rolled his eyes. "Fuck *me*," he said.

"Go upstairs," I said. "*Quick!* I'll try to get rid of him."

After Dennis disappeared into the upstairs hallway, I opened the door.

"Chief! So nice to see you. Come in, come in," I said. I waved to the uniform who was standing guard in my driveway and quickly closed the door. A couple of persistent reporters remained huddled in their vans out on the road.

Chief Larry Hastings was a roly-poly man in his early sixties; he was just a little taller than me and about four times as wide. He had thick white hair, intelligent dark eyes and long, opinionated eyebrows.

When I was little I once asked my father if "Uncle" Larry was a Weeble; the chief had always been round. This made my parents laugh so hard that the memory was etched into my brain. In the twenty-six years since, every time I saw the man, the Chief of the Plymouth Police Department, every *single* time I saw him, the Weebles slogan entered my brain. Usually, it stayed there for days. *Weebles wobble but they don't fall down. Weebles wobble...*

The chief thrust a bouquet of lilies into my arms. "I'm sorry I couldn't get over to the hospital to see you, Sam. Things are a bit crazy right now—"

I grabbed the flowers and led him into the kitchen. "I understand, Chief. Not to worry. How's the case? Did they get anything useful out of the car?" I grabbed a glass, poured the chief some Scotch and handed it to him. I lifted my wine glass toward Turk in the living room. "*This* guy won't tell me anything," I added.

Chief Hastings peered around the breakfast bar. Turk and Barbie and Milo stared back at us with a smorgasbord of expressions. I could see Barbie trying to figure out where Dennis was. Turk was struggling not to laugh. Milo's face remained impassive as he sipped his wine. The Chief looked confused and I was nearly in a panic. I leaned down and pulled a vase out of my cabinet.

"Nice to see you, Chief," said Barbie with a smile. She rose and approached the kitchen and glanced around the room.

Loudly, I cut in. "We were just getting ready to have some dinner. These are so *beautiful*...aren't they pretty, Barbie?" She nodded. As she opened her mouth again, I opened up the tap and ran the water into the vase for thirty full seconds.

"There," I said as I put the lilies in water. I turned back to the Chief. "Um, would you like to join us?" I could almost hear Dennis growling from upstairs. I just hoped he wasn't in my room; I was pretty sure even *he* would notice the cozy aroma of afternoon delight.

The chief downed his Scotch and set his glass on the counter. "Thanks, Sam, but the little lady is waiting." He reached around and squeezed me tight. "I'm just so glad you're all right," he said into my ear. "Some godfather *I* am, huh?" The sharp scent of his cologne filled my nostrils.

"You're a *great* godfather and I'm *fine*, Chief. My friends are all here..." Tears rose in my eyes in spite of myself. I'd almost put the horrific events of Wednesday night out of my mind; now it all came rushing back.

Chief released me and glanced into the living room again. He nodded at Turk. "Didn't know you were friends with Sam, Turk," he said with a shrewd gaze.

"Turk's on my bowling team," said Milo quickly. He grinned. "Raises our handicap considerably."

"*Sheeet*," said Turk.

The Chief watched the both of them for a moment. Finally he nodded. "Right, well, I best be off."

"Thanks again for the flowers, Chief. And tell Nora I said hello and not to worry about me." I walked him to the door.

"Be careful, Sam," he called as he exited. I could see the uniform outside straighten up as the chief walked down my driveway. He might be a roly-poly, but he commanded respect nonetheless. *Weebles wobble....*

I waved once more as he got into his car and closed the door. *Holyshitthatwasclose.* After a few seconds Dennis came down the stairs. He went straight to my bottle of Dewars and poured a few more fingers.

"Where'd *you* disappear to?" Barbie asked with a smile. "The chief was just here."

"*Really?* I was in the can."

Barbie didn't seem to notice the sarcasm. Aren't judges supposed to be smart?

As I walked back into the living room, Turk turned to Milo and said, "*Bowling?* You shittin' me? Dis nigga don bowl."

Chapter 39

"What are we *missing?*" I asked.

Pepper and I were riding shotgun in Milo's pickup; we were heading to Duxbury to welcome Laura home. Grady was already at the hospital.

Milo exhaled loudly. "Do we really know that the Billington link was the *only* connection between the other victims?"

I wracked my brain. "Seriously, we've looked at everything under the sun. Fuller and Cummins didn't have abortions. *None* of them went to Smit's church. They didn't know each other. *I* didn't know *them.* The Billington connection is—*was*—the only thing that made sense…until he came after me. And I guess all of the supposed sins… " I'd finished my family tree early that morning and then spent two more hours double-checking my work. I was not a Billington descendant.

"That means he knows you're working the case," said Milo. "He's scared. We must be closer than we thought." He reached over and took my hand. "This time I am *not* letting you out of my sight. Not until they catch this guy."

I glanced in the side mirror. "Yeah, you and I don't even

know how many cops." Dennis wouldn't tell me how many babysitters there were; I just knew that more than one team was out there watching my every move. I seriously hoped they hadn't bugged my bedroom. For the first time in years I was getting some, and I'd been a little bit vocal about it. I could just imagine the Feebs in their utility van listening.

"If you're right, that means it's someone we talked to," I said. "In person. Clarkson and his crew. Meredith or Zeke Bradley. Their majesties Liz and Charles. By now they know the Sharon Stone cover story was a lie." I'd been headline news for the past few days.

"Someone on the task force," Milo said. He looked over at me. "How do we know there isn't a crazy cop smack in the middle of it?"

Shit. I hadn't even considered that possibility. "Something to run by Dennis later," I said noncommittally. I didn't like to think about bad cops. My parents were cops. My best friends were cops. They weren't perfect *people,* but they were absolutely committed to their work. Nonetheless, it was a possibility that should be explored. Cops-gone-crazy were in the news all the time.

"People aren't always what they seem," said Milo quietly.

"No, they're not," I said.

We rode in silence the rest of the way.

Fifteen minutes later we turned into the Cooke's driveway. As we neared the house, I noticed a dark sedan parked at the end of the driveway. My hands grew clammy.

"Who's *that?*" I asked. Grady's truck was nowhere in

sight.

"Not sure," said Milo. He pulled his truck up to the front of the house.

My babysitters were out on the road; I'd made a point of telling Dennis that I didn't want any intrusions at Milo's house when Laura came home. He was cranky about it, but in the end, he agreed to give us some space. It wasn't even noon; the killer always struck at night.

We gathered up the flowers we'd brought and our backpacks and got out of the truck. Pepper ran gleefully toward the house. There were fish to watch in there, and a Chihuahua in need of grooming. No time to waste. I trailed slowly behind, looking at the sedan. Milo approached the car.

A plump, mid-sized man in a navy blue suit, white shirt and red tie got out. He wore sunglasses, although the clouds were still heavy overhead. A second man exited the passenger side; no sunglasses, he sported fancy, gold-rimmed spectacles. A thin spattering of hair flopped over his pink scalp. A gust of wind grabbed the curtain of hair and made it stand up straight. Dude obviously used hairspray.

I stopped in front of the door and watched. Pepper looked up and meowed. Like me, Pepper isn't always terribly patient.

"Milo Cooke?" asked Sunglasses.

"That's me," said Milo.

"Scott Randolf, Justice Department Investigator."

Milo was quiet for a moment. "*And?* My mother's coming home from the hospital today; she'll be here shortly."

"*And* we need you to come with us," said Hairspray.

Milo stared at the two men, his arms weighed down by a dozen roses and his backpack. "And if I say *no?* As I mentioned, now really isn't a good time."

"There's *never* a good time when you do what we do," said Sunglasses. "But if you don't come with us now, times *could* get worse." He paused. "However, cooperation is always appreciated."

I dropped the flowers I was holding and walked towards the sedan, fishing for my gun in my backpack. Where *was* the damn thing? Finally I found it.

"Do you have some identification?" I yelled, pulling my nine out of my bag. I held it down at my side.

"Whoa, hey, no need to get uptight," said Hairspray. He held his hands up by his face.

"*I* think it's actually a perfect time to get uptight," I said. "You two are sitting here, waiting for us, when we pull in. We don't know who you are. I was *kidnapped* by a serial killer just a few nights ago, in a car just like that one by the way, and now you want my boyfriend to just *go* with you? And leave me alone here? You do realize there are at least two cops standing guard at the end of the driveway *right now*? You upset me, even a *little*, my fragile psyche might just break. I might just get twitchy. *So*, I suggest you explain yourselves just a little bit better. *Right. Now.*"

"Sam," said Milo.

Sunglasses pulled off his shades. Slowly. He put his hands up by his ears. "We don't know anything about any serial killer," he said. He had small, piggish eyes and he squinted now in the daylight.

"Are you *sure*? 'Cause I'm just a little leery of strangers right now. You might be too, if you'd been thrown in a trunk and then nearly drowned." All of the tension and emotion of the past few days was like dry kindling to the fire that was growing in my belly. They couldn't just barge in here and take Milo. Not *now.*

"You mean to tell me you haven't heard about the Pilgrim Slayer? And you supposedly work in law enforcement? *Hello?* My *cat* made the news."

"Sam!" Milo said loudly.

I turned to him.

"*Stop.* This is something else."

I faltered. "What do you *mean,* something else?"

"We need to talk with Mr. Cooke about a Justice Department matter," said Sunglasses. "I'm sorry about your…trauma…but this relates to a case that's a few years old. Just put the gun away and I'll show you my credentials."

I stood there stunned. I looked at Milo but he was staring at the ground.

"Just put the gun away, Sam," he said. "*Please.*"

Forty minutes later, Grady's truck came down the driveway. Pepper and I were sitting on the kitchen door steps. I wiped my eyes and gathered up the flowers Milo and I bought. I stood and walked over to the passenger door and helped Laura out.

"Where's Milo?" she asked.

"I don't know," I said truthfully. Her bright smile faded like new jeans in bleach.

Chapter 40

"Mrs. Trimble? It's Sam. Would you and Mr. Trimble do me a *really* big favor?" I listened. "I'll be over in a few minutes."

I ended the call and took one last look in the mirror. I had on brown pants, a black hoodie, and a navy blue stocking cap. Not the best outfit for a *Vogue* spread, but it just might get me out of my house and over to Mrs. Trimble's without alerting the babysitters.

I had a stupid sit-com streaming on my laptop, just in case the house was bugged. I trusted Dennis, but I wasn't at all sure that he—or his DC-based colleagues—trusted me. I double-checked that my nine was loaded, threw it into my backpack and slid the pack onto my shoulders.

I'd already turned off all but one of the interior lights; I crouched by my slider and stared out around the beach. I didn't see anyone. I watched for two more minutes and then slipped out the door and ran in a crouch down my deck stairs to the sand. I lunged underneath the deck and waited in the bushes for another few seconds. When no one tackled me or shined a blinding light in my face, I made a break for the Trimble's back door.

Thankfully, Mrs. Trimble was waiting and opened up

right away. I hurried away from her door.

I sat down, clear of the windows, in the living room. She shuffled after me in her house slippers and peered down at me with those distorted, unflappable eyes.

"Can I borrow one of your cars for the night?" She raised her eyebrows. "I have to get out of here; I haven't had a single moment of privacy in *days*. It's making me crazy. They follow me every time I leave."

She cocked her head. "You want to ditch the cops? Or the reporters?"

Both. I smiled. "Will you help?"

"Roger," she yelled.

Ten minutes later I was lying beneath a musty wool blanket in the back of Mr. Trimble's Jeep Liberty. I heard the garage door go up and we backed out. Mr. Trimble paused at the end of the driveway and said, "'Night, officer." Something was said in return and Mr. Trimble laughed and then we accelerated down Taylor Ave.

Five minutes later he parked. About ten minutes after that I heard a car pull in beside us. Thank *God* Mrs. Trimble still drove. I'd have to rethink my position on senior citizens and drivers' licenses.

"All clear, Sam." Mr. Trimble got out of the car and opened the back hatch. I crawled out. "Be *careful*," he said with a stern gaze.

"*Thank* you," I whispered. I rushed to the driver's door and climbed in, then pulled out of the empty shopping plaza and headed toward town.

I'd spent the afternoon trying not to lose my mind. After Grady brought me and Pepper home, I paced and cried and agonized over Milo and the case and the seemingly out-of-control life I was now living. Two short weeks ago, I was fine. Okay, I was broke, but I'm used to that. Despite sustaining myself with unhealthy quantities of Great Value brand Mac 'N Cheese, Pepper and I had maintained a simple, straightforward, mostly pleasant existence. Maybe I heard my dead father's voice a little too frequently and maybe I conversed a little too much with a cat, but all in all, I'd thought I had it—more or less—together.

Now I was completely off the rails. I was in over my head on a murder case that was *way* out of my league. I'd been kidnapped and nearly died. I was falling in love—*Shit!*—with a man who, it was now clear, had his own baggage. Baggage that attracted the attention of the United States *Justice* Department for crying out loud. This wasn't a little carry-on bag, we were talking a huge, one-hundred-dollar-over-sized-fee piece of luggage.

What the hell was I supposed to *do*?

Finally, I'd pulled on a jacket and called Pepper out for a walk on the beach. When all else fails, that's always been my bridge back to sanity. I trudged across the damp sand with two not-so-undercover cops stumbling after me in their loafers. I fumed. I cried some more. ("Focus on what you *can* control, Sam," said Dad. "Not what you can't.")

"I can't control *anything*!" I'd shouted. The cops gave me a funny look but I didn't care. I walked to the end of the beach and stared out at the horizon. Finally, I took a deep breath. It was cold and grey, but the beach is my Zen zone. The rhythmic sound of the waves, the sharps and flats of the gulls' cries. The smells. I forced myself to breathe through my nose. *Focus.*

What *could* I control? Not Milo or his problems, whatever they were. Not Laura's health. I was merely a passenger on the roller coaster ride of my emotional state and then there was the black hole of my bank account.

The *only* thing in which I still had unwavering faith was my ability to hack for information and to figure out puzzles. That's what I was good at; that was why I'd thought I could be a PI in the first place. So what could I do *right now* to give myself a sense of purpose, to achieve some semblance of being at the helm of my own ship?

I'd gone back to the house, climbed up the deck stairs and chuckled at the cops dumping sand out of their shoes. Inside, I made a pot of coffee. Then I sat down with a pen and a blank pad of paper—no computer—and I reasoned my way through every single thing I'd learned about the Pilgrim Slayer murders. About the victims. About the locations. About the suspects. About the timing and the messages and the symbols. About John Billington. About my own abduction and the man in the ski mask.

Four hours later I was done. And I'd come to some conclusions.

I parked and turned off the engine and the lights and sat in the dark, watching. It was almost eight o'clock. The windows were lit up and I could see occasional movement in what I thought was the kitchen. I sipped my coffee and ate some cheese doodles. For all I knew I was on a fool's errand, but I planned to sit and watch until everyone was obviously in bed. Then I'd do it again tomorrow. And the next day and the next. I would watch until I either proved or disproved my theory.

I tried not to think about Milo. He'd texted me earlier. "Won't be home for a few days. So sorry Sam. Will explain everything when I get back. Stay safe and cozy." So much for him not letting me out of his sight. I really didn't know if I was upset *for* him or *with* him, but it was my own damn fault. I'd let him in.

Sighing, I turned on the motor and ran the heat for a few minutes, then turned it back off. I shifted position and bit my cuticles. I ate a few more cheese doodles.

Around nine, a front porch light came on and a small figure hurried through the cold to a Toyota Camry. (I'd spent some more time reading Mrs. Trimble's car magazines.) I sat up straight; my heartbeat accelerated. I ducked down as the car backed out of the driveway and passed me. I turned the key, pulled a U-turn out of my parking spot and followed.

Chapter 41

Paddy Barry's was a tiny little hole-in-the-wall bar on Hancock Street in Quincy. Revelers spilled out the front door, talking boisterously and smoking cigarettes. Loud music barreled out each time the door was opened. Meredith Bradley had squirmed her way inside about ten minutes earlier. I'd snapped a photo of her as she walked down the sidewalk.

I parked down the road a little ways and considered my options. I really wasn't dressed for Saturday night at the pub, but I needed to see who she was meeting. She wouldn't drive forty miles to Quincy just to sit alone in a bar. Would she?

I checked myself in the rear-view mirror. I'd done my face before I left home, but the hat had to go. I pulled it off and fingered the frizz. *Huh.* It actually looked pretty good. Style tip for curly-haired girls: Wear a stocking hat for two hours after drying your hair, remove and finger fluff.

There was nothing I could do about the hoodie or the pants, but no one I saw outside of Paddy Barry's was dressed particularly well either. I grabbed my backpack, exited Mr. Trimble's Jeep and crossed the street.

I walked by the pub on the other side of the road, just to

get the lay of the land. Six or seven people loitered in front of the entrance, but I could see very little through the windows. I crossed back to the bar side of the street at the corner and stopped to think.

I could go in myself, but I was afraid that Meredith, or even worse, her date, might see me. And while I didn't know what the killer looked like, he sure as hell knew what I looked like. It was crowded in there. I might get lucky, they might be tucked away in a corner, but this was *me* we were talking about. I'd walk in and Meredith and the Pilgrim Slayer would look up from their drinks and say, 'Hi Sam.' And then I'd shoot him and kill him and then I'd go to jail. The end. I didn't like that story.

I watched the smokers. Six guys, mostly younger, and one girl, talked and laughed, and punctuated their sentences with aggressive tokes of their cigarettes. The girl was the nucleus, the men all vying for her attention. *Of course.* The Margie Method. My outfit was hardly sexy, but the pants cast my ass in a reasonably favorable light and for once I had pretty good hair. I approached the group.

"Dude, *what* are you talking about? The band is totally chill."

"Dude, they don't even come *close* to the NumChucks."
Seriously?

"I kind of like them," said the girl.

Dude Number One beamed at her and said, "Come on, let's go back in. We're missing out." She dropped her cigarette, smashed it under her shoe and followed him through the door.

"I'm *totally* into the NumChucks," I said to Dude Number Two. "David Colter is a friend of mine."

He turned to me and grinned. "No way."

"Way."

"Man, that is *sweet*. Can you get me free tickets?"

I smiled. "I can always ask," I said coyly. We chatted for a few minutes about the musical group that I'd privately renamed the Numb Nuts.

"Can I bum a smoke?"

"Sure." He handed me a cigarette and pulled another out of the box for himself. He held his lighter up for me and I bent over and inhaled.

It took me a few tries to align the end of the cigarette with the flame, but finally the tip glowed orange and harsh smoke coated the back of my throat. I coughed violently for about ten seconds. I gasped and then laughed. "Wow. Sorry, it's been a while, but it smelled so good." *Not!*

He took a huge hit on his own cigarette and blew smoke rings.

"So, anyway, I was wondering if you could help *me* out?" I smiled what I hoped was an alluring smile.

He looked at me, took another hit and said, "What's up?"

"Okay, see, there's this guy in there. I think. And he's been dating a friend of mine and I keep telling her he's a player and he's totally seeing other women, but she doesn't believe me. But I think he's here with this woman tonight." I showed him the picture of Meredith Bradley.

"She's kind of old looking," he said.

"Yeah, well, my friend is actually almost forty."

"*Forty?*" He looked me up and down again as if to confirm that he wasn't wasting his time on a Baby Boomer.

"She's a really great person but she has no clue. Can you just go in and see if this woman is there with a tall guy? And take a picture on my phone?"

Dude Number Two took another big drag and exhaled. I sucked some smoke into my mouth, swished it around there for a few seconds and blew it out.

"You really gonna get me tickets to see the NumChucks?"

"Dude, get me proof that this guy's an ass, and I will *so* get you those tickets. I'd do it myself, but he *knows* me. Here." I took my phone back from him. "Give me your number." He gave it to me and I created a new contact for Dude Number Two. "I'll call David tomorrow."

He dropped his cigarette butt and ground it out. I gratefully followed suit.

"Yeah, sure, I'll have a look."

I set the phone to camera mode and handed it to him. "Make sure you get a clear shot of his face," I added.

I paced back and forth. Ten minutes passed and still no Dude. I ventured a glance through the window, but I didn't see him or Meredith Bradley. I wandered back to the corner. DumbShit was probably in there doing Jaeger Bombs and arguing with Dude Number One about the band. But he had my phone.

Another ten minutes crawled by. *What the fuck!* The smoking crew had already turned over twice.

I was pacing back toward the corner when he tapped me on the shoulder.

"Yo, check it out. That him?"

I stared at the picture for a few seconds. I looked up at Dude Number Two with a big grin and then I squealed and hugged him.

Chapter 42

"Wassup, Nance?" Loud noise muffled his voice; I figured Dennis was at the Trap. There hadn't been another killing since the night I was taken; he was probably blowing off some steam. With Barbie. Or Eileen. Or God knows who. Rather, as Turk would say, God knows whom.

"Dennis, are you sober?" I asked in a sharp voice.

"Mostly," he said. "Why?" His voice sharpened up now too.

"I'm going to text you a picture. Aaron Stevens is the Pilgrim Slayer. *Almost* positive. You need to get a team over to his house. I'm in Quincy. I'm going to tail him home."

"*What? You're where?* What about your handlers?"

"Um, well, I kind of sneaked out."

"JesusHChrist, Sam. I—"

"Dennis, *listen!* I'm really right this time, I *know* it."

He was quiet for a moment; it sounded like he'd gone outside. "How?"

"Look, you have to trust me, but just to be sure, I'm going to hang around here and when he leaves I'm going to listen. He's here with Meredith Bradley. I know his *voice,* Dennis. That will be the final proof. I'll tail him in case he doesn't go home, but you need to get the team ready."

"Fuckin' A, Sam. You're *sure.*"

"Ninety-five percent. Once I hear his voice I'll be certain."

"And you're alone up there."

"Uh...Yeah, but I've got my nine right in my pocket."

"What the hell are you doing tailing people by yourself?"

"I...look, *later!* Are you with me? He won't see me; I'm standing across the street. In the shadows. When they come out, I'll follow them. And then I'm going to follow him home. *Be there!*" I ended the call and texted Dennis the photo taken by Dude Number Two.

The minutes crawled. The air was cold, but adrenaline warmed my blood. My mood swung from terror to elation to cold and calculating. I was standing in a walkway across from Paddy Barry's; I had a clear view of the door.

At nearly midnight, Meredith Bradley stepped out of the bar. She walked toward her car. Where was he? Was he staying on alone? Did he go out the back door? Then Bradley stopped; she'd moved just past the smoking section and now she stood waiting.

I put my hand in my pocket and fingered my nine. I had to get close enough to hear Stevens' voice, but this was the man who tried to *kill* me four nights ago. I'd gotten my hat from the car and my hair was tucked up inside. I pulled it lower now, around my face, and raised my hood. Still, if Aaron Stevens saw my face, I would need my gun.

A minute later, he came out. He stepped past the smokers and smiled at Meredith, who took his arm. They strolled north on

Hancock Street. I recognized his gait. He was tall and powerful. I had no doubt now, but for Dennis and the courts, I needed to hear his voice.

When they'd gone about twenty feet, I ran across the street and slowed to a fast walk. I was wearing sneakers and I moved soundlessly. I narrowed the gap to about ten feet. My hands were sweating in my pocket. I heard Meredith laugh. We were almost to the spot where she'd parked her car. Head down, I continued walking. I was only about six feet behind them now.

"Well, my dear, you've been lovely as always. And so helpful. I can't thank you enough."

A roar flooded my eardrums. I envisioned him coming into my house pointing a gun at me. Bagging Pepper. Throwing me into the canoe. Only now I imagined him with a face. I pulled my head back into my hood as far as I could, sped up and passed just three feet behind the Pilgrim Slayer.

When I got to the next intersection, I stepped behind a utility pole and peeked out. I watched Stevens climb into an expensive looking car and I memorized the plate number as he pulled out onto the street. Then I ran.

Fifteen minutes later I still hadn't caught sight of Stevens' car, which I thought was a Lexus, although I wasn't sure. Had he gone toward Boston? The only logical route back to Plymouth was down Route 3. I'd already passed Meredith Bradley's Camry, and she left a few minutes before Stevens.

I'd called Dennis back with the plate number right after I got to my car in Quincy; theoretically the Staties would be on the lookout for Stevens as well. There were few other cars on the highway. I slowed down a bit and kept my face angled away as Meredith Bradley cruised by.

The night was dark and I'd come to a section of highway where there were no homes or commercial buildings. No overhead lights. Just dense forest. I saw a pair of headlights in my rear-view mirror, approaching rapidly. A chill gripped the back of my neck. A few seconds later, the car was directly behind me. The driver put his brights on and I squinted into the mirror. Then he rammed into me.

I gunned it and pulled the steering wheel sharply to the left. The car behind me accelerated and clipped my right side as I swung back toward the right lane. I was doing about 80 now; I wasn't sure how much higher the Jeep Liberty would go. I continued to swerve back and forth, trying to avoid Stevens—it had to be Stevens, right?—but his engine had a lot more power than the Jeep's.

He accelerated again and caught me square on the back left quarter panel. The Jeep's back end skidded and then the wheels left the road. The Jeep flipped once down the berm between the north and southbound lanes, throwing me into the armrest. The SUV continued over and then jerked to a stop as it hit a tree. I was hanging upside-down by my seatbelt and it felt like I'd cracked some ribs. The airbag had deployed, but now it was deflating. In a daze, I tried to unclasp the seatbelt, but my weight made it impossible to release. I reached for my backpack, which was lying on the roof of the Jeep on the passenger side. I stretched and almost had hold of it when I felt something hard and cold against the side of my head. I recognized that feeling.

"We meet again, Miss Warren," said Aaron Stevens.

Slowly I turned my head toward the window. Stevens was

crouched down, reaching through the broken window, and his all-too familiar gun was pressed against my temple.

"Did you really think I wouldn't be watching you? You shouldn't have underestimated me, Samantha. Or perhaps you simply overestimated your own abilities." He shook his head and smiled faintly. "A fatal mistake, I'm afraid."

Where were those State Troopers? Didn't *anyone* see my car leave the road? I licked my lips and raised my eyes to his.

"I may have underestimated you, Stevens, but I identified you. I've already called the police; they know who you are. You can kill me, but they'll still get you. It'll just strengthen their case against you. Not that four counts of murder and one of attempted murder isn't enough." I stared into his eyes. ("Keep him talking, Sam, but don't piss him off!" said Dad.)

Stevens appeared unbothered. "Yes, I fear I may have to leave this delightful community and continue my work elsewhere. But I don't like unfinished business. *You* are unfinished business, Miss Warren." He smiled. "Your little trick with the neighbors was painfully obvious, although obviously *not* to the policemen out front. I followed you from your home to Meredith's. That's when I decided to call her and ask her to meet me in Quincy for a drink." He grinned. "She jumped at the chance to see me again; the poor woman is smitten. And then I followed you as you followed Meredith all the way to Quincy. Ingenious rather, don't you think?"

For Christ sakes, I'd set my own trap. Where were the cops? How could I keep him talking rather than shooting? I was pretty sure he wouldn't waste too much time, not after what happened on Semour's Island.

"Yes," I sighed, "You outwitted me. Again. But can I ask

287

just one question before you shoot me? I just really want to understand." I looked at him with raised eyebrows. "*Why?*"

Stevens looked around to make sure there were no cars approaching. In all likelihood, a passing car wouldn't even see us. It was late, dark, and we were well off the road beneath dense pines. Someone would have to be looking off to the side at just the right moment to even notice the crashed car. I bent my head forward to try and relieve the pressure; I'd been hanging upside down by my seatbelt for several minutes. Blood was pounding in my temples. I prepared myself for a bullet. At least it would be fast, no doubt better than being strangled by a noose. I was surprised when he spoke again.

"Why?" he said in a loud voice. "*Why?* Weren't my messages clear? The people of this nation are on a path straight to hell. It was my duty, my duty *to God,* to take action." I looked over at him. Beads of sweat were forming on his upper lip, although the night air was cold.

"Over the past thirty years I've watched as American morals have been systematically flushed down the toilet. Abortion was legalized. Not only is it legal, today it seems most women consider it their *right,* like some perverted form of birth control. They commit *murder* so that they can run around fucking like goats. Unmarried, immoral…and the gays! Parades and public demonstrations so that they can marry? Marriage is a contract between a man and a woman and, most importantly, with God! The people of this country—the *women* in this country have gone so far astray…and meanwhile God-fearing men like Charles Smit are reviled; their messages ignored. They—"

"Charles Smit? You know him?" *Keep talking, keep*

talking. Stevens' voice had gotten louder throughout his tirade.

"*Of course* I know him. I attended his church for many years. *Many* years. But Charles' church wasn't having any affect. No one was paying attention. I stopped going a year ago and began work on my own plan. To implement the will of God. To bring America back to its righteous roots. To steer God's children back onto the path to heaven."

He smiled. "And it's working. It's *working.* My actions in Plymouth have captured the collective mind of the nation. As the journalists write more about these women, as the people come to understand their evil forebear and their many sins, righteous Americans will understand. My desperate actions will be vindicated. And like the Saints before us, we will rise up and create—*recreate*—a nation founded in *God.*"

The guy's a fucking nutter. ("Keep him talking Sam!)

"But... *I* haven't had an abortion... I'm not gay," I said. "I went to church at Sight Ministries just last *week.*" I cringed at my pathetic claims. They were true, but it felt wrong to give credence to Stevens' appalling views. But maybe I could make him believe that I was on his side.

"Nice try Samantha. But our little talk is over. My work is too important; it must continue. I think you already know that your snooping is what brought me to you in the first place. You should have stayed out of it." He glanced over his shoulder again.

I jerked my elbow up hard toward his gun, crying out at the pain in my ribs. The gun fell inside the car, landing on the roof just by my head. Stevens scrambled to grab it and I swung my head toward his, head-butting his nose. He sat back and then lunged toward me, wrapping his large hands around my neck and squeezing. So I would go by strangling after all. Stars appeared as my vision faded.

Crack! The rifle report was unmistakable, even in my stupor. Stevens' hands loosened and he slumped gently off to the side.

Chapter 43

I opened my eyes and looked up at the ceiling. After a few minutes, I braced myself for the pain and then pushed myself up off the bed. I couldn't put it off any longer; I had to go. I made my way slowly to the bathroom, did my business and then shuffled back into the bedroom. I eyed the bed and then the clock. It was nine o'clock. I didn't think I would be able to sleep more, and getting in and out of bed was proving quite painful. I shrugged on my bathrobe and stepped carefully down the stairs to the kitchen. I put a fresh filter in the basket and scooped in the coffee grounds. A pot of water later, I hit 'brew.'

Through the kitchen window I could see a herd of reporters holding umbrellas. I sighed as a flash went off. Now my Sunday morning day-after-catching-a-serial-killer look—bedhead, no makeup, bruised neck, large purple egg on my forehead and tatty old robe—would make the papers. I wandered into the living room and peered out at the water.

It was raining softly. Not an angry storm; the sky and the water and the sand were all gentle shades of grey. A perfect Sunday for curling up by a fire with a good book, although I wasn't sure I would be able to curl for at least a few weeks. I had two cracked ribs. Who knew such small bones could cause so much pain?

I felt strangely melancholy. I had done it; I'd solved my first big case. A *huge* case. For all I knew, the Pilgrim Slayer would prove to be the biggest case I ever solved. It's not like we get a new serial killer in Plymouth every six months.

The notoriety would no doubt bring new clients to Sam Warren, P.I.; theoretically that was a good thing. I might even be able to upgrade to brand name macaroni. But after I was treated at the hospital and gave my statement to the police, Dennis had brought me home at four in the morning to an empty house. I missed Milo.

Pepper rubbed my legs and stared up at me as he issued a squeaky, extended meow—the one that meant "I need kibbles."

"I'm sorry, Pep, are you hungry? I know the house isn't empty; *you're* still here. Come on, let's get our coffee and kibbles."

I was adding cream to my coffee when Dennis and Turk pulled into the driveway. I ushered them in out of the rain and Turk held up two large Dunkin' Donuts bags. "Munchkin? Sausage egg bagel?"

I grinned. "All of the above. I'd hug you right now, but then you'd have to take me back to the ER."

"You're welcome," said Turk.

Dennis grabbed plates and we went into the living room where he divvied up the goodies. He looked rough. As he slumped into the couch, he rubbed his hand through his thin hair, making it stick up oddly on the side. Even Turk was a little rumpled. That *never* happened.

"Have you guys even been home yet?"

"Nah, there was a mountain of paperwork to do, and we

sat in while Brueger was interviewed. Took two hours and that was just a preliminary. Fucking IA guy kept asking why he didn't issue a warning."

IA was Internal Affairs. Officer Brueger was the Statie who shot and killed Aaron Stevens as he tried to strangle me. He'd seen Stevens' Lexus on the shoulder, recognized the plate and snuck down the berm with his rifle. He saw me elbow Stevens and the ensuing struggle. When it became clear that I was losing the battle, he fired. The whole thing took about ten seconds.

It was standard procedure for an officer to be investigated following a fatal shooting; Brueger would be at a desk with no firearm until the department determined whether or not the kill was justified. As far as I was concerned there was no question about that, and the cops had photos of my neck to prove it. I made a mental note to find out what Brueger's favorite drink was and deliver a big bottle. Or ten. Maybe one a month for the rest of his life.

We ate quietly for a while. I was listening to the rain on the windows, staring at my Munchkins and trying to decide which to eat next when I noticed Dennis and Turk looking at me with grins.

"What?"

"Should we tell her?" Dennis asked Turk.

"Don know, she be in pain already. Maybe we best wait."

I looked at them both, puzzled. Finally, I couldn't stand it. "Tell me *what?*"

Dennis stood and positioned himself in front of me. Turk came and stood by Dennis, hands clasped behind his back. Dennis looked down at me with a smile. "Miss Warren, in recognition of your assistance in identifying the Pilgrim Slayer, the Plymouth Police Department and Board of Selectmen would be honored if you would join us at police headquarters tomorrow at noon for a press conference to formally announce the capture and death of Aaron Stevens, aka the Pilgrim Slayer." He paused. "*And* to present you with a check for ten thousand dollars."

I'd forgotten about the reward. I squawked and jumped up. I threw my arms around Dennis' neck, crying with both joy and pain. I eased my arms down and stood on tip-toe to deliver a kiss to Turk's cheek. Then groaning, I sat back down in my chair. "Oh, ow, that hurts," I said, laughing.

"I done tole you we should wait," said Turk.

"See ya tomorrow, Nance," said Dennis with a salute. "Or is it *Miss Drew* now?" After he and Turk left, I stood behind the closed door for a minute and then I clapped my hands. If my ribs weren't broken, I'd have done a few cartwheels. Ten *thousand* dollars. Tomorrow. *Praisethelordhallelujah!*

I went back to the living room and lowered myself down into my chair. Pepper jumped up on my lap; absently I stroked his neck and chin.

The police had found plenty of evidence at Stevens' home; there was no question he'd been the killer. But then I already knew that. The jury was still out as to whether or not Meredith Bradley knew what Stevens was doing with the information that she, with her son's help, had clearly provided. Meredith hadn't yet been located; her son was being held, but they weren't getting much out of him. Social Services was working with law enforcement to see what the autistic young man knew.

I honestly had no idea who the killer was when I set off Saturday night, but I'd been certain that Bradley was the link. Between her son and herself, they had the know-how and the access to everything the killer needed to choose his victims.

Meredith Bradley. The poor woman was no doubt astounded when such a handsome, charming man showed interest. I could relate. Her self-esteem was in for a major blow when she learned that she'd been used, if she didn't already know. But I didn't feel *too* sorry for her. One way or another, she was obviously the one who told Stevens that Milo and I were on his trail. Her loose lips nearly cost me my life.

I stared at the empty fireplace. No fire warmed my hearth and there was no Milo to build one. Sighing, I stood and hobbled over to my pile of Duralogs. I placed one in the fireplace and held my lighter to the bright yellow paper. Milo had teased me mercilessly when he first saw my cache of fake wood, but I was never much of a Scout. I didn't know how to get a perfect fire going the way that he could.

I sighed again. I couldn't believe that in my moment of glory, *pain* and glory, the man I'd fallen for was fifty miles away doing God-knew-what with Sunglasses and Hairspray.

I thought some more about Meredith Bradley and how Aaron Stevens preyed on her insecurities. What if Milo was never really interested in me at all? What if he just wanted me for my hacking skills? I knew exactly what types of crime the Justice Department handled; they were pretty bad. Mike Milken bad. John Gotti bad.

I could hack the DOJ, I supposed, and find out exactly what was happening with Milo, but I didn't want to know. Not yet. I just wanted to revel in my investigative victory for one day;

when it came to Milo I was keeping my head planted firmly in the sand. He said he would explain everything when he got back. I would wait.

But had I been completely wrong about him?

Chapter 44

"Well, Pepper, what do you think? Good enough for national news?"

Pepper didn't reply.

I stared at my reflection. I was wearing my red dress and heels and I'd spent extra time on my face. The egg on my forehead where Aaron Stevens' nose had connected was still swollen, but I'd hidden the purple with makeup. The wonder-hat had come off just a few minutes earlier and my frizz was styled to the best of my limited ability. My ribs were taped as tightly as possible; I couldn't breathe very well, but I could move around more or less normally.

I turned and sat on the bed next to Pepper. "You should really be there too, you know that?" He stared at me with those round, yellow eyes. "You kept me going that night on the island." *You and Milo.* I scratched his chin and kissed his head. I rose and tottered down the stairs.

I pulled my long coat out of the closet. It was cold outside, but the rain had ended overnight. *Thank God.* For once the press could take pictures that wouldn't later reduce me to tears. I looked at my backpack but decided to leave it home. There would be plenty of law enforcement at the press conference; I didn't need my gun and I wasn't about to spoil my outfit with that ratty old bag. Maybe I would do some shopping—*if* there was anything left once I paid off my credit card bill and the overdue property taxes.

I stepped outside and smiled for the reporters. I waved and got in the car.

I pulled into the Plymouth Police Headquarters driveway and tried to maintain an attractive smile as dozens of cameras zoomed in. The parking lot was mobbed. As I eased the Mini through the crowd, I saw Dennis and Turk and the Chief standing in a parking space right in front of the brick building. Dennis waved me over and they made room for my car.

"There she is, Miss Plymouth herself," said Dennis as I exited the Mini. I carefully hugged each of them, self-conscious of the cameras.

"So, first you're a victim, and then a few days later you solve the mystery—a mystery our senior detectives, hell, the FBI, couldn't solve." Chief Hastings squinted at me with those sage eyes. "Not bad for a rookie PI," he added with a smirk. Dennis and Turk were, all of a sudden, very interested in the gravel beneath their shoes.

"Guess I just got lucky, Chief," I said with a smile.

"Mmm hmm. *Real* lucky. Lucky to be alive." He frowned at me.

Drops of sweat ran from my armpits down my sides.

"Lucky for *us*, I guess," he added and put his arm around my shoulders. "Come on, let's get this over with."

We walked over to a podium that was set up outside the main entrance. The two suits from the FBI were there and Dennis, Turk and I took our places beside them.

"Good afternoon, everyone," the Chief began. "I want to start off by saying that an enormous amount of round-the-clock effort went into solving these terrible crimes and that without the cooperation of state, local and federal officers...."

I zoned out. These things were always so boring. I was just waiting for the part where they gave me ten thousand dollars. I stared out into the sea of faces.

In addition to the press, a lot of citizens were there too, which surprised me. But then, it was a sensational crime spree and people are naturally curious about all things gruesome—whether Charles Smit liked it or not.

A twinge of sadness cut through me. The one face I *really* wanted to see was missing. ("He'll be back, Sam," said Dad. "And I'm the proudest father alive, er—in *spirit*—on the planet right now.") My eyes blurred for a moment.

The tall pink FBI agent took his turn at the mike and then Dennis said a few words about how the investigation would continue until all of the necessary evidence had been compiled and catalogued. "But we have no doubt at this time that Aaron Stevens was the serial killer who terrorized our town for the past two weeks. And, I can assure you, he'll cause no further harm." There was applause as Dennis backed away from the podium and Chief Hastings came forward. For a roly-poly, he was very light on his feet. *Weebles wobble but...*

"And finally, last but most certainly not least, I'm proud to recognize today a remarkable young woman—*my* Goddaughter—Samantha Warren. After surviving her first encounter with Aaron Stevens, Sam came to some remarkably astute conclusions. Her actions late Saturday night, in all likelihood, prevented Stevens from fleeing to another town where he intended to continue his murderous spree. Thanks to Miss Warren, Aaron Stevens, or as you all like to call him, The Pilgrim Slayer, will never kill again." He paused. "Did I mention she's my Goddaugher?" The crowd chuckled. He turned to me. "Sam, would you join me?"

I walked quickly to the podium and grabbed it. I was *not* going to fall off my heels on national television. Chief put his hand on my shoulder and whispered, "Relax." We smiled for the flashing cameras for a few seconds.

He reached under the podium and pulled out a check and raised it for the crowd to see. "This is a check in the amount of ten thousand dollars made out to Samantha Warren as a reward for her invaluable assistance in making America's Home Town safe again." He turned to me, but instead of handing me the check he turned back to the mike. "Oh and, by the way? Sam's my Goddaughter." He grinned and the crowd laughed loudly. I rolled my eyes. *What a ham.*

He handed me the check and said into the mike, "Let's all show Sam our appreciation." He backed away and clapped his hands together; the noise grew loud as the crowd joined in. *Jeeeesus.* My cheeks flushed; no question they were now the same color as my dress. I waved and stepped quickly back. Turk patted my shoulder and Dennis mussed my hair.

"*Hey!*" I said and tried to smooth it down. But the crowd kept applauding and I just couldn't wipe the grin off my face.

The Chief and the other officers took questions from the press for about twenty minutes. Finally, the reporters cleared out, rushing off to file their stories and chase the next ambulance.

A number of citizens came up to me and shook my hand and thanked me. It was surreal. Alan Perkins came over to me and said, "Thank you for helping to find the man that killed my wife." We both teared up. I knew only too well what Anna Fuller had suffered. Her widower didn't need to know the details.

Finally, the crowd thinned out and I noticed Liz and Charles Smit standing off to the side. *Shit.*

They approached and Charles stuck out his hand. "May I?"

I shook his hand, unsure of what to say.

"I want you to know, Liz and I understand why you may have had some…suspicions… about me and my congregants. *Sharon.*" The smile didn't quite reach his eyes. Then Smit frowned. "I always knew Aaron was enthusiastic about the ministry, but I never dreamed…" He raised his eyes. "You must understand that I would never condone such…Our doctrine is…conservative, but…" For the first time in his life, Charles Smit couldn't quite find the right words.

I nodded. "It's all right. I understand." I would never understand Smit's doctrine, but I did believe that his horror over Aaron Stevens' actions was genuine.

Liz extended her hand. "I am *sincerely* so grateful. To think I was working side-by-side with that man for all this time. Oh, it's horrifying." She shook my hand firmly. "*Thank* you."

I looked her in the eye. "You're very welcome."

She nodded and clutched Charles' arm and they walked away. Liz Smit wasn't so bad after all, I decided, but her husband was still creepy.

I turned around, scanning the parking area for Dennis and Turk. I found them over by the doors, mingling with about a dozen people, including Judge Barbie. I laughed. She got points for persistence if nothing else.

I yelled to Dennis and waved my goodbyes. I was ready to go home and change out of my ridiculous shoes. And then Pepper and I would take a ride to the bank. *Hot dog!*

Chapter 45

The sun had just set; a few wisps of pink and mauve remained on the horizon, but soon it would be black outside my windows. I was eating a bowl of Trix next to the fire. Another Duralog fire. Pepper was curled up on my lap and, had it been just three weeks earlier, I would have been perfectly content. But now things were different.

I hadn't heard any more from Milo, but Grady had come by earlier to check on me and to tell me that Milo was expected back the next day. Grady was still angry, but he couldn't—or *wouldn't*—tell me much.

"Kid fucked up, Sam. That's all I know right now," he said bitterly. "Thank God Laura was already on the mend; this might have done her in."

We talked for a few minutes, but it was awkward and he didn't stay long.

"Tell Laura I'll come for a visit in a day or two," I called after him. He threw his arm in the air in response without a backward glance as he walked down my driveway to his truck.

Taylor Ave was blissfully free of both reporters *and* cops. It was really over, at least as far as I was concerned. Dennis and

Turk would be busy with the evidence, probably for weeks, but I didn't need to even think about Aaron Stevens any more. I tried not to, but that left my mind free to think *way* too much about Milo Cooke. I raised my bowl to my lips, drank the sweet remains of the milk and set the empty bowl down on the floor. I stared into the flames, stroking Pepper.

I must have fallen asleep. When I heard the knock at my door, I opened my eyes and blinked in the dark room. My Duralog was half gone. *Mrs. Trimble?* She doesn't usually knock. I turned on the lights, went to the front door and squinted through the peephole. Meredith Bradley was on my front stoop. *Shit.*

I rushed back to the living room and grabbed my phone. I sent Dennis a text; I *really* hoped he wasn't celebrating somewhere with Barbie. Or Eileen. For good measure, I copied Turk and the Chief. I padded silently back to the door and stood behind it.

Bradley knocked again.

I peered out. She was wearing a heavy winter coat with the hood up. Her nose and eyes were red. Her hands were in her pockets.

I opened the door an inch with my foot wedged against the bottom.

"Hello," she said. "Could I talk to you for a minute?"

"The police have been trying to find you," I said.

"I know."

I waited, but she said nothing more.

"Why do you want to talk to me?"

She shivered.

I wanted to keep her there, but what was under that coat? In her pockets? She was a small woman, but...

"Just a minute," I said and closed the door. I ran to my desk, pulled out my nine and checked the cartridge.

I went back to the door. She was still huddled there. I opened it a few inches again. "Before I let you in, you need to know that I'm armed. If you're here on some kind of revenge mission..."

She gave me a sad smile. "I'm not going to hurt you."

About three minutes had gone by. How soon would backup arrive? "Take off your coat and lay it on the ground."

She did as I asked.

"Raise your arms and turn slowly around."

She was wearing a brown turtleneck with jeans and loafers. The sweater wasn't snug, but I didn't see any bulges.

Sighing, I opened the door, my nine at my side.

She walked past me into the living room.

"Have a seat," I said, waving my nine toward the couch. I sat down in my chair, the gun resting on my lap and my finger on the trigger.

"This is nice," she said, gazing around. For crying out loud, was I supposed to offer tea now?

"What do you want, Meredith?"

Staring at the fire, she asked, "Is Zeke all right?"

"I...uh...I mean, Social Services is involved. I'm sure they're taking proper care of him, but...he's probably pretty scared."

She nodded and looked back at me. "I've never left him before. Ever."

I stared back at her. Her short greying hair was limp and her face was wan.

"So, why did you? Leave him."

"I saw the police at Aaron's house. After I got home Saturday night. I was so *happy*, you know?"

I waited.

"I put on high heels and a new nightie under my long coat and drove over to his house." A tear rolled down her cheek. "I've never done anything like that before." She wiped her face.

Where was this going? Five or six minutes had now passed; a patrol car couldn't be too far away. I hoped.

"He was using you, Meredith. You *and* Zeke."

"I know." She sighed. "Maybe I always knew. But for five whole months he made me feel like…" She shook her head. "Ever since he was born, all I've ever *done* is take care of Zeke. Find him the best tutors, take him to therapy. Work with him every night after working all day. For the first time in my life, I had something that was just for me. Now it's gone and… it's worse than before." She looked at me. "Now I know what I was missing."

I heard tires skidding on my driveway.

"I'm sorry," I said.

I heard running out front and then footsteps pounded up the deck stairs. I went to the slider, never taking my eye off her, and pulled the broom handle out.

"I'm really very sorry."

I opened the door and two uniforms aimed their weapons at her.

I lay awake in bed for a long time after the police took Bradley away. I knew *exactly* how she felt.

Chapter 46

The air was cold but the sky was clear and my breath clouded my sunglasses as I huffed down the beach as fast as my aching ribs would allow. I had on my new favorite hat with Dad's hoodie and my black leggings. It felt good to work my muscles and empty my mind and absorb the beauty of the sea. I'd woken in a dark mood, but the walk helped.

A bunch of gulls were swooping and diving near my house; their shrill cries were harsh in the early morning calm. I saw one land and then take off with a crab in its mouth. A few seconds later the gull dropped the poor thing and the entire flock dove, vying to peck through the crab's cracked shell. Compared to him, I was having a *great* day.

I walked up onto my deck and leaned against the railing to stretch my calves. A few seconds later Mrs. Trimble appeared on the stairs.

"Good morning, Sam," she said, her voice as screechy as ever. "I made you a coffee cake. It's probably not as good as the chocolate cake I threw on that reporter but…"

I laughed. "Morning, Mrs. Trimble. I'll have to start running more if you keep bringing me cake."

She set the pastry down on my picnic table. "So, I saw the cops were here again last night…"

Ahh. The *real* reason for her visit.

"Yeah, it was nothing major. Meredith Bradley turned up; I just talked to her until the police came. She was seeing Aaron Stevens. She's an important witness."

"I see." She stood there looking at me. "Haven't seen Milo in a few days."

Me either. "He's been in Boston," I said.

"Hmm."

I didn't elaborate. I walked over to the picnic table and smelled the coffee cake.

"This smells great—"

"Speak of the devil," Mrs. Trimble said.

I looked up. Milo was coming through my slider.

I felt a thrill.

"Hi," he said. He had on jeans and a black turtleneck and his brown waves lay softly around the collar. *Yum.*

"Hi." I pulled off my hat and ran my fingers through my hair.

"Well, I guess I'll leave you two alone." Mrs. Trimble hobbled down my stairs.

"Thanks again for the coffee cake," I called. She lifted a hand and waved and disappeared into her house.

Milo walked up to me and put his arms around me. "God, you feel good," he said.

I inhaled sharply. "My ribs," I said.

He loosened his grip. "Oh, sorry, Sam. Dad told me." He

looked down into my eyes with concern.

I pulled away from him and picked up the coffee cake. "Let's go inside," I said.

He followed me into the kitchen and put coffee in the maker. I sliced the coffee cake and put two portions on plates and sat down at the breakfast bar. A few minutes passed, during which I studied his back. And his butt. Just a little. He poured the coffee, stirred in cream and sugar and sat down beside me.

I waited.

"I guess you had your moment in the sun. I'm really sorry I missed it, Sam." He looked at me and put his hand on mine. "I'm really proud of you."

I smiled a little. "Thanks. So, are you going to explain what's going on?"

He sighed and took a bite of coffee cake. "This is good."

"Milo!"

"Okay, okay. Sorry." He grabbed a napkin and wiped his mouth.

"Why's your dad so pissed off?"

"Phht." Milo waved his hand like he was shooing a fly. "He's mad because I paid mom's hospital bills. I thought they'd be grateful, but Dad was insulted. Thinks I'm trying to show him up. It doesn't have anything to do with my…situation. Not really."

"Sooo. What *is* your situation? I need to know what's going on Milo."

"I know. Okay." He cleared his throat. "Okay."

I waited.

"So, when I was at Harvard, I was in this investing club."

I knew it.

"Met a lot of guys. We were all so cocky." He looked at me. "I was gonna go to Wall Street and make millions. I was never gonna look back at this little shit town or my Dad the lobsterman. I was an ass. We were all asses.

"So, this one guy, Phil; he was a couple of years older than me. He got a job at Goldman Sachs. I had an investment account; I'd saved up a few thousand dollars and was starting to trade some. I was doing all right; the first year I turned three thousand into seven thousand. I thought I was the shit.

"Anyways, one night a bunch of us are out and Phil shows up; he's in town for some Harvard alumni thing. We had a few drinks and all night he's telling me how much money he's making; how great life in New York is. And he gives me a few stock tips. 'Sure winners' he says. So I bought some, and about three weeks later one of them announces a buyout. I tripled my money. I called him up and thanked him, and from then on we stayed in touch. For about a year, he'd call me every so often and give me his latest hot tip. I made a *bunch* of money."

"How mu—"

"A *bunch*. Just listen. So one day I'm leaving campus and I run into this other friend of ours and he says, 'Did you hear about Phil? He got busted for insider trading.'" Milo sighed and looked at me. "I was *shitting* myself. Turns out I had been trading on insider information; I just didn't know it. By this time I had more than two hundred grand in my trading account—that's *after* paying the taxes, which I always did."

Holy shit. "Two hundred *grand?*"

"Yeah. I stopped trading after that and kept my head low. I finished out the semester and that's when I decided I needed a break. That's when I came home."

"So, you really didn't know?"

"I really didn't, Sam. But I probably should have. There were just too many home runs…but I was high on the buzz. Now DOJ wants me to pay back the money I made off the insider trades *and* they want me to testify against Phil. He's looking at five years at least. Maybe ten."

I thought about that for a minute. "Are you going to do it?"

"Yeah, I am. At first I felt bad, but you know what? My only real crime was being stupid. Phil knew *exactly* what he was doing and he pulled me into it." He turned to me. "The trial's in New York in a couple of months. I'll probably have to be there for a few days."

"How much do you have to pay back?"

"Just over a hundred."

"*Thousand?*"

"Yeah."

Wow. And I was excited about the four thousand dollars in reward money I had left. We ate some coffee cake.

"Where do I fit in?" I asked.

He blinked. "What do you mean?"

"Why did you want to go out with me?"

He laughed. "Because I *like* you, Sam. A lot."

"Are you still trading stocks?"

"Here and—" He stopped and stared at me. "Do you think I want to *use* you?"

I looked down at my plate.

"Sam." He took my hand again. "Look, all that shit's in the past. It's like I told you the other night. I'm not that person. Not anymore. I'm going to pay my dues and testify and move on." He leaned over and kissed my cheek. "I really hope you'll give me a chance."

I leaned back and looked him square in the eye. Finally I nodded. "Okay."

Chapter 47

"I'll be back in a few hours," said Milo. He leaned down and kissed me softly.

I smiled up at him. "I've heard that before."

"Ouch. Guess I deserve that."

"Go on, have a nice dinner. Tell Laura and Grady I said hello." I closed the door behind Milo, still smiling.

I put some hot water on to boil and walked over to my desk. Time to pack up the Pilgrim Slayer case. I pulled the photos and documents down from my bulletin board and sorted them into various files. When I heard the water boiling, I went back into the kitchen and poured some into a mug and added a teabag. Blowing into the steam, I gazed out the window.

Injun Bob was heaving himself out of his minivan. Stunned, and more than a little wary, I watched him plod up my driveway. He raised his eyes to mine and caught my gaze, then nodded. I went to the door.

When I opened it, we looked at each other for a few long seconds. He nodded again, as if confirming something to himself. Finally, he broke the silence. "You needn't be frightened of me."

I flushed and smiled. "I'm not frightened. Do I look

frightened? Why would I be frightened of you?" I was, in fact, a little frightened.

"May I come in?" he asked.

"I—uh, sure." I opened the door and pressed myself against the wall so that he could pass. "Just have a seat in the living room," I said. "Would you like some tea?"

"Tea would be nice."

I poured another mug of hot water. "Herbal or regular?" I called from the kitchen.

"Herbal, please."

I grabbed the teabag and sugar bowl and placed everything on the breakfast bar. "Here you go," I said. He was standing at the door looking out at the ocean. His khaki pants were baggy over hiking boots; on top he wore an enormous red hoodie. The signature beret was perched over his long grey-black hair.

Slowly, he turned and joined me at the breakfast bar. He eased himself into one of the stools and studied my face. "Aren't you going to ask me what I'm doing here?"

"Well, yes. I was wondering…What should I call you?" I didn't want to let 'Injun Bob' slip; he might not appreciate the nickname I'd assigned.

"Rob. Call me Rob. I came because I need to share with you what I've learned since our first meeting."

I raised my eyebrows and took a sip of tea.

"In short, I believe you to be a member of my soul family." He placed his tea on the counter and gave me an intense look. "I've been getting messages, signals if you will, ever since our first meeting."

I opened my eyes wide and then laughed, but he held up a

hand and said, "Hear me out."

"But you can't be ser—"

"I'm very serious." He took another sip of tea. "I sensed you at the Plantation that day, when I was in the research library. After the second murder."

I blushed and looked down.

"You were there; I knew you were there. I didn't know how I knew, but after I left the building, I followed the path a little ways up the hill and then stopped and watched. A few minutes later I saw your…interesting departure through the window."

My jaw dropped.

"I began to pay attention, to try and hone in on the signals. I had some dreams."

I took a step back from the bar. Now I really was frightened. I'd been hunting a crazy killer but it seemed I'd gone and found myself a crazy stalker at the same time.

He raised a hand. "I am not here to hurt you. On the contrary, I'm the one who alerted the state police to your location a few nights ago." He set his mug back down and studied my face. "I had a vision, a very strong vision. I clearly saw what was happening to you. I called; I told them what mile marker you were near. I may have even saved your life."

"But…but that's crazy." My thoughts were jumbled. "How could you know? I mean, Breuger said he saw Stevens' car…and anyway, you said your third eye's blind." Is that where the band got its name, I wondered hysterically.

"There are things we don't understand in this world," he said. "Please sit down. Let me explain it to you as best I can." I hesitated. He patted the seat of the bar stool. "Sit, Samantha

Warren." Finally, I relented.

"Okay," I said once I was seated. "Explain."

"The first time I saw you, at the Plantation, I surprised myself by calling out to you. I don't go out of my way to talk with strangers. Especially not white strangers. Except when I'm working; there, it's my job." He turned in the stool and faced me. I worried that my Ikea bar stools wouldn't hold up under Bob's—er, Rob's—substantial weight.

"I forgot about you after that, frankly," he said with a smile. "Until that day in the research library. I was in there talking with Stevens, asking him about his research—little did I know, by the way, what he was really up to—but I kept seeing your face. I didn't even know your name, but our encounter in the parking lot kept coming back to me. Puzzled, I left. As I said, I walked away, but I had an almost uncontrollable urge to go back. Instead I stood and watched. Sure enough, you came sliding out the window a few minutes later." He smirked. "Graceful," he added.

I blushed again.

"After that, I tuned in. I've had these psychic moments before, but this was stronger. The night you were taken to that island, I felt a profound sense of unease and I knew it was related to you somehow, but I still didn't know your name or how to respond." He took another sip of tea. "It was a very unpleasant night."

For me too, I thought.

"After that you were all over the news. I learned what I could about you; searched for you on the Internet. Read up." He paused. "NSA, huh? That surprised me."

I shrugged.

"I continued to follow the case. I opened my mind to your signals, and over the next few days, they intensified. I began to receive clear visions. Not constantly mind you, but often enough to take notice."

Shit. Had Injun Bob been tuning in when Milo and I got cozy?

"Saturday night I was in bed asleep, when the vision came to me very strongly. It was like a dream at first, but at the same time I knew it wasn't a dream. It was real. I got up, went to the gas station at the corner and made an anonymous call. Then I went home and sat up, waiting. I meditated; I needed to know whether or not you were all right. It was overwhelming. And then, maybe fifteen minutes later, a sense of calm descended. I knew you were okay; I knew the threat had passed."

He fell silent and I pondered his claims. I'd had the mental dialogue with my dead father for a few years now, but I'd always believed there was a rational explanation. Like the one my shrink provided, that it was simply my subconscious mind. But this was different. I'd never even seen this man until a few weeks ago.

"You haven't really explained," I said. "You've described some very difficult to believe scenarios, but you haven't explained. And you said 'soul family.' What exactly is that?"

Rob laughed. "You're right. Well, it may or may not satisfy you, but here's how I've explained it to myself." He leaned back. The chair back held up.

"You recall I spoke to you of spirits when we first met? That's real, Sam. I know you were skeptical, but I have experienced the spiritual world on numerous occasions in my life. You simply have to open yourself up to it. But what is a spirit, really? It's the energy of one who has left the physical plane. But those of us still here, in the physical plane, also exude energy. We experience the energy of those around us, every day. But for some reason, and I have a theory on this, the connection between me and you is very strong. Our energies are connected."

"But Rob," I interrupted. "After we met, the only time I thought about you was as a suspect."

"You haven't opened your mind, that's all."

"But I have, I—" Suddenly, I was embarrassed to mention my ongoing mental Father-Daughter talks.

"I'm aware of the link you have with your father, Sam." Rob turned and looked out toward the beach. "You're in touch with him, aren't you?" He waited.

"I guess…"

"He reached out to me too, Sam. Saturday night. I think he facilitated my vision; I think he knew you were running out of time." Rob turned back to me. "I think that there's a connection between my ancestors and yours. I know your family dates back to the early settlers. I've concluded that at some point, our families were linked. Perhaps my ancestor saved one of yours. Perhaps it was the other way around. I really don't think we'll ever know, but I firmly believe that at some point over the past four hundred years, our families were close. Hell, we could even be related. It doesn't really matter. What matters is that you understand and that you not be afraid. Maybe, you'll even find a way to embrace this connection we have."

Rob stood. "I know I've given you a lot to think about and I don't have any intention of inserting myself into your life uninvited. I just thought you deserved to know what I experienced. I do hope we can be friends someday, but that's entirely up to you." He walked toward the front door. "Just remember, Sam. I'll be there to help if you need it." With that, he let himself out.

Milo's breath had evened out; his arm felt heavy on my side. As much as I loved having Milo with me in bed and his strong arm around me, my ribs weren't ready for the weight. I lifted his arm and rolled onto my back.

I stared at the ceiling, running Injun Bob's story through my mind. I was never going to get used to calling him Rob. Could it be true though? That we were linked, psychically? I hadn't told Milo about his visit, much less his crazy tale. And yet…his story seemed plausible. He could have just seen me that day, falling through the bushes outside the research library at Plimoth Plantation. But there *had* been an anonymous call to the state police Saturday night, made from a location that was very close to the address the DMV had on file for one Robert Hopkins. When it came in, however, Sergeant Brueger had already seen Stevens' car and was seconds away from firing on Stevens. So, though I didn't think Injun Bob was lying, I wasn't convinced there was some mystical connection either. And he didn't actually save my life. But what about his visions? Could we be somehow connected in a non-physical plane? It was a lot to accept, but as I fell asleep I saw his smiling face on the back of my eyelids.

Chapter 48

"Got nice weather for it anyway," said Grady. "You two enjoy; this little fella will be happy as a clam keeping watch over the fish." He scratched Pepper's chin. Pepper generally didn't like to be held for long, but in Grady's arms he seemed relaxed.

Laura smiled from Grady's side. "He's always welcome, and Lady could use a bath anyway," she added, laughing. Some color had returned to Laura's cheeks and her cough was nearly gone.

Milo put his hands on my shoulders and turned me around. "Thanks you two," he yelled over his shoulder as he pushed me toward the car. "We'll see you tomorrow night." Leaning down, Milo whispered in my ear. "Unless I can convince you that we deserve a whole week away?"

Milo opened the door for me and I climbed into the passenger seat. My sore ribs made shifting uncomfortable; I was letting Milo drive the Mini out to Provincetown for a well-deserved weekend getaway.

"Sadly, I don't have a six-figure bank account like some people," I said. "I need to get back to work next week. I have three appointments with potential clients," I added with pride. All those bad-hair shots in the papers had been good for something.

I turned on NPR and Milo and I laughed through an hour of Car Talk. Finally, I turned it off. "If I laugh any more, my ribs aren't going to heal," I said. Traffic was light and we were rounding the elbow of the Cape; in another forty-five minutes or so we'd arrive at the tip of Cape Cod, where John Billington and another forty men had signed the Mayflower Compact nearly four hundred years earlier. It seemed fitting. Milo had booked a bed and breakfast for the night. I made a mental note to work that into my next conversation with Mrs. Trimble.

"About your work, Sam..."

"What?" I was thinking about the four-poster bed and decadent breakfast that awaited.

"Well, I was thinking." Milo cleared his throat. "I mean, we make a pretty good team, right?" He glanced over at me.

I sat up straighter and looked at Milo. "What are you trying to say, Milo?" I had a pretty good idea.

"Well, you know, I have a lot of financial expertise. You could expand your business to include forensic accounting and..." He sighed. "Dear Sir or Madam. Attached is my resume for your consideration. In addition to an MBA from Harvard University..." He laughed and chanced another look at me.

Stalling, I said, "You don't have your MBA, actually."

"I'm going to take my last course next semester. I already called my advisor."

"That's good." I looked out the window. The sky was that crisp blue that comes only with turning leaves and falling temperatures.

"I'd like to be your partner, Sam. I'm even willing to invest; we could rent an actual office. Advertise in Boston. Like I said, financial investigation would be my specialty. Law firms are always looking for dirt on public companies after they file class action law suits. I know some people. I could bring in business. And we could work together on the tough cases. And I can keep my eye on you."

I thought about it for a few more minutes. We were approaching the Wellfleet Wildlife Sanctuary. Did I really want a partner?

"Do you think it's a good idea for us to work together if we're dating?" I asked.

"I do. Look, we don't have to be together 24/7. We can work independently on some cases and together on others." He paused. "I mean, right now I want to spend every minute with you, Sam. But I know what you mean, what's worrying you. I'll give you your space if you need it." He reached over and took my hand. "I hope you won't need too much though," he said and squeezed.

"And what if we break up. Are—"

"We aren't going to break up."

I looked over at him. "You sound awfully sure about that."

"I am," he said. "But I'm willing to take it slow until you're sure too."

Wow. I was thrilled but also terrified. I stared out the passenger window, afraid to let Milo see my eyes. ("Go for it, Sam. I approve," said Dad.)

"Sam?"

I leaned my head back and closed my eyes and then squeezed Milo's hand. I opened my eyes and smiled. "*If* I were interested, just how much would you be willing to pay for half of my business?"

Saturday night in Provincetown is an experience you won't soon forget. Milo and I were walking along Commercial Street, holding hands and watching the drag queens and entertainers that paraded up and down the strip. P-Town is sometimes called the Key West of the north; it has more same-sex couples per capita than any other city in America. Even though it was off season, plenty of colorful characters were out. It might be fun to bring Charles Smit here some time, just to watch his reaction.

We found an upstairs pizza joint and sat outside under the heat lamps. We sipped our drinks and watched in amusement, laughing out loud at the personalities. There was a man in a long blond wig and a pink ballet tutu with hairy white legs running around the street, doing the occasional arabesque and making kissy faces at some of the more flamboyant queens.

Our pizza came, and as I bit into a slice, I noticed a young male couple walking along the street below. They weren't in drag, but they were holding hands and at the corner, they stopped and kissed. I set my pizza down and leaned closer.

"Sam, don't stare," said Milo.

I shook my head and smiled. I was getting ready to tell him that I *knew* the guy when my text message alert went off. I pulled my phone out of my pocket and read it. The message was from Dude Number Two. "Got those tix 4 me?" it said. *Shit.*

"What is it?"

"Tomorrow I need to make a call for some concert tickets."

"Concert tickets?"

"For Dude Number Two. So he can see the Numb Nuts." I laughed out loud and Milo just shook his head. I would explain later.

"See that guy down there, the one in blue stripes kissing the guy in the brown hoodie?"

"The ones you were staring at? Yeah."

"His name is Andrew Mattison. Remind me to show you my report on him sometime."

Sam Warren, Private Investigator *Extraordinaire*.

Richelle Elberg

When I was eight, I told my parents I was going to live in a log cabin in Maine and be an author when I grew up. (I wanted to be Laura Ingalls, but by the ocean.) Somewhere along the way I decided a business degree might pay better, and, having obtained said degree, I spent twenty years writing articles and doing financial analysis on the telecom industry. Got married, had the customary two children and bought a house. Traded up for a better house. *Et cetera*.

A few years later (okay, forty years later – sheesh) I'm revisiting that childhood dream. My first novel, *Impunity*, was published in 2011. It's a suspense thriller set in the White Mountains of New Hampshire and the Boston suburbs.

In 2012, I spent three months living on White Horse Beach in Plymouth, writing *Saints & Strangers*. Sam is a lot like me, except she's younger, prettier, cooler and carries a gun. Okay, maybe she's not that much like me. But *Saints & Strangers* is just the first of many rollicking adventures that will put Sam – and her hunky friend Milo – to the test.

Turn the page for a taste of the sequel – *The Second Peirce Patent*.

www.richelleelberg.com

Excerpt from *The Second Peirce Patent*
Book 2 in the Sam Warren, Private Investigator
Extraordinaire, Mystery Series

Chapter 1

"I might have a case," I said into my cellphone as I pushed through the glass doors of the Pilgrim Hall Museum and skipped down the stairs. "A *good* one." I pulled my sunglasses out of the frizz and positioned them on my nose. It was late May in Plymouth and the weather was finally starting to act like it. The air was balmy and a brilliant tangerine sun warmed my face.

A healthy Memorial Day Weekend crowd was forming on the sidewalk along Court Street, despite the early hour, so I turned right and followed a narrow paved path toward the museum parking area out back. "There's been a painting stolen from Pilgrim Hall; Dennis is asking the Chief to okay me for the work right now."

"That's great, Sam!" My PI partner—and boyfriend—Milo Cooke, was working one of those incredibly boring (though amazingly profitable) financial cases in Boston. In fact, Milo had been carrying the financial load at our young investigative firm

THE SECOND PEIRCE PATENT (EXCERPT)

for a couple of months now; Robin was starting to outshine Bat Girl, which really didn't sit well with me (aka Bat Girl. *Inside joke*). The prospect of a new, potentially lucrative, case in my bailiwick put a bounce in my step.

"So, a painting was stolen from Pilgrim Hall? Crazy. Which one?"

"*The Landing of the Pilgrims*, by Henry Bacon," I replied. "Not to be confused with *The Landing of the Pilgrims* by Henry Sargent. Which hangs right next to Bacon's version," I added. "Or rather, did."

Nineteenth century artists, particularly those named Henry it seemed, had been devoted to envisioning the Pilgrim's arrival in America—never mind that more than 200 years had passed and precious little accurate detail surrounding the event survived. There were, the museum director had explained, at least half a dozen known works with the same title. Most of them worth a mint.

"The Bacon painting is the one showing that young girl—I forget her name—stepping onto Plymouth Rock. The Sargent is that huge piece that they've been renovating. They're spending two hundred grand on it; there's a big reception planned for the unveiling in about two weeks. Loads of bigwigs will be there. The governor. Senator Jordan. You get the idea. The new museum director is losing her shit."

I continued. "But with those two shootings earlier this month, Dennis and Turk are hoping the Chief will let them sub it out; they're not interested in searching for a 150-year-old piece of canvas when gangbangers are shooting up the town. They're asking the Chief to let me consult." Which meant, basically, let me have the case. "Dennis called me over here around 8. He's talking to the Chief now."

That balmy sun was growing warm so I wandered toward the tree line at the back of the parking lot. Milo was speaking in tongues, something about fiduciary obligations and due diligence. Finally, I cut him off. "Milo, I don't speak Wall Street. Just tell me, is the case going well?"

He laughed and my heart melted a little. I love Milo's laugh. I love everything about Milo Cooke, although I haven't quite worked up the nerve to tell him so.

"It's going well. In fact, tonight, a couple of the lawyers invited me to go sailing with them in the Hahbaahh. So, yeah, I think they're pleased with my work." I smiled. Milo had the Harvard accent down. Of course, as he was a recent graduate of the august institution, I guess that shouldn't have surprised me.

A dull humm was coming from behind the trees where I'd sought shade. Curious, I ambled in that direction as Milo described the sailing club to which his yuppie lawyer friends belonged.

"They said it's only about $600 a season, Sam. We should check it out. We can sail as much as…"

A heavy, wet vomit smell invaded my nostrils as the humming grew louder. I stopped, looked around, and then continued toward the noise. "Milo," I whispered, but he didn't hear; he was still going on about sailing. I pulled my hoodie up and pressed it over my mouth and nose. I scanned my surroundings, but there was no one in the parking lot, or on the nearby street. I took another cautious step. Must be a dead animal, I thought, as Milo described the regatta he planned to see over the weekend. *A raccoon probably. Just a raccoon.*

The buzz grew louder. I was now standing beside a large maple tree. I took another step and, holding my breath, peered around the trunk.

"Milo!" I yelped as I jumped back, gasping. That was no raccoon. Shaking, I stumbled back into the parking lot. I fell against a parked car, turned around and puked. Right down the driver side door.

"Sam?" Milo waited, then yelled, "Sam!"

"Sorry, Milo," I gasped into the handset. "I gotta go." Then I turned and ran across the lot toward the museum door.

The back doors to the museum were locked. Frantic, I peered through the glass, clutched the handles and shook the doors. Hard. Inside, a uniform hurried toward me with an angry expression on his face. "Museum's closed," he yelled through the glass.

"Open up!" I shouted. I shook the doors some more. "Get Dennis and Turk!" I didn't recognize the officer; several had been called in to keep watch around the perimeter of the museum once the missing painting had been discovered.

The cop's face turned red. "Stop shaking the goddamn doors!"

I slapped the glass right in front of his face and he jerked back. "Get Detective Sheffield!" I shouted. "There's a body out here!"

His eyes opened wide. *Finally.* "You say there's a body out there?" He cupped his hand around his ear like an old deaf man.

JesusHChrist. I nodded my head up and down with exaggerated motion. "Yes! Get Detective Sheffield and ...Turk!" I couldn't for the life of me remember Turk's last name.

The uniform turned and jogged toward the main gallery, leaving me peering between my hands through the window. Thirty seconds passed, then sixty. What the fuck was taking so long? I glanced back toward the trees where I'd seen, and unfortunately, smelled, the dead man.

Another wave of nausea rolled through my gut. I inhaled sharply through my nostrils and turned back to face the door. I'd seen photos of horribly murdered bodies before, when I worked the Pilgrim Slayer case with Dennis and Turk last fall. But I'd never seen an actual body—a *murdered* body—up close. Saliva filled my mouth and I was afraid I would vomit again. I spit onto the sidewalk and looked frantically through the window. What was taking them so long?

My phone rang and I nearly jumped out of my sneakers. Milo.

"OmyGodMilo! There's a body, I found a body. A man's body. You were talking about the regatta or whatever it was, and I nearly fell over a dead man. Shot in the head. Right behind Pilgrim Hall!" I caught my breath. "Oh, Milo. It's so gross! The smell is—"

"Are you safe, Sam?" Milo's voice was calm, but had an edge.

"Yes, I mean, I don't know. I'm locked out of the museum; I yelled at the uniform inside to go get Dennis and Turk but they're not here yet. I'm standing by the back door." Again I hooded my eyes with my hands to peer into an empty hallway.

THE SECOND PEIRCE PATENT (EXCERPT)

"Milo, he was shot in the head. His brain was spilling out the back of his head." Abruptly, I gagged again.

"Sam. Listen." Milo raised his voice, but only a bit. "I want you to walk toward people. Now, Sam. Okay? Can you see any people?"

"No, but there were loads out front." I turned and stepped toward the parking lot. "Just, just stay on with me, okay? I'm walking toward Chilton Street."

"Good, Sam. Walk quickly."

"Chilton, Mary Chilton. That's the name of the girl. In the painting. Stepping onto Plymouth Rock."

"Who?"

"Mary Chilton was the young girl, the first Pilgrim to set foot on land."

"Sam! Are you near people yet? Save the history lesson."

"Almost, sorry." I was just trying to remove the image of fresh brains from my own. I rushed toward the sidewalk, turned right and jogged up Chilton toward Court Street. At the corner, a young couple with two toddlers in a double stroller studied a tourist map. I stopped next to them and stood gasping and staring back toward the trees behind the museum.

"Ummm. Can we help you?"

Apparently I was standing a bit closer than is generally accepted amongst strangers. "Sorry," I said. Again. "Oh, your babies are just adorable." I leaned over and crossed my eyes at the children. The little girl screwed up her face and started to wail.

"Sam?" Milo was still on the line.

The woman glared at me and pulled the screaming baby out of the stroller.

THE SECOND PEIRCE PATENT (EXCERPT)

"Sorry." I glanced once more toward the back of the museum and then hurried over to the steps in front, where I sank down and rested my forehead on my knees.

"Sam!"

Weakly, I brought the phone back to my ear. "I'm here."

"What the hell are you doing? Jesus, Sam! Are you out of that parking lot?"

"Yes, I'm sitting on the front steps. In front of the big columns." Pilgrim Hall Museum is housed in a Greek Revival structure with six large granite columns in front. Wide, white stairs climb from Court Street up to the entrance.

I looked around. Cars and pedestrians streamed by. The young couple was hurrying away from the crazy redhead who'd scared their children, but there were still plenty of people about. "I'm safe. I think. Should be. There are at least a dozen people nearby."

"Good." Milo exhaled loudly.

After 30 seconds or so of silence, I said, "Okay." I took a deep breath. "You don't have to stay on any longer. I need to find Dennis. I'm okay now."

Just then I heard Dennis' voice; he was shouting my name from somewhere behind the building. *Shit.* "Gotta go, Milo, I think Dennis is freaking out because he can't find me." I stood and walked back toward the corner.

"Call me back when you can, Sam. And be careful!" Milo clicked off.

As I reached the corner, I could see Dennis standing on the sidewalk, down near the trees, bellowing. Sighing, I jogged back toward him and the putrid dead man.